Troublemaker

Also by Trice Hickman

Dangerous Love series

Secret Indiscretions
Deadly Satisfaction

Unexpected Love Series

Unexpected Interruptions
Keeping Secrets & Telling Lies
Looking for Trouble

Playing the Hand You're Dealt

Published by Dafina Books

Troublemaker

TRICE
HICKMAN

WITHDRAWN

Dafina
Books

Kensington Publishing Corp.
www.kensingtonbooks.com

DAFINA BOOKS are published by

Kensington Publishing Corp.
119 West 40th Street
New York, NY 10018

All Kensington Titles, Imprints, and Distributed Lines are available at special quantity discounts for bulk purchases for sales promotion, premiums, fund-raising, and educational or institutional use. Special book excerpts or customized printings can also be created to fit specific needs. For details, write or phone the office of the Kensington special sales manager: Kensington Publishing Corp., 119 West 40th Street, New York, NY 10018, attn: Special Sales Department, Phone: 1-800-221-2647.

Dafina and the Dafina logo Reg. U.S. Pat. & TM Off.

ISBN-13: 978-0-7582-8727-4
ISBN-10: 0-7582-8727-5
First Kensington Trade Paperback Edition: August 2014
First Kensington Mass Market Edition: September 2016

eISBN-13: 978-0-7582-8728-1
eISBN-10: 0-7582-8728-3

10 9 8 7 6 5 4 3 2 1

Printed in the United States of America

Acknowledgments

I start every book the same way, and this one is no different. I want to begin these acknowledgments by honoring The One who sits most high. I give praise and thanks to God for blessing and guiding me through storms so that I may bask in the rainbow that is life

Each book I write is an exercise in discipline, dedication, and stamina. Completing a novel requires hours upon hours of uninterrupted time, along with a tremendous number of sleepless nights, endless amounts of coffee, along with the love, support, and understanding of the people around you. I'm fortunate to have all these things in abundance.

There are many people to thank who have helped me along this journey

Thank you to my family and friends. I have the greatest parents (Reverend Irvin and Alma Hickman, your love and faith sustains me), siblings (Melody and Marcus, you two are my aces!), aunts (way too many to name, so know that I love you all!), uncles (ditto what I said about aunts), cousins (ditto about aunts and uncles to the 10th power), and friends (I'm blessed with an abundance of individuals in this category who are just like family) in the world.

Thank you to my girls who are always in my corner and show me love; Vickie Lindsay, Sherraine McLean, Terri Chandler, Kimberla Lawson Roby, China Ball, Lutishia Lovely, Tiffany Dove, Cerece Rennie Murphy, Tracy

Wells, Kim Riley, Tammi Johnson, Yolanda Trollinger, Marsha Cecil, Melody Vernor-Bartel, and the one and only Barbara Marie Downey.

Thank you to my publishing family at Kensington; my amazing editor, Mercedes Fernandez, my super fly publicist, Adeola Saul, and all the marketing and sales folks who work hard to get the word out.

Thank you to my phenomenal agent, Janell Walden Agyeman. Words cannot express how much your guidance, wisdom, and friendship mean to me. Thank you for being my champion and operating with professionalism and integrity in everything you do.

Thank you to all the bookstores, libraries, specialty shops, and retailers who have purchased my books and hosted book signings for me. Thank you to the bloggers, book festival organizers, and literary professionals who support writers and the work we do!

Thank you to the faculty, staff, students, and alumni of Winston-Salem State University. You have supported me from the very start of my career. There's no love like RAM love!

And last but certainly not least: Thank you to every single book club and individual reader who has supported me by purchasing my books, reading my work, and helping to spread the word. You are a powerful force and without you I wouldn't be able to do what I do. I appreciate you more than you know!

Peace and many blessings,

Trice Hickman

Chapter 1
Allene

"You can never go wrong doin' right," Allene Small whispered to herself as she thought about the events that were about to unfold. She couldn't count the number of times she'd repeated those words during the nine decades she'd lived on earth, or in the six that she'd spent as a spirit waiting to reemerge into the world she'd once known.

Allene had enjoyed a rich, full life in her day. She'd experienced ups and downs, joys and heartbreak, and eventually, the calm peace that living ninety-eight years had brought her. She'd been widowed at a young age, outliving her beloved husband and eventually all her siblings and her children, as well as some nieces and nephews. She'd witnessed fiery crosses burning in the night, emblazoned with hatred and fear. She'd endured oppression before joining activists who fought for justice, civil rights, and social change. She'd watched one decade roll into the next as presidents and heads of state came and went, by consequence of elections or death. And she'd seen men ride in horses and buggies, fly planes in the sky, drive motorized vehicles along busy streets, and then miraculously walk on the moon.

Allene felt grateful and blessed to have lived long enough to experience things that many had not. She was also thankful that for as long as she could remember, she'd known an invaluable truth most couldn't fathom—that there was life after life. The peace she'd found in that knowledge had comforted her during times of trouble.

Now as she sat in her trusty old rocking chair, surveying the colorful flowers that graced the large wraparound porch where she'd been sitting all morning, her heart held excitement and caution about what she knew lay ahead. She took a deep breath and inhaled the sweet fragrance of the rose, azalea, and magnolia bushes flanking the front of the house. "This old place sure 'nuff has stood the test of time," she said with a smile. "Isaiah and Henrietta would be right proud, God rest their souls."

Allene loved being back in Nedine, South Carolina, the small town where she'd lived out the best parts of her days. She looked out as far as her eyes could see, noting that while some things had changed, so many had remained steadfastly the same. The large, white placard displaying THE SMALL PROPERTY in black calligraphy still towered at the edge of the road a few hundred feet away, announcing to visitors that they had reached the grounds of the grand residence that her son, Isaiah Small, had built from the ground up.

At the time, Isaiah's had been one of the largest homes in Nedine as well as the two surrounding counties, and today it proudly continued to hold that distinction. This was a huge feat for a black man, then and now. After Isaiah died, Allene had moved from her tiny house a few miles up the road, and settled into the quiet comfort of living with Isaiah's devoted widow, Henrietta, whom Allene had loved as her own daughter.

After Henrietta passed away, John, Isaiah's and Henrietta's son, cared for the house with great love and attention. Even though John had moved away to Raleigh, North Carolina, to start a banking empire and carry on in his father's successful footsteps, he'd made sure to preserve the family homestead where he'd been born and had many fond memories of growing up. Several times a year, John, along with his wife, Elizabeth, and their daughter, Victoria, would return to Nedine to make sure the house was well maintained and that any necessary repairs were made.

Once John's age and declining health prevented him from making trips to his beloved hometown, he'd hired a property management company to oversee the upkeep. After his death, his daughter, Victoria, had picked up the torch and seen to it that her father's birthplace was kept in good order. Allene was proud that her son's legacy was still intact, along with much of the land, rental properties, and other real estate holdings that had been passed down from one generation to the next.

"They're all gonna be here soon. Even the ones who ain't supposed to come," Allene said with reserve. "But then again, I reckon that ain't such a bad thing, 'cause nothin' happens by mistake. There's a plan for everything, we just gotta play it out to the end."

Allene nodded to herself as she looked up into the gray, stormy sky. It had been raining nonstop since early this morning. Heavy at times and light at others. Allene felt happy every time she heard the pitter-patter sound and the fresh smell that God's liquid glory created in its wake. She remembered back to the days she'd spent in her tiny home, and how she'd loved to listen to the rain dance atop her roof and beat against her windows. The natural rhythm had been soothing, and always made her feel a sense of peace—as if whatever had been wrong could be made right by the water that came and washed things away.

Allene wished so badly that the rain could clear out the troubles awaiting her family. Having the gift of prophecy, she was able to see some of the challenges that were on the horizon, and the struggles her loved ones were surely going to face. She wanted to intervene by warning them of what was coming, and tell them what they needed to do in order to avoid the problems heading their way. But age, wisdom, and experience had taught her that some things couldn't be interfered with, or manipulated. Only time, patience, and living through the situation could rectify whatever was wrong.

This was why Allene knew that choosing to do the right thing would never lead her down the wrong path. She'd been a witness to situations that had borne out that evidence time and time again, and she knew without a doubt that bad intentions could easily lead to devastating consequences. Conversely, she also knew that if one had good intentions and did what was fair and just, regardless of the circumstances, things would eventually unfold into a favorable outcome.

Allene knew that some of her family members were carrying heavy burdens, and to her disappointment, one in particular was plotting a hidden agenda, heading in the wrong direction by ignoring what was right. "Lord, help me guide Alexandria so she can help our family," she whispered aloud, looking up into the sky. "I waited a mighty long time to come back, and now, I'm ready. I just hope they're ready, too."

It had been nearly a year since Allene had first made her spirit form known to anyone in the land of the living. She'd reached out to Alexandria, her great-great-granddaughter, because she'd known it was time to make contact. Alexandria was a special young woman, who, like Allene, and Allene's great-grandmother before her, possessed the gift of prophecy.

The gift of prophecy was a precious ability that had been passed down through the generations, only by way of the female members of their family, dating back to the Akan people of Ghana, West Africa. The gift was a sacred and valued treasure that people both revered and feared within Allene's family, as well as the outside community.

During Allene's lifetime, her gift had allowed her to foretell events in advance of them happening. She could discern good from bad in the blink of an eye. She could sense when danger was approaching or when peace would prevail. She knew people's thoughts without ever having to engage them in conversation. And she could accurately declare good fortune or disappointing loss for those seeking her advice on any given situation.

Now as a spirit in the land of flesh and blood, she possessed those same abilities along with the added benefit of being able to exist between two worlds. Allene walked within the supernatural realm, able to communicate with others who shared the gift, like her great-grandmother, Susan. Even though she was able to see family and friends who'd passed on, she couldn't communicate with them unless they possessed the gift of prophecy. The living world was much the same way, only there, things were more complicated because life was still happening, unfolding in real time, which always presented challenges.

After years of patiently watching and waiting, Allene was glad when the time finally came that she could return to the world she'd once known. She was there to help Alexandria, who had struggled with her abilities for most of her life, but had now come to terms with the extraordinary gift she'd inherited. Just as Susan Jessup had been Allene's guide on her life's journey, it was now Allene's turn to do the same for Alexandria.

Allene continued to watch the sky and listen to the rain fall as she thought about what was going to happen two weeks from now. She could see the blessings, as well as the trouble that was going to ensue once everyone gathered under one roof. Tempers would flare and hearts would be hurt by deception. Long-held secrets were going to be revealed, weaknesses would be exposed, and a devious plot to steal and control was going to be uncovered. Allene could also see that there would be heated moments and tension between family members and friends.

"Sometimes people just got to go through things in order to make a change," Allene said to herself.

She knew that hearts, minds, and loyalties would be tested when her family came together for a grand celebration two weeks from now, and unfortunately, someone was going to meet their demise before the weekend came to an end.

"I'll see you soon, baby girl," Allene whispered into the air, sending words of love and comfort to Alexandria. "You just hang in there and know that everything's gonna be all right."

Chapter 2
Alexandria

Alexandria smiled as she stretched her long, shapely legs across PJ's buttery-soft leather sofa. "Now that I've finished cooking, it's time to relax," she said aloud. She ran her fingers through the mass of thick curls atop her head and let out a deep breath of relief, glad she was finally able to relax after her long day. She'd been busy from the moment she'd stepped out the door this morning with a coffee mug in one hand and a toasted bagel in the other. Her life had been more hectic in the last year than she could ever remember. So much was changing so fast, but with that change she felt the hope and excitement of new possibilities that lay ahead.

She breathed a sigh of relief when she thought about the fact that this Friday would be her last day of work at a job she'd dreaded since the day she'd started. She was an attorney, on the fast track, employed with the prestigious downtown Atlanta law firm of Johnson, Taylor, and Associates. Alexandria had worked there since she'd interned with them while still in law school. Now, six years later, she was ready to step out of what she'd been academically trained to do, and take hold of the direction in which her heart had always led her, which was to pursue her passion as a writer and spoken-word artist.

Alexandria thought about her promising future as she lay on her back and flipped through one of her many bridal magazines. Even though her wedding day was just one month away, and all the major details had been planned to a tee, she still couldn't resist looking at pictures of happy couples, replete with bountiful flowers and their wedding parties in tow, all overflowing with nuptial bliss.

Alexandria smiled every time she thought about how happy she was and how much her life had significantly changed since this time last year. It seemed as though it were just yesterday that she'd broken up with her old boyfriend, Peter, and in less than twenty-four hours, fate, along with her grandma Allene's sage advice, had led her down a completely different path to peace, understanding, and true love. Now she was engaged to PJ, her childhood best friend who'd walked into her life and changed her world.

She could still remember her grandma Allene's words. *Speak what's in your heart. Say what it is that you desire, and watch it walk into your life.*

Alexandria had heeded those words and still lived by them today. She knew that speaking what she wanted, and then trusting and believing with indomitable faith that her desires would be met in abundance, was the reason PJ was in her life. As she looked at the beautiful gowns of silk and tulle, she raised her hand in the air, as if in praise, and gave thanks for her blessings. "Amen," she said quietly.

She was thankful for this joyous time in her life, and she planned to savor every moment because she was all too aware of the trouble that was lying in wait on the other side. Gritty realities and unpleasant truths were about to surface, not just in her life, but in the lives of family and friends whom she loved. She knew the road ahead was paved with detours, rough patches, and a few hazard signs. But she also knew she'd get through them thanks to her faith, her grandma Allene, and the amazing gift of prophecy she now embraced.

"Thank you, Grandma Allene," Alexandria whispered. "I love you for showing me the way."

As soon as her words floated into the air, Alexandria knew that her grandma Allene's spirit had entered the room. Whenever she felt a warm breeze, a gentle, unexplainable tug at her arm, or smelled the unmistakably sweet scent of magnolias—which had just wafted by her nose—she knew it was her great-great-grandmother communicating with her.

Alexandria inhaled the fragrant, uniquely Southern scent that always made her feel safe and at ease. That sense of comfort and security was very different from the turmoil and strife she'd experienced in the past whenever she thought about her gift.

Communicating with spirits and having premonitions were abilities that had burdened Alexandria since she was five years old. She'd always felt different and out of place, constantly trying to navigate where she stood in a world filled with uncertainty. Her lack of grounding and understanding of her gift had made her afraid of the supernatural powers she possessed. But all that had changed last summer when Allene had contacted her for the first time.

Initially, Alexandria had been leery, and she hadn't wanted any part of the mysteriously frightening world that had been haunting her since she was five years old. Many times she could remember waking up in the middle of the night, drenched in sweat and covered with fear, terrified of the voices that belonged to spirits from another world that she couldn't see or touch.

She also recognized that the ability to know what was going to happen in a given situation before it took place wasn't always a good thing, and it had quickly become a heavy weight on her shoulders. She'd worried about things that kids her age didn't have to deal with. She'd witnessed accidents, death, and destruction, and it had made her fearful of doing something as normal as dreaming at night because of what she might see. She'd often stood helpless with her knowledge, not knowing what to do or in whom to confide, so she'd learned how to ignore her gift and block out visions whenever they threatened her peace of mind.

But once her grandma Allene had come into her life and shown her the beauty of her gift, along with the strength and infinite possibilities it held, a new world had opened up to her for the first time.

She'd been hoping that her grandma Allene would soon make contact with her again. She missed hearing the old woman's comforting voice and the soothing, down-home Southern accent it carried. Allene hadn't communicated with her in nearly three months, which had initially alarmed Alexandria. But then she remembered Allene's promise—that she'd always be there to guide and protect her. Alexandria knew she'd have to wait patiently and trust in Allene's words, which were solid and rooted in love.

The one thing that Alexandria longed for more than anything was to talk with Allene face-to-face, instead of speaking in whispered tones through visions that always seemed to end much too quickly. During one of their talks, Alexandria had asked Allene to appear to her in the flesh.

"Grandma Allene, I want to see you. Can you come visit me?" she'd asked.

"I'd really love to, baby girl," Allene whispered to her from a faraway place. "But that's a very difficult thing to do. I only know of one other spirit who's been able to travel from our world to yours, and that's my great-grandma, Susan Jessup. She came to me once, while I was living," Allene said with a smile in her voice that was mixed with sadness. "But after that one time I never saw her again until I passed on and joined her in the spirit world. Travelin' between worlds can be dangerous. Life and death is on two different sides, and once you cross over that's where you stay."

Allene explained that travel between the spirit world and the world of the living was no easy feat. Only a select handful of highly skilled individuals, all of whom had possessed the gift when they'd been alive, were able to exist between realms.

Although Allene was an apparition, and in her world she could float across a room, walk through walls, and defy space, she was limited in her abilities once she left the spirit realm and came to the time and place where Alexandria existed. She'd been ninety-eight years old when she'd passed away, and upon her return to the living world, her nearly century old bones would revert back to their fragile state, the same as when she'd taken her last breath. Gravity and the earth's other elements could work against her.

"I did come to see you one time," Allene had told her. "It was last year, shortly after I first made contact with you. I came to your mother's house and sat right in between you and her at the table in her big fancy kitchen."

"You did?" Alexandria said in shock.

"Yes, but I was only able to stay a short while. I wasn't

fully prepared for how much it would take outta me. But it was worth it 'cause I got to see two generations of my family. Bein' in the presence of you and your mama was a joy."

"But if you're a spirit why do you get tired?" Alexandria asked. "I thought you were impervious to physical ailments."

Allene shrugged and then nodded. "I used to think the same thing about spirits until I became one. God sets up everything 'xactly the way it's 'sposed to be. Can you imagine how much devilment spirits could cause if all of us could freely walk among the living, and do whatever we wanted without fear of harm, hurt, or danger to our bodies?"

"You've got a good point," Alexandria said in amazement.

"I'm one of few who can do it, and even though I only visited for a short spell I was overjoyed to see you and your mama."

"I can't believe you were sitting next to me. . . . I wonder why I didn't feel your presence."

" 'Cause I didn't want you to. I was there to observe."

"I didn't know you could cloak yourself like that."

"I could then, but I doubt I'd be able to do that now. Your abilities have gotten much stronger. I don't think I could hide from you if I tried."

"Grandma, I really wish it wasn't so hard for you to come visit me. I want to see you. I miss you."

"Aww, I want to visit with you, too. But it's difficult, baby girl, and I see why my great-grandmamma only came to visit me every once in a blue moon, and when she did, it was only in my dreams. Even though I'm in spirit form, I still have to use human energy to travel from my world to yours."

"I've been able to glimpse into your world through my visions, and sometimes I can see you just as plainly as if you were sitting next to me," Alexandria said with excitement. "Maybe if I concentrate hard enough I can come to where you are."

"No, baby girl," Allene said with caution. "You can look back into the past, and you can see things that's gonna happen in the future. But the only way you can step into my world is if you pass on."

Alexandria nodded as she listened to her grandmother's voice. Knowing what she was going to say next.

"Just like you and I both know," Allene said gently, "that won't happen for another seventy years. But don't worry. I'm gonna always be with you—even when you can't see or hear me, I'll be near. I'm gonna protect and guide you."

As Alexandria looked around the room and thought about the conversation she'd had with her grandma Allene, she came up with an idea. She set her magazine to the side, lay perfectly still on the sofa, closed her eyes, and concentrated. She took deep, calming breaths to ground herself in preparation for what she was about to do.

Slowly, an image formed before Alexandria's eyes that made her smile. She could see Allene sitting in an old rocking chair on the front porch of a large, beautiful home set against the backdrop of luscious flowers, shrubs, and tall trees. Rain was coming down by the bucketful, and she could see that Allene was enjoying the downpour as she looked up into the stormy sky.

Suddenly, Alexandria gasped when she realized that something very strange was happening. Usually, when she communicated with Allene, it was through whispered words held together by a time and place she couldn't touch—the spirit world. But now, it was different. Alexandria opened her eyes quickly and gasped again. "You're here," she said aloud. "Grandma Allene, you're here in my world."

"Yes, baby girl. I'm here," Allene whispered in a voice that sounded as strong and as clear as if she were sitting next to Alexandria on her sofa.

"But how? I thought making a trip here was too difficult."

"That's true, it's a challenge. But Susan helped me to focus, and with time, patience, and practice, I'm here. I had to come."

Alexandria swallowed hard, fighting to hold on to the vision of Allene that she could see when she closed her eyes. But it was no use because, slowly, everything started to fade to black. She could no longer see Allene, but she could hear her with perfect clarity. "How are you Grandma?"

"I'm just fine, and I feel real good."

"Oh, thank goodness. I want to see you. I miss you so much."

Allene sighed. "I know, and I miss you, too, baby girl. I can't come to you, but you can come to me."

"Where are you?"

"I'm where you and the rest of our family needs to be. I'm where it all began."

Alexandria took a minute to think, and then it came to her. "I know exactly where you are!" she said with excitement.

"Yes, and I want you to come here and bring the rest of our family with you, too."

"Why do you want me to bring our family?" Reservation was lodged in her throat as she waited for what she sensed was going to be an answer that would bring about more questions.

"Because . . . it's time to bury the past and start new beginnings."

"That sounds promising and complicated at the same time."

"I reckon it can be. But like I always say, you just gotta hold on and trust that everything's gonna work out like it's 'sposed to."

"So this means I'm going to finally get to see you?"

"Yes, baby girl."

Just as Alexandria was going to ask another question, Allene's voice drifted away as quickly as it had come. She was gone.

Alexandria wasn't ready to let any part of Allene go, so she fought to hang on to the magnolia scent that was starting to fade. Even though she was disappointed that her conversation with Allene had been so brief, she felt good knowing that her grandma was in her world, and that they'd finally be able to share the same time and space.

"I'm looking forward to seeing you very soon, Grandma Allene." Alexandria smiled, feeling that besides her upcoming wedding, seeing Allene was going to be the highlight of her year. But as she blinked and opened her eyes, her joy quickly turned to worry. She sat up straight and brought her hand to her mouth as she thought about what Allene had said. *I had to come.*

In that instant, Alexandria knew that her grandma Allene's visit wasn't going to be the joyful reunion she'd fantasized about.

Chapter 3
Victoria

"How can two small words cause so much trouble?" Victoria whispered aloud as she stared at the name flashing across her cell phone screen. Her body stiffened against the soft fabric of her high-back office chair while she bit down on her ruby-colored lower lip; a nervous habit she'd developed when she was a teenager. The name PARKER BRIGHTWOOD flashed at her like a warning light, and she knew that a call from him was something for which she needed to brace herself.

She sat forward, propped one elbow on top of her large mahogany desk, and debated whether she should answer his call or let it roll into her voice mailbox. She knew she'd have to talk to him sooner or later, so rather than avoid and ignore him—a costly mistake she'd made in the past—she hit the talk button.

"Hello, Parker."

"Are you okay?"

"Yes, I'm fine. Why do you ask?"

"Because you sound so formal. Not like your usual self."

She wanted to ask him how he could possibly know what she usually sounded like. After all, it wasn't as if they talked on a regular basis. Those days had ended many years ago. But she also knew that as much as her life and circumstances had changed in that long span of time, a few delicate, if not complicated, things hadn't, and Parker was one of them.

"You sure you're okay?" he repeated.

"I'm sure. Now how can I help you?"

He chuckled. "There you go again, talking to me like a greeter in a department store."

"I have to keep things on a business level with you."

"Oh, and why is that?"

She took a deep breath. "Because you don't know how to act."

"Well, since you're the consummate purveyor of proper etiquette, maybe you can give me a few lessons. I'm a very good student and I catch on pretty quick, but you already know that, don't you?"

She smiled on the other end, despite not wanting to.

They were both quiet for a short pause. Victoria could hear him breathing through the silence on the other end, and she imagined the sly grin that was no doubt spread across his lusciously soft lips, which carried a perfect tint of pink. She was almost pulled in for a moment, but she quickly regained her focus. "I don't have all day, Parker. What do you want?"

"Victoria, I think you're losing that gracious Southern charm that always made you so lovable, and I might add, irresistible."

"Get to the point or I'm hanging up."

"Okay, okay. I want to know if I can add two more guests to the list for the reception?"

Victoria reached for her silver-plated pen and softly tapped it against the top of her desk as she let out a small sigh. She knew that Parker's question was nothing more than an excuse to talk to her. When he'd called last month asking her the very same thing, she'd told him then that according to the guest list which she'd spent hours meticulously creating, all in preparation for the final headcount for his son's and her daughter's wedding next month, there was room for up to five additional guests.

Ever since that bright, sunny afternoon one year ago when her daughter, Alexandria, had happily told her that she'd reconnected with PJ, her childhood best friend, who happened to be Dr. Parker Brightwood Sr.'s son, Victoria had known that trouble was waiting to find her.

A storm cloud of memories had rushed back into her life that day, but unlike her encounters with Parker from the past, she now knew she'd have to handle him, and their dealings, in a very different way.

Rather than rehashing the fact that she'd already answered his question last month, and pointing out that his phone call was basically a ruse to engage her in conversation, she simply went along with the flow. "Yes, Parker, that's fine. You can bring two more people. Anything else?"

He chuckled again, this time in a slow, seductive tone. "Damn, that was easy. If I'd known you were going to be so accommodating I would've asked for more . . . much more."

His smooth, deep, and sexy voice hadn't changed over the years. And even though his words were laced with dangerous innuendo, coming from his mouth, they sounded as good and as sweet as apple pie. Silky seduction was part of his undeniable charm, and it had worked on her more times than she cared to remember. Victoria knew she couldn't be drawn in by his sexiness or the natural chemistry they'd always shared. She had to use her head and shut things down before they had an inkling of a chance to get started.

"I know exactly what you're hinting at, Parker. And I'm not having it. We're too old to play these ridiculous cat-and-mouse games."

"Who's old, and who's playing games?"

Victoria pressed her hand against her left temple. "Bring whomever you want. Just make sure you all show up on time."

"Are you upset?"

"No, I'm irritated."

"Have you been having a rough day?"

"Not until you called me with this foolishness." Now she couldn't hold back any longer. "You knew full well when you dialed my number that you could invite more guests because we discussed this last month when we talked. You didn't have to call me today."

Parker cleared his throat. "Victoria, I have a hectic schedule and a very busy practice at two hospitals. Sometimes it's hard to keep everything straight. I know we've talked about this before, but I honestly wasn't sure if I'd reached the headcount you gave me, so I wanted to check with you before extending an invitation to two of my colleagues."

"Uh-huh, right . . ."

"It's true."

"Sure, Parker. Whatever you say."

"Listen, I'm being straight with you. I have no reason at all to lie. You know I don't play games."

"Sure, you don't."

"Damn, I don't remember you being this cold."

"Put on a jacket and get used to it."

Parker laughed, then lowered his voice. "You're really something else."

"Are you finished?"

"No, I have one more question."

Victoria sighed, not sure she wanted to hear what he had to say, much less answer to it. "Go ahead."

"I want to know what's wrong with me calling you? We're going to be in-laws . . . family, in a manner of speaking. A phone call is much more personal than an email. I can get personal with you, can't I?"

Victoria squirmed in her chair. "Get personal? What's that supposed to mean?"

"Anything you want it to."

"Parker, I don't have time for this. Like I said, bring whomever the hell you want to bring, and as I told you at the beginning of this conversation, don't call me again with any more foolishness."

Parker's deep voice took on an even deeper tone. "Our children's wedding day isn't foolishness."

"You know what I meant."

"I know what you just said."

Victoria stood up and walked over to her office window, pacing back and forth in her black patent leather peep-toe heels. "Of course the wedding isn't foolishness. It's going to be the single biggest day of Alexandria's and PJ's lives, and I know without a doubt that it will be the start of a happy future for them both. What I'm talking about is the way you're always dropping hints and alluding to things . . ."

"Alluding?" Parker interrupted her in a surprised voice. "Victoria, we go way back, and you know me. I don't allude, I take action. I might flirt, but I don't drop hints. I'm direct and I say what I mean."

"Then why are you calling me during the middle of the day with this?"

"I thought I already explained that."

Victoria took a deep breath, continuing to pace back and forth.

"I hear you taking those deep breaths," Parker said. "Just calm down and stop pacing back and forth in front of your window. Relax."

Victoria stopped in her tracks. He knew her too well, even after all these years. She walked back to her desk and sat down. "You're right. We're going to be in-laws soon. We'll be seeing each other at the holidays and other occasions as the years go on, so I want to get something straight right now."

"Okay, I'm listening."

"I'm happily married. Our children are getting ready to be happily married. And from what I hear, hopefully you will be happily married, too. So please stop this flirting or whatever you want to call it. This isn't right and it needs to end with this call."

Parker cleared his throat and let out a small laugh. "That's really interesting. I don't know who you've been talking to, but I can assure you that marriage isn't on the table for me. However, I couldn't agree with you more about PJ and Alexandria, and I wish them nothing but the very best. I love Alexandria like the daughter I never had, and I have no doubt that she and my son will enjoy many years of happiness."

Victoria wasn't about to tell him that PJ had been the source of her information, or that he wasn't a fan of his father's significant other, and now she regretted making the comment. "I'm happy to hear that, Parker, and I'm glad we understand each other."

"I think we always have."

"Okay, well, you take care and I'll see you at the wedding."

She didn't give him a chance to respond. She hit the

end button and leaned back against her chair as she let out a deep breath. She thought about the wise saying that Alexandria had told her grandma Allene had whispered to her one evening. *You can never go wrong doing right.* Victoria knew that Parker was anything but right, and if she wasn't careful with him, she could find herself going in the wrong direction.

Parker had broken her heart in what seemed like another lifetime, and the poor choices she'd made with him years later had nearly cost her the happy marriage she'd talked about moments ago.

"This time I'm going to do the right thing. I'm not going to make the same mistake a third time."

But even as Victoria spoke those words, a small voice told her to hold on tight for the bumpy road ahead.

Chapter 4
Alexandria

Even though the end of Alexandria's conversation with her grandma Allene had left her knowing there was some sort of trouble looming on the horizon, she felt overjoyed to have been able to connect with the wise old spirit. She was especially excited about the prospect of actually having face time with Allene, which she knew was a rare and special privilege. She was drawn from her hopeful thoughts when she heard keys rattle in the doorknob.

"Hey, baby," PJ said as he walked through the front door.

If there was one thing that was guaranteed to make Alexandria feel happy and peaceful all at once, it was seeing the big smile on her fiancé's face when he greeted her at the end of a long day. Dr. Parker Brightwood II, or PJ, as everyone had called him since he was a baby, made her feel as if she were looking at sunshine and rainbows whenever he stepped into a room.

No matter what challenges she faced or mountain-high obstacles that sometimes presented themselves, PJ's loving presence could melt them all away. Not only did he have a smile that could make toothpaste envious, his smooth, baby-soft skin, curly black hair, deep brown eyes, subtle dimples, and muscular frame made her feel the heat of his passion, especially in the bedroom.

But the thing that endeared him to her most wasn't his extraordinary good looks, or his incredible lovemaking skills that always pleased her. What had captured her attention, drawn her in, and made her want to be his wife were his gentle spirit and compassionate heart. He was a good man and one of the most sincere human beings she knew. From the first moment they'd reconnected last year, she'd known he was the one.

He could wow her with his intellectual prowess just as easily as he could make her laugh at his silly jokes. He was the type of man who could thoroughly enjoy a lazy afternoon lying around the house, then switch it up by dressing in his dapper best to hit the town by nightfall. She also liked that he was a man's man—rugged, responsible, hardworking, loyal, and honest. He made Alexandria feel loved, safe, and protected, not just by the words he spoke, but by the proof in his everyday actions.

Alexandria set her wedding magazine on the coffee table and smiled back at him. "Hey, honey, how was your day?"

"Busy, but very, very good. How about yours?"

She paused and accepted PJ's soft kiss on her lips as he bent over the sofa. "My day was pretty routine until I heard from Grandma Allene. She contacted me this afternoon."

"Really?" A mixture of excitement and caution coated PJ's voice. "It's been a while. Is everything okay?"

Alexandria knew that the concern in his voice was justified because whenever Allene contacted her it was usually to warn or advise her of some sort of impending trouble. And because it had been a few months since Alexandria had heard from Allene, there was a good probability that something bad was about to happen.

"I'm not sure what's going on," Alexandria responded, "but Grandma Allene's going to help me through whatever is ahead, which I think must be pretty big because she's here . . . in our world."

"Ali, what do you mean, she's here in our world?"

"You know how I usually talk to her through whispers when she contacts me, or when I'm able to reach back and see her in another place and time? Well, when I saw her today it wasn't in a different realm, it was in the here and now. When I asked her where was she, she said she was where it all began, and that means she's in Nedine."

PJ shook his head from side to side in disbelief. "She's in South Carolina?"

"Yep. At the house my great-grandfather built, our family homestead."

PJ stared at Alexandria in amazement. "Even though I've witnessed you say and do some pretty incredible things, I'm still blown away by all this. Ali, it's so mind-boggling."

"I know. Sometimes I feel as shocked and bewildered by it as you do."

PJ sat down beside her on the sofa. "Why's she in Nedine? Why didn't she come to you here in Atlanta?"

"She said that Nedine is where everything started, and she wants us to come there because, and I quote, 'It's time to bury the past and start new beginnings'."

PJ tilted his head in confusion. "I don't understand. What does she think you and I need to bury from the past?"

"I think the *we* she's talking about is my family." Alexandria closed her eyes for a moment, concentrated, and then smiled with the knowledge that she was right. "Yes, she was definitely talking about my family. That's why she wants me to bring them with me when I go there."

"When does she want you to come?"

Alexandria closed her eyes again and took a deep breath, seeming to almost meditate. "Soon. Like, in two weeks . . . yes, definitely in two weeks."

"You do realize our wedding is only four weeks away?"

"Yes, honey, I know. But I'll still have time for a quick weekend trip to South Carolina before our big day."

PJ leaned in and held Alexandria's hand. "Okay. If this is what Grandma Allene wants us to do, I'm all in."

"You mean you'll go with me?"

"Of course." PJ gave her a soft smile. "We're a team. You're going to be my wife and that means supporting you in whatever you do. Just say the word."

Alexandria returned his soft smile with a big one of her own. "This is why I love you so, and sometimes I feel like I need to pinch myself to make sure I'm not dreaming."

"Pinching hurts—how about a kiss? It's much softer and more fun." He leaned into her and delivered a gentle kiss to her lips.

"That's nice." Alexandria felt warm and fuzzy. But her tingly feeling didn't last long because in a flash she thought about her family. "Somehow I'm going to have to convince my mom and dad to come. And Christian will definitely need to come along, too," she said, referring to her younger brother who'd just graduated from Morehouse College a few months ago and was now living in New York, about to enter Columbia's business school.

"You mean we'll have to spend the weekend with your brother?"

Alexandria fully expected that reaction from PJ because she knew how her brother could be. Despite his upper-class background and fine education, Christian had a reputation for being a bad boy. He loved to party and have wild fun with even wilder women. But what pushed him into the limits of danger, and why PJ treated him with cool reserve, was the fact that Christian had begun to dabble in two things that were sure to lead to trouble—gambling and drugs.

"I know you don't care that much for Christian, but he's family and he's going through a rough time right now. Maybe this trip will be good for him."

"I hope so."

Alexandria let out a sigh. "I know he can be a bit much to deal with, but he's growing and he's still trying to find himself."

"Ali, he's a grown-ass man and he knows exactly who he is and what he's doing. You know I don't judge, but given what he's into, I'm very uncomfortable spending any length of time with him."

"I understand, and at times I feel the same way. When I spoke with him last week I told him that he needed to get his life in order. He's entering grad school and if he's not careful he'll ruin his future behind the mess he's doing."

PJ shook his head. "I've seen so many brothers with promising futures get caught up in that world. Drugs are dangerous, period, and I hope your brother realizes that before it's too late."

"So do I."

"Your parents have been very patient with him. They're good people."

Alexandria nodded. "I'm really blessed to have a good family, and I'm so glad you get along with them."

"Me too. They've welcomed me with open arms,

even the ones I don't know very well, like your Uncle Maxx," PJ offered. "Didn't he grow up in Nedine with your grandfather?"

"He sure did." Alexandria loved her uncle Maxx. He was her dearly departed nana Elizabeth's brother and her grandpa John's best friend. He was in his late nineties, and though age had slowed him down from the wild lifestyle he'd led up into his eighties, his mind was still sharp and he still got around fairly well on his own. His days were now spent taking short walks in the park with his great-grandchildren in Dunwoody, a picturesque suburb situated outside the Atlanta city limits where he lived with his grandson.

"Do you think Uncle Maxx should come, too?"

"Yes, I do." Alexandria smiled. "Although he's related by marriage, he's still family, and Nedine is his home. I just hope he's up to making the trip. When Mom and I visited him a few weeks ago, he seemed to be slowing down."

PJ nodded. "Uncle Maxx is a true character. He's done so much and had so many experiences, I guess it's finally time for him to take it easy. I'm sure if he's up to it he'll come."

"You're right. I'll call my mom tomorrow to get the ball rolling so we can set some plans into motion."

"This is a lot to process, especially on an empty stomach," PJ said as he took a deep breath and inhaled the aroma of food. "Can we talk about this over dinner?"

"You hungry?"

"Starving. And something smells good, too."

Alexandria loved that PJ enjoyed her cooking. "I made shrimp scampi, roasted new potatoes, and steamed asparagus."

"You worked all day at the office and then came home and made dinner?"

"Well, I have to admit, I left a little early. I wanted us to enjoy a hot meal together."

"What did I do to deserve you?"

Alexandria smiled. "Apparently something really, really good."

"I know that's right. I hit the jackpot."

"I can't believe you still have an appetite after everything I just told you."

"A man's gotta eat. Besides, you can't fight the devil on an empty stomach."

Alexandria dropped her playful smile and sat stock-still. Her hands trembled slightly as her eyes blinked quickly. "What did you just say?"

"Oh, that's something I heard one of the nurses at the hospital say this morning. Her name is Ms. Brown. She's an older lady and she has all these unique sayings. I thought it was interesting and kinda true. Not that your family is the devil or anything."

Alexandria looked at him with wonder. "That's one of my grandma Allene's sayings. I've heard her repeat those very words in visions."

"Get outta here. . . . Do you think it means something?"

Alexandria didn't want to alarm PJ, but she also didn't want to hide the truth from him. "Yes, I think it does. Grandma Allene always says that coincidence is God's way of remaining anonymous. Nothing happens by chance, everything is part of a plan. The fact that she contacted me today and the nurse at the hospital repeated one of her sayings . . ."

"Do you think Ms. Brown has the gift or something?"

"I'm not sure, but I believe her saying that in front of you was intentional. You were meant to hear that so you could repeat it to me." Alexandria took a cleansing breath to calm herself. She didn't want PJ to think something bad was about to happen, because she honestly didn't know what all this meant. Things were happening so fast.

But the one thing Alexandria was certain of was that her grandma Allene was going to help her find the answers to her questions. In the meantime, she had to figure out a way to get her family down to Nedine in two weeks, and in the present, she needed to arrest PJ's worries. "I'll get to the bottom of this later. Like you said, you've gotta eat, and I have some food in the kitchen to feed you."

PJ smiled. "I like the sound of that. Feed me, baby!"

Alexandria put on a smile. "Right this way." She took PJ by the hand and led him to the kitchen, all the while saying a soft prayer of protection for her family.

Chapter 5
Victoria

It had been over an hour since Victoria hung up the phone, and no matter how hard she tried to concentrate on the work in front of her, she was still thinking about her conversation with Parker. "That man really knows how to push my buttons," she said in a huff.

He was her old lover, and once upon a time he'd been her dream come true. He was the man she'd fantasized about spending her life with. He was a part of her youth that had been both bitter and sweet, exhilarating and frustrating. And ultimately, their relationship had ended on a sour note, leaving her hurt, and both of them damaged in ways that still lingered today.

"Why can't the past stay back there where it belongs?" Victoria whispered to herself. She picked up a sheet of paper off her desk, leaned back in her chair, and started fanning her face. She didn't know if the hot flash had been brought on because of menopause, or if the very thought of being entangled with Parker again was making her feel intense heat. Either way, she didn't have time to go through more changes in her life, especially if they involved complications.

She wiped her glistening forehead with a Kleenex. "I've gotta get myself together." She reached down, opened her desk drawer, and removed her compact from inside her cosmetics bag. "I know I probably look like a hot mess," she said to herself as she peered at her face in the small mirror. She powdered her nose and made an appraisal of her looks, and she had to admit she liked what she saw.

For a woman in her early sixties, Victoria knew she looked damn good. She'd always been tall, slender, and shapely, and now as she was cruising into her senior years she'd still managed to hold on to her figure, evidenced by heads that still turned when she entered a room. She looked closely in the mirror, examining the small lines at her eyes that were barely visible, and she ran her fingers across her supple skin, which still glowed thanks to her dedicated skincare regimen and the good fortune of being blessed with extraordinary genes.

Satisfied that she looked presentable enough for her meeting in one hour, she put away her compact, tucked a few loose strands of her silky chin-length bob behind her ear, and took a deep breath. She felt like her old self until her mind fell back on Parker again. "Damn it!" she hissed. "I can't let him do this to me again, especially with the troubles I already have at home."

She shook her head as she thought about the way her life had been two decades ago. She had loved Parker deeply, but he'd cheated on her, breaking her trust along with her heart. Once they had gone their separate ways, she'd married, but he hadn't. Years later, they had been reunited when their kindergarten-age children had ended up in the same Jack and Jill chapter, as well as the same classroom at a prestigious private elementary school. And that was when the real trouble had begun.

From the moment Victoria and Parker had seen each other, it had been impossible for either of them to deny the intense chemistry and unfinished business that still lingered, like an itch they couldn't scratch. A casual smile had turned into a lunch, which had led to a late-night visit to her office, and before Victoria had known what was happening, she'd almost slept with Parker one weekend while her husband, Ted, had been out of town on business.

She was pulled away from her troubling thoughts by the buzzing of her phone, alerting her that a text message was coming through. She bit down on her bottom lip when she saw that it was from Parker.

Parker Brightwood: I hope your day gets better. See you next week.

Victoria let out a deep, frustrated breath. "The wedding isn't until next month. Why is he coming to town next week?" she wondered aloud. "Maybe he meant to say next month but just got things mixed up." But she knew he didn't. Parker was a methodical man, steeped in the precision of details down to the tiniest degree. His work as a heart surgeon and his personality as a highly competitive, driven man, had made him that way. As he'd told her during their conversation, everything he said or did was intentional, so she knew he meant exactly what he'd typed in his text message.

"He can come to town all he wants, but he won't be seeing me," Victoria said as she quickly typed a reply."

VST: No need to see me unless it's wedding-related.

She waited for her phone to vibrate and sure enough a minute later Parker had sent another text.

Parker Brightwood: It is. Will be in town for business. And want to go over cost of rehearsal dinner.

VST: Text or call your question.

Parker Brightwood: This requires face to face. Heading to a meeting. Will message you later.

Victoria stared at Parker's response and shook her head. "Damn it. He can never leave well enough alone, and I can already see that he's going to cause trouble."

This would make Parker's fifth visit to Atlanta over the last six months, and his frequent trips were starting to fill Victoria with worry. He'd moved back to his hometown of Washington, D.C., over twenty years ago, and although PJ had returned to Atlanta to complete his pediatric residency at Emory University Medical School, according to what Alexandria had told Victoria, Parker rarely came back to the Peach State for visits. "PJ usually goes to D.C. to visit his dad, especially since all their family is there," she'd said, "but Mr. Brightwood sure has made a point to come here more often since PJ and I became engaged."

Victoria remembered the suspicion in Alexandria's voice when she had mentioned Parker's visits last month. It was no secret that Alexandria, as well as PJ, was well aware of their parents' complicated past. But Victoria wasn't about to offer up any commentary on the subject.

Victoria didn't like the fact that ever since Alexandria and PJ had started seeing each other, Parker had been adding to his frequent-flyer miles traveling back and forth to Atlanta. And now that the happy couple's pending nuptials were drawing near, it seemed as though he was making it his business to show his face as often as he could. Victoria wondered if Parker had plans to move back to the area. "Lord, I hope not," she said to herself as she thought about the prospect. "God, I know you have a lot more pressing issues to deal with than mine, but please, please hear me and keep Parker in D.C. where he belongs."

As Victoria thought about her past, her mind drifted to Ted. She reached over to the edge of her desk and picked up the pewter frame that held a photo of him and her when they'd celebrated their twenty-fifth wedding anniversary a few years ago. Aside from giving birth to her children, Victoria knew that marrying Theodore Thornton was undoubtedly the single best thing she'd ever done, and with the exception of her late father, John Small, he was the best man she'd ever known.

Just as she was about to call Ted, her cell phone rang again. She looked at the caller ID, shook her head, and chuckled. "Hey, Samantha. How are you?" Victoria greeted with a smile in her voice.

Samantha Baldwin Jacobs was the wife of Victoria's best friend, Tyler Jacobs, and in the seventeen years that she and Tyler had been married, Samantha had also become one of Victoria's closest and most trusted girlfriends.

Samantha had once been a hellcat who'd gone through men as if they were disposable products for her personal use. She had possessed a rebellious streak that landed her in drama-filled, and sometimes dangerous, situations. She had partied nearly every night of the week, regardless of the fact that she'd had a young son whom she'd let her best friend and her parents raise for the first five years of his life. Simply put, she'd been out of control. But all that had stopped when she'd fallen in love with Tyler. He'd shown her what true love was, and helped her grow and mature into the responsible mother, wife, businesswoman, and friend she was today.

"Hey, girl, how's it going?" Samantha asked.

"My day was swimming right along until your cousin called me with some nonsense."

"Oh, Lord. What's Parker up to now?"

Victoria paused for a moment, knowing she had to

carefully measure her words. Although she and Samantha were the best of friends, and talked freely about any and everything, no matter how delicate the subject, Parker was Samantha's first cousin—her favorite cousin to be exact—and Samantha valued and protected her family like a pit bull. Over the years, Samantha and Tyler hadn't seen eye to eye when it came to Parker either. Tyler had never liked the man, and after Parker had cheated on Victoria and broken her heart, Tyler officially had no use for him.

Victoria struggled with the fact that Parker was entwined in her life in more ways than she cared to acknowledge. Over the years, she'd managed to keep her memory of him at bay by never discussing him with Samantha or Tyler. She'd made it clear that her ex-lover and his life's happenings were none of her concern, and ushering him into her life in any way would serve no one. Just because he was a part of Samantha's life, that didn't mean he had to enter her world.

But the minute that PJ and Alexandria had fallen in love, Parker had been back on the scene in Victoria's life, front and center. And not only was he in her life again, he was about to become part of her family.

Victoria leaned back in her chair, carefully choosing the words she was going to say. "He wanted to know if it was okay to invite more guests to the wedding reception."

"What's wrong with that?" Samantha asked. "At least he's trying to be considerate. Hell, some people just show up and don't give a shit about inconveniencing anybody."

Victoria shook her head. Samantha had changed in many ways, but the one trait she couldn't break was her predilection for cursing. She could put a Hells Angel to shame and not think a thing of it. "True. But here's the thing. . . . He already knew he could invite more people because I told him so when Alexandria, PJ, and I talked with him about the guest list on a conference call last month."

"Oh. Well, maybe he just forgot. You know how busy he is, juggling his practice and all the activities he's involved in with the D.C. social scene."

Did they rehearse that line? Victoria wondered. "Samantha, I know you love your cousin, but sometimes . . ."

"Girl, I know how Parker is, and I know he probably called just to talk to you because he still has a thing for you after all these years."

"I just think he likes to irritate me."

"Uh, Victoria, who do you think you're talking to?"

"What do you mean?"

"You don't have to play coy and pretend with me. I know the deal, and I know that Parker still has a 'lil somethin'-somethin' on his mind when it comes to you."

Victoria didn't want to lie and say he didn't, but she also didn't want to cosign what Samantha had just said. She sat quiet on her end and continued to listen.

"Girl, I'm just gonna tell you the truth. I confronted Parker about his feelings for you right after PJ and Alexandria got engaged, because I knew it was gonna be trouble. When I told him outright that I suspected he still had feelings for you and that he needed to let it go, he didn't deny it," Samantha said, making a *tsk*ing sound as she spoke. "It's just straight-up sad because he's way too old for this shit, carrying a torch and what not. But it is what it is."

Samantha had just created silence on the line.

"Hello? Victoria, are you still there?"

"Yes, I'm here. I'm just taking a moment to process what you said."

"I know you're not going to admit it, but you can't deny that what I just said isn't true. Now the question is, how do you really feel about him, and how are you going to handle him being an extended member of your family?"

Victoria had often thought about Parker over the years. But her trips down memory lane nearly always ended with an uncomfortable feeling and no real closure. Now, her daughter and his son were going to be husband and wife, making him her in-law. It was a thought that often left her feeling as though a rock were lodged in the pit of her stomach, especially given the fact that her husband couldn't stand Parker. Ted had made it clear that he'd be civil toward the man for Alexandria's and PJ's sake, but because of their past he would never trust Parker, and he certainly wasn't welcome in their home.

Victoria crossed her legs and fiddled with her note-pad. "Parker and I have a history that can't be denied. But that's all it is as far as I'm concerned. Period. I'll treat him the way I do any other person I know, with as much courtesy as I can, as long as it's extended to me in return. Nothing more and nothing less."

"That sounds like a prepared statement."

"Like you said, it is what it is."

"All right. I guess that's your story and you're sticking to it."

Victoria was starting to grow weary. "I'm sorry I mentioned his name. Can we move on to something more interesting and less annoying than the topic of your cousin?"

Samantha laughed. "Fine with me. I was getting tired of hearing your denial anyway," she said with a sigh. "Besides, I have a question to ask you."

"I'm going to ignore that smart remark. Sure, ask away."

"Can you make me a chocolate cocoa cake? I've had a rough week and I sure as hell could use a pick-me-up.

There's nothing in the world like your chocolate cocoa cake with a cold glass of milk."

"Sure, but I have plans tonight. I can bake it tomorrow and bring it over if you like."

"Not only are you a great friend and a beautiful, accomplished, and fantastic woman, you're a saint!"

"Now you're putting it on way too thick," Victoria said with a laugh. "What's going on, Samantha? You're obviously stressed. Is it work?"

"Puh-leez! You know I don't even let Lancôme stress me like that."

She had to agree that what Samantha had just said was true, and it was one of the many qualities Victoria admired about her. Samantha had been employed with Lancôme for over twenty years, and was now a regional vice president of sales. She worked hard and she'd built solid relationships with customers that had ensured her longevity and steady climb within the company. But for as long as Victoria had known Samantha, work had never been one of her top priorities because that slot was reserved for her family and friends.

"I can handle work with my eyes closed and my hands tied behind my back," Samantha said, letting out a heavy breath. "It's that son of mine that has me about to eat a bottle of Valium. He's got all these fast-ass girls blowin' up his cell phone day and night. The little heffas even call the house looking for him. And now, this latest mess he's gotten himself into . . . I tell you, I'm at the end of my damn rope."

"Samantha, I don't want to assume anything, because you do have two sons, so which one are you talking about?"

"Good point. Girl, it's Chase. That boy is about to make me lose my religion."

Victoria wasn't surprised. CJ, short for Carl Junior,

was Samantha's oldest son, and the model of what a young man should be. Even though his biological father was an unscrupulous drug dealer who'd been in prison for most of CJ's life, he was the exact opposite of the man whose DNA he shared. CJ was responsible, dependable, trustworthy, and kind. He'd graduated with honors from Howard University and was about to enter Georgetown Law School this fall. He'd never given Samantha or Tyler a moment's trouble beyond normal teenage growing pains. But Chase, her younger son . . . he was a different story.

"If I didn't know any better, I'd swear that that crazy, sorry-ass Carl Jackson was Chase's father instead of Tyler."

"Samantha, you should be ashamed of yourself for saying that."

"Why? Hell, it's true and you know it."

Victoria chose to remain silent on that comment. "Okay, so tell me what's going on? What did he do now?"

"I'm surprised Tyler hasn't already told you. But then again, he's so mad he can't see straight. And you know it takes a lot to get your best friend upset. He even left the house this morning without making a cup of coffee."

Victoria stopped fiddling with her notepad when she heard the strain in Samantha's voice as she spoke about Tyler. Victoria had seen a missed call from Tyler earlier that morning. She'd been in a meeting when his number had flashed across her cell, so she'd let it go to voice mail. She'd planned to call him later today. "Samantha, tell me what's wrong."

"Are you sitting down?"

"Yes, and you're scaring me. What in the world has happened?"

"Chase got a girl pregnant."

"What?" Victoria shook her head.

"I know, girl." Samantha let out a deep breath filled with frustration. "Tyler's appetite is gone and my skinny ass is eating everything in sight. I feel like I'm the one having a baby."

"Oh, Lord."

"I don't know if the Lord has anything to do with this situation goin' on right here."

Victoria sucked in a deep breath. "Is it Heather?"

"Who?"

"I thought that was Chase's girlfriend's name."

"See, that's a damn shame. The boy has so many little hoochie mama wannabe girlfriends that no one can keep them straight. Not even me."

"Wow."

"This lovely young woman's name is LaMonica."

Victoria bit down on her lip. "I've never heard you or Tyler mention her."

Samantha huffed in frustration. "That's because I was hoping she'd go the hell away."

"You don't like her?"

"Sad thing is, I've never met her. I've only heard him talk about this girl. She doesn't even live in Atlanta. This little heffa is all the way up in D.C."

Victoria's eyes bucked wide. "As in the nation's capital?"

"You got it."

"How in the world . . . ?"

"It's such a long story that I don't know where to begin. And to be honest, I'm still unclear about all the details of how they hooked up in the first place."

"Okay, well, do you know how far along she is?"

"Chase just dropped this bomb on us last night, and apparently the girl is four-months pregnant. I know that my son is irresponsible and that he's made some pretty stupid mistakes, just like a lot of sixteen-year-olds do.

Hell, just like I did. I guess this is my payback for the messed-up shit I put my parents through when I was growing up."

"This isn't payback for anything. Children are a blessing, no matter how they come into this world, and if you're going to be a grandmother, you better change your thoughts about it right now."

"Grandmother!" Samantha screamed. "Damn it! I'm not ready to be anybody's freakin' grandmother, and I'm not gonna be raising anybody's little crumb snatcher either. "

"Samantha, stop yelling and calm down."

"I can't, I'm too upset!"

"Well, you're gonna have to do something because you can't get all worked up like this."

"That's easy for you to say. Neither one of your kids ever gave you a teenage-pregnancy scare."

"No, but I had my share of challenges raising Alexandria and Christian and there were a few times I almost lost it. No parent goes through the process unscathed," Victoria said. "But right now, for Chase's sake, you have to get your emotions in check. You have to move forward and decide what you're going to do as a family now that he's going to be a teenage father."

A few moments of silence hung in the air before Samantha spoke again. "You're right. I'm just so angry and I feel like this is all my fault. Maybe I should've been stricter on him and been more watchful over what he's been doing."

Victoria couldn't remember ever hearing the type of emotion that was choked in Samantha's words. Sure, she cursed like a gangster and she had a temper—which could flare up if one attempted to mess with her family—but rarely did she let things affect her to the point of hurt feelings. She was tough like steel and rough like sandpaper.

But Victoria knew that even the hardest badasses had a soft spot when it came to their children.

"This isn't your fault, Samantha. Chase is a child, but he's also old enough to know what's right and what's not. You and Tyler have worked hard to instill solid values in him, just like you did with CJ. Each child is different, I can tell you that from raising my two. Alexandria and Christian are worlds apart."

Samantha exhaled loudly in agreement. "You can say that again."

"Exactly! So don't feel like you've done anything wrong. Just pray that from this point forward you all can work together to make this situation right."

"There ain't nothing right about two teenagers having a baby."

Victoria knew that in Samantha's current state of mind, nothing she said was going to calm her friend, so she decided on a different approach. "I'm sorry about all this, but I know you guys will get through it. I'm going to make you that chocolate cocoa cake you want and bring it over tomorrow night so we can talk. Okay?"

"Okay, girl. Thanks. I really appreciate you."

"No problem. I'll see you tomorrow."

Just when Victoria thought her worries were complicated, she got a reminder that everyone was going through something. If Samantha was this hurt and upset, she could only imagine how Tyler must be feeling.

Victoria knew she needed to call her best friend and talk to him, and maybe even take him out for a drink. But right now she had to put her priorities in order, which meant heading off trouble before it started. She knew she had to clear the air with her husband about the subject that always caused tension between them: Parker Brightwood. Whenever his name came up, Ted would become noticeably irritated and distant.

Victoria quickly sent Tyler a text message letting him know she'd meet him for coffee the next morning so they could talk. "I'm going to pray hard for them," she whispered. She logged off her computer, reached for her handbag, and headed down the hallway.

She sent a text to Denise, who was her longtime friend and loyal office manager, and asked her to conduct their afternoon meeting without her because she wouldn't be back in the office today. She walked with purpose as she slipped out the back door and headed to her car, which was parked in the lot adjacent to her building.

"Out of all the men in this big wide world, why in the hell did my daughter have to fall in love with Parker's son?" Victoria mumbled as she sat behind the wheel of her silver Mercedes Benz and started the engine.

She knew what she had to do, so she stepped on the gas and headed home. She planned to cook Ted's favorite meal, make sure he was nice and relaxed, and then have a serious heart-to-heart about the two things that had been weighing down their marriage for the last six months—Parker Brightwood, and the fact that her and Ted's sex life had slowed to a snail's crawl.

Chapter 6
Samantha

Samantha parked her car in the garage and turned off the engine. She sat for a few moments enjoying the silence of being alone. She wanted nothing more than to have the house all to herself tonight, but that was truly wishful thinking. Tyler was out conducting a crime prevention forum across town with his non-profit organization, Youths First Initiative, and would be home in a few hours, but she was sure that Chase was in his bedroom with the door closed, blasting hip-hop music at an annoying decibel.

Reluctantly, she got out of her car and entered her house. She placed her keys on the brushed nickel hook beside the door, and listened for the deafening beats she'd have to tell her son to turn off because there would be no music, TV, or phone calls for him for the rest of the week. But when, after a few minutes, she didn't hear any noise, she became suspicious.

Samantha walked out of the kitchen and over to the

edge of the stairs. "Chase, are you up there?" she called out. When she didn't get an answer, she went up to his room, turned the knob, and walked inside. His bed was made, the room was quiet, and there was no sign of activity. "Where is he?"

She immediately became worried and started to panic, picturing Chase out doing any number of things that made her heart beat fast with anxiety. "Let me call that boy and see where he is," Samantha said as she walked back down to the kitchen and dialed her son's cell phone.

A deep, husky voice, much too manly for a sixteen-year-old greeted her. "Sup?"

Samantha pursed her lips. "Excuse me? What kind of way is that to answer your phone?"

"Oh, sorry, Mom. My bad. What's up?"

"Where are you?"

"I'm at Brad's, remember?"

"And why are you there?"

"I told you last week that I was spending the night and you and dad said it was fine. As a matter of fact, I gotta go."

"Whoa, whoa, whoa! Not so fast. After the news you gave your father and me last night, you don't need to be sleeping under any other roof except this one."

"But you said I could."

"That was last week, and before last night."

"I talked to Dad a little while ago and he said it was all right. It's cool, Mom. Relax."

Samantha couldn't believe that Tyler would allow their son to operate with a business-as-usual attitude, especially considering Chase's predicament, and she wondered if her son was lying. But as she thought about what he'd said, she knew Chase had to be telling the truth because the boy knew better than to lie on his father. However, whether he was really at Brad's house was a different story.

"Mom, I've gotta go."

"Why're you rushing me off the phone?"

"Brad's mom is about to order pizza and then we're gonna watch a movie."

Samantha was so upset she wanted to scream. She couldn't believe her son's laissez-faire attitude. He needed to be home on punishment, sitting in his room alone—no friends, no pizza, and no movies—feeling remorse while he contemplated his future and thought about what he'd done. Instead, he was enjoying a fun summer night with a friend.

But Tyler had already said it was okay, and she didn't want to contradict her husband. Still, she wanted to confirm that Chase was really where he said he was. "Put Brad's mother on the phone."

"What?"

"You heard me," she said as she rested her hand on her barely there hip. "Put Brand's mother on the phone so I can talk to her."

"She's getting ready to order pizza for us, Mom."

"Uh-huh, I heard. Put her on the phone right now or I'm coming over there."

Samantha could hear Chase huffing and puffing and giving her back talk on the other end of the line. She didn't care how much he grumbled or complained, she was going to make sure that he was really at Brad's, and not over at some girl's house or out getting into any other kind of teenage mischief. A minute later, Susie Vartron, Brad's mother, came to the phone, greeting Samantha in a chipper voice that never seemed to lose its enthusiasm even at the end of a long day.

Samantha felt a wave of relief wash over her body, allowing her to release the tension that had been gripping her shoulders all day. She thanked Susie for keeping an eye on her son and assured her that she and Tyler would get together with Susie and her husband for dinner in the coming week.

"At least Chase told the truth and he's in the home of a responsible adult," Samantha said, allowing herself to breathe easier. She stood in the middle of her kitchen and looked from one side of the room to the other, trying to figure out where she'd gone wrong with raising her son. She'd never been one to stress over situations, especially ones she had no control over. But ever since last night, when Chase had broken the news to her and Tyler that his girlfriend, LaMonica, was pregnant, she'd been on edge.

Samantha's entire day had been spent worrying about her youngest son's future. What impact would this have on his schooling, finances, social life, and mental state? She reached into the cabinet for a glass and then searched the refrigerator for the bottle of pink Moscato that had her name on it. She poured herself a glass and drank it down as if it were spring water.

"Lord, give me strength," she said as she walked up-stairs with her handbag on her shoulder, her empty wine-glass in one hand, and the open bottle in the other. She kicked off her shoes and plopped down onto her soft bed, staring at a framed picture on her chest of drawers that had been taken four years ago. She and Tyler were seated on a red velveteen settee while CJ and Chase stood be-hind them bearing big smiles. CJ had been in the first se-mester of his freshman year at Howard University, and Chase had been entering middle school. "Those were good times," she said aloud.

With what felt like a Herculean effort, Samantha re-moved her clothes piece by piece, shedding her stylish corporate suit, and pulled on her silk bathrobe. "I need a nice, relaxing bath," she said with a deep breath of exhaustion. She walked into her spa-like master bathroom and turned on the hot water to her Jacuzzi tub. She walked over to the vanity, looked at herself in the mirror, and nearly jumped back when she saw the tired, haggard-looking woman who was staring back at her.

"Damn, I look like a hot ass mess!" she said with horror as she examined her face.

Being a fashionista, beauty expert, and employee of a renowned cosmetics company, Samantha prided herself in her physical appearance and she put a lot of work into perfecting her look. She knew she wasn't naturally pretty, nor did she have the kind of body that turned heads. Her facial features were average, her light yellow skin was prone to break-outs, her coarse, sandy brown hair needed constant care, and she fought to keep weight on her rail thin frame. She clearly understood her flaws, but she also knew exactly how to fix them.

Primer, concealer, and foundation had been her best friends since high school, and over the years she'd mastered the art of applying them so well that her skin looked dewy soft, and smooth. Her small eyes, flat nose, square jaw, and high forehead were nothing to rave about, but once she applied eye shadow, mascara, lipstick, and blush, she created facial contours that were model worthy. Her coarse hair used to be disguised by expensive weaves and wigs, but now she wore it in a sophisticated pixie cut that shined as a result of regular deep conditioning, hot oil treatments, and weekly salon visits. And instead of wearing body-enhancing garments to give her the illusion of curves she'd never had, she made her thin, boy-shape body stand out by rocking slim pencil skirts paired with expensive stilettos that highlighted her toned, mile-long legs.

But as Samantha looked at herself in the mirror and examined her skin, which appeared rough and sallow, and peered closely at her eyes, which carried a tired, beaten-down expression, she was a long way from the glamorous woman who usually stepped out into the world with confidence. She shook her head in frustration. "That boy's trying to make me a grandmother, and I'll be damned if I'm not already looking like one."

She walked back out to her bedroom, poured herself another glass of wine, picked up her phone and dialed her best friend, Emily, as she headed back into the bathroom.

"Hey, Samantha," Emily said after picking up on the second ring. "Is that water I hear in the background?"

"Yes, girl. I'm running a much-needed bubble bath."

"You must have the house to yourself tonight."

"Yes, but only for a little while. Chase is spending the night at a friend's so he'll be gone, and Tyler's conducting a community forum across town, so he'll be back in a few hours."

"Lucky you. I can't remember the last time I had the house to myself for a few hours."

"Girl, me either," Samantha said as she took a sip of wine.

"Ed and the kids are always here. I'm not complaining, but I sure do miss my me time. It's so important for us to have time to ourselves."

"You can say that again, and I'm savoring every minute of mine."

"I'd so love to trade places with you right now."

Samantha shook her head, wishing they could do exactly that. Samantha and Emily had been best friends since their freshman year at Spelman College. They'd been roommates and formed an instant bond, tying them closer than any two blood sisters could ever be. They even shared the same birthday, but aside from that they were opposites in almost every way one could imagine.

Emily had grown up an only child in a modest home

tucked inside a working-class neighborhood. She'd been raised by her widowed mother, a school teacher with a kind heart who'd passed along her sweet nature and kind ways to Emily.

Samantha's upbringing had been drastically different, hailing from an old-money, Washington, D.C. family in the famed Gold Coast community. She had an estranged brother whom she hadn't seen in nearly twenty years since he'd moved to Paris with his male lover, and she was daughter to an uncaring socialite mother whom she loathed. But her heart and love were rooted in her nurturing father, who was a prominent attorney. Other than her husband, Samantha's father was the best man she'd ever known.

The two women's unique backgrounds and personalities served to complement one another. Emily's calm demeanor softened Samantha's bold, often over-the-top personality. And Samantha's wild and free spirit helped bring Emily out of her shy, timid shell. They valued, protected, and loved each other to no end. But their long-standing friendship had been tested many years ago by an unexpected and shocking betrayal.

Shortly after celebrating their thirtieth birthday, Samantha had found out that her meek and quiet friend had been having an affair with her father.

In Samantha's eyes, her father, Edward Baldwin, could do no wrong. Ever since she was a small child she'd been a daddy's girl. Conversely, she'd always had a mutually hateful relationship with her mother, and to this day they barely even spoke. But she'd loved Ed with all her heart, and the betrayal and deception she'd felt from him and her best friend had rocked her to her core.

Both her father and Emily had kept their affair a secret from her, sneaking around right under her nose. Once Samantha discovered the truth and the level of their deception, it had devastated her and Emily's friendship, and distanced her from her father, causing her to drift apart from both of them for nearly a year without so much as speaking. But time, love, and maturity had healed those wounds. Samantha and Emily had become pregnant around the same time, and when Samantha realized that life with Emily had made her father the happiest he'd ever been, she'd started to come around.

Today, Emily and Ed were still in love, happily married, and raising two children, Elise, who was sixteen, and Phillip, who'd just turned thirteen last month. Emily had chosen Samantha's middle name to give to their daughter, and it had filled Samantha with joy.

Samantha was glad that after all she and Emily had been through over the years, their friendship was still rock-solid. As a matter of fact, both women could honestly say that they were closer now than they had ever been. Healing from the hurt had been hard, but it had made them wiser, stronger, and better women from the experience, and they vowed never to keep another secret from each other, ever again.

"If I was in your shoes," Emily said, "I'd be taking a long soak in the tub, too, and I'd be sipping some wine at that."

Samantha took a deep breath. "My glass is in my hand as we speak. But trust me, you don't want to trade places with me right now."

"Samantha, what's wrong? You don't sound good and I can hear stress in your voice."

"I don't even know where to begin."

"You're scaring me. Tell me what's going on?"

Samantha could imagine Emily—with her flawless nut-brown-colored skin, beautiful, cover-model-looking face, and body that looked as though it belonged to a young twenty-something hottie—sitting on her couch with the phone pressed against her ear and worry enveloping her body.

"It's Chase," she said.

Emily let out a deep sigh. "Oh no, not again. What's he done now?"

"He got a girl pregnant."

There was silence on the line as Samantha waited for Emily's response. "Hello? Emily, you still there?"

"I'm here," Emily said. "I'm on my way to the kitchen. I need a drink."

"Why do you think I'm sippin' right now?"

"I'll be joining you as soon as I open a bottle."

The two friends talked and sipped as Samantha gave Emily the details from the previous night.

"I'm still stunned," Emily said. "It's just hard to believe that Chase has been having a relationship with a girl he met up here last spring? How in the world can a sixteen-year-old maintain a long-distance relationship when most adults can't?"

"Emily, please pull off your rose-colored glasses. This isn't a long-distance relationship. He banged the girl while we were up there on spring break a few months ago and now she's four months pregnant."

"But you said that Chase said she's his girlfriend."

Samantha sucked in her breath. "That's the term that he used to make it sound better. That boy has I-don't-know-how-many little so-called girlfriends running around Atlanta. He's rarely mentioned her name until last night."

"I know you're furious, disappointed, and worried all at once. I know I would be."

"Yes, and the thoughts that have been going through my mind . . ." Samantha let out another deep breath. "I should've never let him out of my sight while we were up there visiting."

"Don't beat yourself up. Chase has always been the

type of child who's done what he wants to do, regardless of what anyone tells him. You and Tyler have tried over and over to help him make better decisions. CJ has tried and Ed and I have tried. Even Elise tried to talk to him while you guys were up here. This is on Chase and no one else."

"I was the same way, stubborn as hell when I was his age. I got into all kinds of trouble because of my mouth and quick temper. And yeah, I was boy crazy and I got around, but pregnancy wasn't even on my radar. How hard can it be to put on a damn condom? I know for a fact that he has them because I've found them in his room when I'm in there snooping."

Emily sighed. "That falls in line with making good decisions and being responsible."

"And my son doesn't do either. I can only imagine what kind of girl this LaMonica is."

"Did you say LaMonica?" Emily asked, drawing in a sharp intake of breath.

Samantha cut off the running water that had filled the tub, set her glass on the vanity, and stood completely still. "Yes . . . oh Lord, do you know who she is?"

"Is her last name Carpenter?"

"I don't know. I was so upset when Chase was telling us that I don't remember what he said her last name was. But I do know that she lives in Crestwood and she's a year older than he is."

"Lord have mercy, it's a small world," Emily said. "This has to be the same girl."

"You know who she is?"

"Yes, and she's friends with Elise. They're in the same Jack and Jill chapter as well as this year's debutante cotillion."

Emily proceeded to tell Samantha as much as she could about LaMonica Carpenter.

LaMonica was an attractive seventeen-year-old who looked more like a college senior than a high school junior at the private school she attended. She was a straight-A student and had been inducted into the National Honor Society last year. Her mother was a high-ranking employee in the federal government, and her father was a successful businessman who was running for a seat on the city council.

A funny feeling came over Samantha and she was hoping it was just a combination of frayed nerves and an over active imagination. "What are her parents' first names?"

"Millie and David. They're our age and they both went to Georgetown. Do you know them?"

Samantha's head was swimming. *This can't possibly be,* she thought to herself.

"Do you know them from your days here in D.C.?" Emily asked again.

"Uh, I'm not sure."

"They're a very nice couple and LaMonica seems to have a good head on her shoulders. But . . ."

Samantha knew that "but" was code for bad. "Spill what you know."

"I hate to talk negatively about the girl, and I'm only going on what I've seen from afar, but she's always seemed a little too streetwise and grown for my taste. You know, the kind who has something up her sleeve. Slick, as you would say."

Samantha shook her head, pulled off her robe, and slid down into the warm bubbles. "Now it makes sense why Chase was interested in her."

"I probably shouldn't say this, but I just have to ask . . ."

"What?"

"How do you know this baby is really Chase's?"

The thought had crossed Samantha's mind as she was thinking about it earlier today, but she'd been so flustered she'd barely had time to process it thoroughly. And now, if LaMonica's father was who Samantha thought he was, she didn't put anything past the girl. "That's a good point. All we know is what Chase has told us, and all he knows is what she's told him. That's why I can't wait to speak with LaMonica's parents this weekend. Trust and believe, Tyler and I are gonna get down to the bottom of this."

Samantha and Emily talked a few minutes longer before Emily was pulled away by after dinner kitchen cleanup. Samantha lay back in her Jacuzzi tub and tried to relax, but she couldn't. All she could think about was her son and the child he possibly had on the way, and how it would change everyone's lives. She prayed it wasn't Chase's baby, and if bad luck had it that it was, she prayed even harder that her suspicions about LaMonica's father were wrong.

She closed her eyes and exhaled, but then shot straight up when she heard her name.

"Sam, I'm home," Tyler called out as he walked into the bathroom. "I had a long day and I'm so glad to be back."

"Me too. Why did you tell Chase it was okay to stay at Brad's house tonight? That boy should be here, on punishment."

"Sam, the damage is already done. I let him stay with Brad because you and I need tonight, alone. We need to talk, and be together, then tomorrow we can bring Chase back into the fold when our heads are a little more clear."

Tyler's words and presence had relaxed her more than the warm bubbles and wine. "You're right."

He reached over and took a sip from her glass. "You know I prefer my Ketel One, but this isn't half bad."

Samantha smiled wide. She'd initially wanted the house all to herself, but now she was glad that Tyler was home, giving her the steady reassurance and comfort she so desperately needed. They locked eyes with each other and she didn't have to say another word. He removed his shirt, then his pants and boxers, and slid down into the tub behind her, cradling her back against his chest.

"It's gonna be all right, Sam. We're gonna get through this."

Samantha didn't want to ruin the wonderful moment, but as she lay relaxed into the comfort of Tyler's chest, she had to ask him the question that was on her mind. "Do you remember what Chase said LaMonica's last name is?"

Tyler nodded. "Carpenter. Why?"

"Oh, nothing, I just wanted to make sure."

Right then another rock landed in the pit of Samantha's stomach. *How in the hell can this be happening?* she thought. Her past was coming back to haunt her in the form of David Carpenter, the handsome football player she'd briefly dated in college. They shared a secret they'd each sworn to take to the grave. They each had dirt on the other, which had sealed their "I'll never tell" deal. But now that the game had changed and the stakes involved her son, Samantha knew she'd use the information she had against him in order to save her son, even if it meant sacrificing herself.

Chapter 7
Alexandria

PJ created a relaxing mood by cuing up music from his latest jazz playlist, then he set the table and poured the wine while Alexandria prepared their plates for dinner.

Last month, Alexandria had moved out of her apartment across town and into PJ's luxury condo, which had more room. With their nuptials just a short time away, they'd decided to move in now rather than have to go through the hassle after a busy wedding and honeymoon. Being with him and living in the same space had given her a small taste of what married life was going to be like and she knew she was going to enjoy it.

Alexandria loved evenings like this that gave them a chance to bond over a good meal and conversation. "A happy stomach equals a happy home," her mother always told her. She knew that PJ's appetite was always ready, and she planned to satisfy it, in and out of the kitchen. As she looked at him, she knew she couldn't ask for a more loving fiancé, and without a doubt, he was going to make an even better husband and father. "Thank you, baby," she said with a smile.

"For what?" he asked as he finished lighting the candles on the table.

"For simply being who you are. I love that I can drop crazy stuff on you, and you just roll with it like it's no big deal. I know this last-minute trip to Nedine wasn't in the plans, but you're still willing to rearrange your schedule at the hospital so you can go with me."

"As much time as I put in at work, they know they owe me."

"Yeah, but you still didn't have to offer to go, especially under the circumstances."

"You said that this is about family, and there's nothing more important than that."

Once they settled in at the small dining room table, they were ready to eat.

"When do you want me to book our flight to Nedine?" PJ asked as he took a bite of his shrimp scampi.

Alexandria sipped her wine slowly. "I'm thinking next Friday morning. I need to talk to my mother tomorrow and see when she, Dad, and hopefully Christian can fly out, if at all. I'm also going to call Uncle Maxx and see if he's up to making the trip."

"Okay, just let me know and I'll handle it."

"Thanks, honey," Alexandria said as she and PJ tapped their wineglasses together for a toast. "How's Gary doing?" she asked. Gary Mosley, the adorable five-year-old boy whom PJ had been treating for the last three months, was one of the hospital's Boarder Babies, which was part of a national program at hospitals across the country. Boarder Babies were children who either had been abandoned in the hospital at birth, or had been dropped off at its doors by parents who could no longer handle the responsibility of caring for their child. These abandoned children were boarded and cared for by the nurses and doctors, who relied on grant funding, and in most cases, their own wallets, to cover the financial costs of keeping the children healthy and safe.

Gary had been abandoned three months ago by his drug-addicted mother, who'd been in and out of rehab for years. One of the nurses had found him near the back entrance one night, lying on the ground, barely alive, wearing nothing but a pair of soiled underwear and a dirty T-shirt. He was badly malnourished, dehydrated, and whimpering in pain. Gary was so small he looked more like a three-year-old than his five years.

After a thorough examination, the doctors had discovered that little Gary needed a kidney transplant in order to save his life. Miraculously, he'd received a new kidney within a few months of being placed on the list. PJ had been an instrumental part of the surgical team, and had grown attached to the little boy, as had Alexandria, who came by the hospital and visited him every chance she could get.

"He's making great progress," PJ said. "He asked about you this afternoon. He said, 'Where's Miss Ali? I want Miss Ali to come and see me.' "

Alexandria smiled. "Awww, I miss that little guy. I would've stopped in after work, but I had so much running around to do. I wonder if it'll be okay to swing by there tonight. Maybe I can read him a bedtime story before he goes to sleep."

PJ looked at his watch. "I don't see why not. I know he'll light up when he sees you walk into his room."

"How much longer do you think it will be before he's ready to leave the hospital?"

"At least another month. But even then, I'm really nervous about it."

"Because of where he'll go and what will happen to him . . . ?"

PJ nodded. It was a sobering reality that neither he nor Alexandria wanted to face. Over the past several months Gary had become a significant part of their lives. Each day, they either visited his room or talked with him by phone, and each night they prayed for him, speaking affirming words for his healing. From the moment Alexandria had heard PJ talk about the sick little boy who'd been abandoned in a state of near death, she had known that there was something different and special about Gary Mosley.

Initially, Alexandria had wanted to look into the future and see what it held. would Gary get a kidney in time? If he did, would he survive? And if he survived, what would happen to him once he was well enough to leave the hospital? Would he be put into the foster care system, relegated to a childhood filled with bad memories like her paternal grandmother had experienced? Or would one of his distant relatives step up to claim him and give him a happy life?"

Those questions were constantly at the forefront of Alexandria's mind whenever she thought about Gary. She knew she could use her gift to easily find out the answers and put her anxiety at rest, but she decided against it. She was learning how not to be so attached to the outcome of things, but instead, to savor the journey of getting there. She was exercising patience, allowing herself to be content with discovering new experiences and unexpected joys each day. Going through Gary's journey with him had already proven to be a rewarding endeavor, and she was looking forward to what was next to come.

She still remembered the first time she'd seen Gary. After listening to PJ talk about the little boy for a few days, she had decided it was time to go by the hospital and pay him a visit. She'd brought him a pack of crayons and a coloring book, along with a cherry-flavored lollipop. Gary had been asleep when she'd slipped into his room. She'd stood beside his bed and instantly fallen in love. He was small, and fragile, and helpless. He reminded her of how she'd felt as a child when spirits would bombard her with their voices at night.

She'd pulled up a chair beside Gary's bed and watched him as he slept, taking shallow, labored breaths. Even though he had been a very sick child whose health was hanging in a precarious balance, he'd looked beautiful and bright in Alexandria's eyes. His deep, chocolate-colored skin had been taut and smooth. His long lashes had extended from his closed lids, making them look almost false, and the shallow rise and fall of his tiny chest had made Alexandria's own heart ache for him as he struggled to breathe.

Even though she'd had to wear protective gloves at the time, she'd put her hand over his, hoping he could feel her warmth and love. She'd waited patiently for two solid hours before Gary had finally opened his eyes, and when they'd looked at each other, she'd known at that moment that he was going to be a part of her life.

"You're a big reason why Gary's recovering so well," PJ said.

"He's a precious little boy and I'll do whatever I can to make his life as complete as it can be."

"Alexandria Elizabeth Thornton, this is one of the many reasons I can't wait to make you my wife."

Alexandria leaned over and kissed PJ. "And I can't wait to get you down that aisle."

* * *

After they finished dinner and drove to the hospital, PJ and Alexandria held hands as they walked down the hall, headed toward Gary's room. "This is really gonna make his night," PJ said, giving Alexandria's hand a gentle squeeze.

"Mine too."

As they passed the nurse's station, Alexandria slowed down when a warm sensation came over her. Ms. Brown was in the area. She could feel her presence, and although she'd never met the woman and had only heard about her today, through PJ, she instantly knew without a doubt that the nurse also had the gift. She looked over to her right and saw a kind-looking lady smile at her and nod.

PJ looked in the direction where Alexandria had trained her attention. "That's Ms. Brown," he said.

"Yes, I know."

Alexandria could see that PJ fully understood what was happening. He nodded. "Go ahead and talk to her. I'll check on another patient, and then I'll head down to Gary's room and wait for you."

Alexandria watched as Ms. Brown slowly walked from behind the nurse's desk and stood over to the side, waiting for her with a look that said she'd been expecting company.

As Alexandria drew closer, she examined every detail of Ms. Brown. At a little over five feet tall, she was shorter than Alexandria had imagined, and her chubby cheeks and soft eyes gave her an almost cherubic appearance. Her dark blue scrubs looked as though they'd been laundered at the dry cleaners, and when she leaned on one leg Alexandria could see the perfectly neat crease running down the front of her pants. She was a meticulous woman, evidenced by the other careful details of her appearance. Her short black hair was streaked with flattering auburn highlights, which complemented her chestnut-colored skin. She gave Alexandria another warm smile and stretched her arms to greet her.

"Hello, Alexandria," Ms. Brown said. "It's so nice to meet you, sugar."

Alexandria bent down and welcomed the woman's embrace, which felt as comfortable and natural, as if she were hugging a loved one she'd known all her life. "It's nice to meet you, too."

Ms. Brown smiled. "I'm glad you received the message I delivered to PJ today."

"Yes. But how did you know about me?"

"I saw you for the first time last week when I came up to bring a new patient on this floor. You were visiting with Gary Mosley and as soon as I saw you I could tell you were special, and that you had the gift. Then today, I woke up with a strange sensation, but in a good way. It was a warm feeling, and I kept hearing a woman's voice inside my head saying, 'You can't fight the devil on an empty stomach,' and somehow, I knew that I needed to repeat those words in front of PJ because that message was meant for you."

"Did the voice you heard have a Southern accent, kind of heavy, yet gentle at the same time?"

Ms. Brown smiled and nodded excitely. "Yes, yes, it did. Almost like I knew her, but I know I don't. This kind of thing has never happened to me, so I knew I had to pay close attention and go where the spirit led me. Do you know who the woman is that contacted me, or why she wanted us to connect through that message?"

"It was my grandma Allene," Alexandria said. She felt a warm tingle on her arm and the smell of sweet magnolias in the air. "She's here with us right now." But as soon as Alexandria's words came out, the scent disappeared and Allene was gone. She knew that this was Allene's way of letting her know without a doubt that she'd orchestrated this meeting.

"She's standing here with us right now?" Ms. Brown asked.

"No, but I felt her presence just a few seconds ago. She wanted me to know that it was indeed her who contacted you."

Ms. Brown squinted her small eyes. "What does all this mean?"

Alexandria wasn't sure of how to answer the question because she really didn't know. Allene had a way of leading her down a road, and then stepping back to let her find her own way down the right path. Alexandria knew that like most everything else, her great-great-grandmother was guiding her and giving her a lesson. She closed her eyes, concentrated, and then re-opened them quickly.

"You just had a vision, didn't you?" Ms. Brown asked.

"Yes. And I want to thank you right now for watching over Gary while PJ and I are gone next weekend, and during our honeymoon."

Ms. Brown nodded. "This is really something. My director just told me today that I'll be working on this floor, and specifically with Gary, for the next month or until he's released, whichever is first."

Ms. Brown went on to tell Alexandria that her gift was limited, and didn't allow her to see into the future, reach back into the past, or communicate telepathically as Alexandria could do. But she could sense things, and in particular, the presence of good or evil. She told Alexandria that she would watch over Gary and make sure that nothing bad happened to him, or PJ for that matter.

"Thank you, Ms. Brown. I'm sure that we'll be in contact from here on out," Alexandria said with a smile.

"We sure will, sugar. We sure will."

* * *

Alexandria was on her way to Gary's room when she saw PJ coming toward her.

"I just finished checking on another patient down the hall," PJ said. "Is everything okay?"

"Yes, Ms. Brown and I talked. She has the gift, and she's going to watch over Gary for us."

"This is pretty amazing. Each time when I think I can't be surprised I'm proven wrong."

Alexandria smiled. "But it's all good. And in this case, it's great."

When they entered Gary's room, walking hand in hand, the young boy looked up and smiled so wide that it made both Alexandria and PJ smile back.

"Miss Aliiii!" Gary said with a happy grin. He maneuvered his small body so he could sit up in his bed. "I knew you would come and see me."

Alexandria leaned over Gary's bed and gave him a kiss on his cheek, which made him grin even harder. She wanted to snap her fingers and make Gary all better, but she knew that time, good medical care, and lots of prayer were the only cures. "Of course I came to see you. How's my little man doing?" she said with a smile.

"I'm good. I ate a Popsicle!"

"You did? What flavor?"

"Red."

Alexandria laughed. "Sweetie, red is a color, remember?"

"Oh yeah, I forgot. It was cherry."

"I'm glad you enjoyed your cherry Popsicle. Are you ready for a bedtime story?"

"Yes! Yes! Yes!" Gary said with excitement. "I like it when you read me bedtime stories, Miss Ali."

PJ pulled his stethoscope from around his neck and

leaned over Gary's bed. "Before you two get all wrapped up in story land, I need to check you out, okay, big guy?" he said, looking at Gary.

PJ examined Gary as Alexandria sat patiently, looking into PJ's face for any signs of decline or improvement in Gary's condition. This was always one of the toughest parts of her visits. Alexandria wished she could take away his pain, but she knew being there and loving him would have to suffice for now.

"You're doing just fine," PJ said. Then he looked over at Alexandria. "Everything's gonna be all right."

He'd just repeated the very words that Grandma Allene had told her this afternoon, and it quieted the last remnants of Alexandria's worries. She was grateful that signs of blessings were all around her, especially given what she knew her family was going to encounter on their trip to Nedine next week.

Less than ten minutes later, Alexandria had only read through half the storybook when Gary drifted off to sleep. She reached over and placed her hand on his, which she was glad felt warm to the touch. She closed her eyes to say a quick prayer, but then gasped when she received a vision she hadn't seen coming. A calm knowing flooded her body, and she felt at ease. She looked down at Gary and smiled. "Good night, my sweet baby."

PJ walked over to where Alexandria stood and looked into her eyes. She nodded, answering his question before he could ask it. They had discussed in great length the fact that they wanted children, and unlike some soon-to-be newlyweds, they wanted to start their family right away. Given PJ's profession and his love for children, coupled with Alexandria's nurturing instincts, they were excited about having kids. They'd also discussed the very real possibility of including Gary in their family plan.

"I guess we better set up a meeting with the hospital social worker and child services so we can start the adoption process," PJ said.

Alexandria nodded. "We're going to be newlyweds and parents all at once."

"I'm fine with that, but are you sure it's what you want?"

"I'm as sure about making Gary our son as I am about becoming your wife."

They stood over Gary's bed for a few more moments before they left his room, walking hand in hand, looking forward to the bold new life that awaited them.

Chapter 8
Victoria

"I can't believe I'm going through this crazy drama again. And the third time around at that," Victoria whispered to herself as she scooped strawberry ice cream out of the container and into the two bowls in front of her. She spread a dollop of fresh, homemade whipped cream atop each dessert, trying with all her might to remain relaxed for the conversation she was about to have with her husband.

Once again, she and Ted were going to have to discuss the one person who had always been a nagging splinter that they couldn't seem to remove from their marriage—Parker Brightwood. But now a new problem that was surely going to add fuel to the already flickering flame had slowly crept up—the surprising and frustrating disappearance of their sex life. Victoria knew she had to approach it with just as much sensitivity and care as the subject of her former lover.

Although Victoria and Ted were in their senior years,

they were both active and healthy, and had still enjoyed a robust, and even adventurous sex life—that is, until a year ago, right around the time that Alexandria and PJ had reunited and started dating. From that moment right up to today, Victoria's and Ted's bedroom activities had gone from a little, to less, to nothing at all. Victoria didn't expect to keep up the activity they'd both enjoyed in their younger days, but she also didn't want to go without sex completely.

She had tried to gently talk to Ted about the state of their love life two months ago while they were lying in bed one night. She'd lit a scented candle, removed her silk nightgown, cuddled next to him, and whispered her desires into his ear.

"V, I'm really tired. I had a long day," had been Ted's response.

Victoria pulled away and tried to keep her composure. "What's wrong?"

"I just told you, I'm tired."

"You don't look at me the way you used to. Are you not attracted to me anymore?" She looked down at the empty left side of her chest where her breast had once been before cancer and a mastectomy had claimed it.

Ted pulled her close to him. "V, you know I think you're the most beautiful, sexy woman on earth. Of course I'm still attracted to you."

"Then why don't you want to make love to me anymore? It's been months. We don't hug. We don't kiss. Nothing."

Ted let out a sigh. "I've been under a tremendous amount of pressure with the company, and trying to figure out what I'm going to do when I retire in a few years has taken a lot more planning than I'd initially thought it would."

"Worry about that later," Victoria said softly, "but take care of me, and us, in the here and now."

Ted kissed the top of her head. "I love you, V."

"Are you having an affair?"

Ted shook his head and looked her in the eye. "No, V. Did you hear a word I just said?"

Victoria trusted Ted, but she also knew that his actions over the last six months were out of character and unlike the man she'd been married to for nearly three decades. Ted was the consummate professional and had always taken care of business, planning and strategizing down to the tiniest of details when it came to ViaTech, the telecommunications company he owned and had grown into an international force. He was already grooming their son, Christian, to step into an executive position at ViaTech once he graduated with his MBA from Columbia in two years.

She understood his drive, and that his many work related pressures could affect his libido. But she also wanted to make it clear that she was ready for their drought to end.

She'd tried to arouse him, only to be disappointed, and she knew she had to get to the bottom of what was wrong. "Do you think we need to go see someone about this, or get you some medication?"

"Medication? I'm fine. I don't have any problems."

"Clearly that's not true. You haven't touched me since frost was on the ground."

"V, let's talk about this later." Ted leaned over and turned off the light on his nightstand, making it clear that the conversation was over.

"I can't believe you just turned off the light and dismissed me."

He sighed. "I'm not dismissing you. I'm just tired."

"Uh-huh."

"I love you, V. I'm still attracted to you, and like I said, there's no one else. You're the only woman who'll ever share my bed and my life." He kissed her good-night before turning over and falling asleep.

Victoria hadn't so much as mentioned her concerns or frustrations about their pitiful sex life since that night about two months ago. Running her business, volunteering with selected charities, co-chairing an upcoming breast cancer walk, and helping to plan Alexandria's and PJ's wedding had kept her busy from sunup to sundown, but one month from now many of her distractions, particularly her daughter's wedding, would be lifted, and she'd be back to square one with an itch that needed to be scratched. She had no intention of continuing down a road that was creating distance between them.

"Here you go," Victoria said as she walked into the den with two bowls of ice cream.

"Thanks, V." Ted smiled like a kid who'd just been given his favorite treat.

Victoria sat down beside him and smiled back. She looked at Ted and was glad that after all the years they'd been together she still found him sexy, fun, and interesting. And best of all, her love and appreciation for him had deepened as each year rolled by into the next.

She studied him closely, admiring the fact that he'd aged well and looked much younger than his driver's license stated. He was tall and still in good enough shape to jog four miles a day. His good looks were now well seasoned like those of a vintage Hollywood heartthrob. His thick salt-and-pepper hair was still surprisingly full, and Victoria loved running her fingers through it. Thanks to the olive undertones he'd inherited from his half-black mother, his skin looked tanned and robust, and his ocean-blue eyes, compliments of his white father, were still beautifully hypnotic with just a few lines around the edges.

"This is the finishing touch to that delicious dinner you cooked." Ted savored another spoonful of ice cream. "I'll have to jog an extra mile in the morning."

Victoria wanted to follow up on his last statement by telling him that the extra mile she wanted him to tackle was in their bedroom, but before she approached that subject she knew she had to handle another delicate matter first. "Parker called me today and . . ."

"Why?" Ted interrupted before she could finish her sentence.

She could see that he was already defensive. "He wanted to check and make sure it was okay to invite more guests to the reception."

Ted looked at her but didn't say a word. She could swear he'd just rolled his eyes, yet another thing that was very unlike him. "But that's not the reason I mentioned his call. I told you because he's coming to town next week."

Ted's jaw tightened. He swallowed his ice cream and clanked his spoon against the bowl. "What's the occasion? Are we involved, or is he coming specifically to see you?"

"No, not really. He'll be here on business and he wants to know the costs for the rehearsal dinner."

"What does the cost of the rehearsal dinner have to do with him?"

Victoria blinked, realizing how far removed Ted was from the planning process. "Honey, he's paying for it. So I guess he has a right to want to talk over how much he's forking out."

Ted shook his head. "He doesn't give a damn about cost. He's just trying to find excuses to see you."

"Why would you think that?"

"Because he's come to town several times over the last six months, and from what I understand, even though PJ's been living here for several years, Parker never traveled to see him the way he does now."

Victoria raised her eyebrow. "And how do you know that?"

"Because I asked Alexandria." Ted was looking directly into her eyes, as though he knew that she knew what he'd just said was true. "I find it strangely coincidental," he continued, "and very suspicious that he has a sudden interest in being here so often."

Victoria wasn't surprised that Parker's frequent visits to Atlanta had not been lost on Ted. But until now she'd had no idea that he suspected Parker might be seeing her when he came to town. From past experience and mistakes, she knew she had to nip this in the bud. "Twenty years ago you had every reason to question and doubt me. I'll give you that. But as I sit here now, in this present time and space, fully and completely in love and devoted to you, and only you, I can assure you that whatever reason Parker has for coming to Atlanta, it's absolutely no concern of mine."

"But his reason for coming is because of you, Victoria."

Whenever Ted referred to her by her given name instead of V, the pet name he'd started calling her when they were dating, she knew he was angry. "I haven't done a thing to encourage his visits. When he comes to town I don't even see him, I just hear about it from Alexandria, like you apparently have."

Ted set his ice cream on the coffee table in front of him, leaned back into the couch, and crossed his arms at his chest. "We need to talk."

"Good. I agree."

"I've held a lot inside and it's really eating at me."

"I can see that."

"I'm happy for Alexandria, and I've grown to think of PJ as a son. He's a fine young man of great character and integrity. We couldn't ask for a better mate for our daughter if we went out and picked him ourselves. I believe he'll be a good husband to her, and for that I'm grateful. But as you already know, I have a problem with his father. The fact that you two have a history doesn't bother me." Ted unfolded his arms and looked directly into Victoria's eyes. "But the fact that you still have feelings for him does."

Victoria bit her bottom lip, a move she made whenever she was nervous, anxious, frustrated, or perplexed. Right now she was all of those things. But it wasn't because there was truth in Ted's words. She was fully aware of the extent of her feelings for Parker. He still owned a small piece of her heart, and she knew he most likely always would. But she also knew it wasn't the part that mattered. It wasn't the part that made her jump for joy, feel full inside, and want to go to the end of the earth and back just to hold on to it. Ted owned that part, and no one could ever take his place.

Victoria knew that her and Ted's love was tested and true. It had held up in sickness and in health when cancer had reared its ugly head. It had survived for better or worse when she'd found out that Ted had discovered his mother was half-black and had hidden that fact from her. There were dozens of other examples of their love that flashed through her mind. They'd shared hurt and pain, but they'd also celebrated joy and happiness, and Victoria knew that no matter what type of lingering attraction she had for Parker, she would never again risk her marriage in order to reach back for a distant memory.

She returned Ted's stare and cleared her throat before she spoke. "I can't control how you feel, but I can control my actions. Everything that I say and do demonstrates my love for you and my commitment to our marriage and our family. After all these years together you should be able to trust in that."

"I love you, so I guess I'll just have to," Ted told her.

"What do you mean, you guess?"

Ted let out a deep breath. "I don't trust him, and I don't want the two of you to ever be alone together."

Victoria couldn't believe her ears. "We've been through too much and survived too many storms to have a squabble over an ex who I made a mistake with a lifetime ago. For our sake and for the happiness of Alexandria and PJ, please let this go."

"Promise me that you won't be alone with him."

Victoria stared into Ted's eyes and could see that he was resolute. She didn't like making promises because, just like life, she knew they were subject to change without notice, depending upon the situation. But she loved Ted with all her heart and she wanted to make peace of things, so she gave in. "Okay, I won't be alone with him."

"Thank you, V."

"You don't have to thank me. Even though there's no cause for concern, I'll do whatever it takes to ease your mind and make you feel more comfortable."

Ted nodded, then picked up his spoon and polished off the rest of his half-melted ice cream.

Later that night, as Victoria lay next to Ted in their king-size bed, she looked over at him and then up at the ceiling. He was fast asleep, but she was wide awake, thinking about the conversation they'd had. She'd decided not to broach the subject of her frustration with their sex life because the topic of Parker Brightwood had been enough conflict to deal with in one night. But she knew they were going to have to tackle the growing issue at some point.

Victoria reached over and turned off the light on her nightstand, hoping and praying that for once in her life, her gut feeling—that although Ted had said nothing was wrong, there was a mountain of troubles he was keeping from her that made her situation with Parker look like child's play—was wrong.

Chapter 9
Alexandria

Alexandria took a sip of her lemongrass tea as she sat behind her desk in her downtown office. She looked at the boxes she'd begun to pack yesterday, which were sitting in a neat row against one side of the wall. Over the years she'd filled the small space with sentimental mementos, gifts, and pictures, all in an attempt to create a slice of comfort in a place where she'd never felt at home. With the exception of the complimentary teas, coffees, and delicious breakfast pastries the firm provided each morning, there was little else she'd miss about her job. "It's time to bury the past and start new beginnings," she said, smiling as she repeated her grandma Allene's words.

As she thought about her future that lay ahead, she dialed her mother's cell phone.

"Hey, sweetie," Victoria answered, picking up on the first ring.

"Hey, Mom, how's your morning going?"

"It's busy but good. As a matter of fact, I just finished talking with your aunt Debbie and she told me to tell you that she can't wait to see you when she comes to town for the wedding. Did I tell you that she's flying in a few days early?"

Alexandria smiled at the mention of her godmother's name. "No, you didn't. But that's great. I haven't seen her since she visited last year."

Debbie Long and Victoria had been roommates in graduate school at the University of Pennsylvania. Their friendship had blossomed despite their differences in everything from physical appearance to personal style. While Victoria was African-American, tall, sophisticated, and pragmatic, Debbie was Caucasian, short, and an artsy-fartsy free spirit who flew by the seat of her thrift-store pants. Their forty-year friendship had helped them survive raising children on both their parts, illness on Victoria's, and divorce on Debbie's, and through it all they'd remained close and had even strengthened their bond through the years.

"She said she might even stay a few days after the wedding just to kick back and take it easy," Victoria said.

"I'm so glad Aunt Debbie's going to be able to make it."

"You know she wouldn't miss your wedding for the world. She's so happy for you, and she's looking forward to watching you walk down the aisle just as much as I am."

"Did she say if Brandon will be able to make it? I haven't seen him in years," Alexandria asked, referring to her godbrother and Debbie's son.

"I don't think so. Debbie said his schedule has been really hectic since he was promoted to head chef at that fancy Manhattan restaurant where he works. But wouldn't it be fabulous if he could prepare a special pastry dish or some nice hors d'oeuvres and have them shipped down here for the cocktail hour before the reception starts?"

Alexandria knew her mother would start talking about the wedding ad nauseam, so she quickly jumped into the purpose of her call. "Mom, I have something very important that I want to talk to you about, and I need you to hear me out, okay?"

"Uh-oh, what's wrong?" Victoria asked with concern.

"I wouldn't say that anything is wrong, but something's definitely about to happen. Yesterday Grandma Allene contacted me." Alexandria could hear her mother's sharp intake of breath, as if anticipating that something bad had already taken place. "Calm down, Mom. . . ."

"Please just tell me what's going on."

Alexandria spent the next five minutes repeating to Victoria what she'd told PJ last night. "So you see, Mom, we need to go back to Nedine. I wouldn't be pushing this if I didn't think it was important, and Grandma Allene certainly wouldn't be here in our world, wanting us to come there, if she didn't think it was necessary. We all need to go."

"What do you think she's referring to about burying the past in order to start new beginnings?"

"I'm not sure, but I think, since she wants all of us there, it will mean different things for each person."

"Do you think our family is in any kind of danger?"

"The only thing that I can say with a fair amount of certainty is that whether we are or aren't, we need to travel to Nedine next weekend. I know Grandma Allene has a reason for wanting us to go, and everything she's led me to has been right on the money." Alexandria knew that her mother worried over her, and that she still felt guilt for not being able to help her deal with her gift when she was growing up. "Mom, I told you this so you'll know what's going on, but I don't want you to worry. It's going to be all right. Grandma Allene won't let anything happen to me or any of us."

"I suppose you're right. I guess I'm a little antsy because so much has been going on lately. It just seems like the devil's always trying to stir up trouble."

"I can't argue with you on that point. And that's all the more reason why we all need to go to Nedine, and especially Christian."

"I worry about him so much. He called a few days ago and I know without a doubt he was either drunk, high, or both."

"Are you serious?" Alexandria ran her fingers through her heavy mass of curls as she thought about how out of control her brother was becoming.

"I'm afraid so. There was loud music and laughter in the background, so I guess he was having a party."

"What did he want?"

"Nothing," Victoria said in a heavy, frustrated breath. "He claims he just wanted to say hi. He mumbled a few incoherent words and then hung up."

During Alexandria's last conversation with her brother a few weeks ago she could tell that something wasn't quite right, and he'd sounded drunk or high, as her mother had just said. She didn't want to use her gift to peer into his life, but she also wanted to know exactly what was going on with her brother.

"I'll have to pack my patience in order to deal with your brother right now," Victoria said. "Your father nor I will tolerate him using drugs, period. And he better not bring any to the house."

Alexandria didn't put it past her brother to do exactly

what her mother had just said, but she refrained from telling her. "I pray that he gets some help. Hopefully next weekend will be a start toward it."

"Wait a minute. . . . I just glanced at my calendar. Do you realize that your wedding is two weeks away from next weekend?"

"Yes, I know. But it's going to be such a quick trip, and all the wedding plans are finalized so there's nothing pressing that needs to be done that can't be taken care of when we get back. Besides, I know you've got everything ironed out to a tee."

Victoria let out a small chuckle. "You better believe it."

"There won't be any problems, Mom. I'm going to focus on the positive side of this trip. I think it'll be a good getaway for us."

"To tell you the truth, your father and I haven't had a getaway in quite a long time, probably a year or two."

"Everyone's schedule is so busy that none of us have taken time to connect and unwind. We can use this trip to bond as a family and come closer together."

"Now that I think about it, it would be nice to have a break and a change of scenery to slow things down before the rush of your wedding. I haven't been back to Nedine since your grandfather passed away six years ago."

"I wish I'd had the strength to travel down there to attend the burial," Alexandria said with a little sadness in her voice. "But it was all I could do to sit in the church at the memorial service you planned. Back then I was still terrified of the spirits that might come to haunt me if I went to Nedine and saw the actual gravesite. But I'm not afraid anymore, and I have Grandma Allene to thank for that."

Victoria's voice filled with the same sadness that had

just overcome Alexandria's. "I wish I could see her, and my parents, too. Sweetie, your gift is a blessing."

Alexandria wanted to tell her mother that at times, her gift could also be stressful and disturbing. But just as she was going to claim a bright outlook on their family trip, she was going to do the same about her gift.

"Yes, I do feel blessed to be able to see, feel, and connect with their spirits."

"Just thinking about the fact that we're going back to the place where my parents were born and raised makes me feel good. I used to love going there as a child. The more I think about it, maybe there's nothing wrong at all. Maybe Grandma Allene simply wants us to enjoy each other as a family. Putting an end to old things and starting new beginnings makes me think about the fact that you'll get a chance to visit your grandparents' final resting place as you prepare to move on to the newness of your upcoming marriage."

"Yes, and speaking of new beginnings, PJ and I visited Gary last night and he's coming along well."

"Awww, that's great! He's such a special little boy and I know you and PJ have become very attached to him."

"More than attached, we love him."

"I can tell by the way you sound when you talk about him. I can't imagine abandoning my own child. Poor thing. What's going to happen to him once he's well enough to leave the hospital?"

Alexandria smiled on her end of the phone. "If all goes well, PJ and I plan to adopt him."

"What?! When did you make that decision?"

Alexandria could hear surprise, concern, and caution all mixed into her mother's question. "I've known it for some time, but PJ and I just decided last night. We know it's a big step and a huge commitment, but trust me, Mom, we're ready. I've seen the vision and we're ready."

Alexandria could picture her mother biting down on her lip as she said, "But you're going to be newlyweds."

"And new parents," Alexandria said with confidence.

"Sweetheart, I know you've got a good head on your shoulders and you think things through before you do them. But are you sure about this? Motherhood adds a new dimension to life that you wouldn't believe."

Alexandria simply smiled. "I've seen that firsthand from your example, and it's an experience I'm ready for."

Victoria let out a heavy sigh. "But it also comes with a whole heck of a lot of responsibility. Children can bring great joy, but they can also bring a lot of headaches, too. And trust me, marriage alone will guarantee you some of that."

"It's going to be all right. Trust me on this."

"You don't know what I know."

"Actually, in some cases I do." Alexandria was referring to her gift, and she knew her mother understood exactly what she was saying. "But I don't have to look into the future to know this is right—I've looked into my heart, and it always steers me right."

Victoria was quiet for a short pause before she spoke. "If there's one thing I've learned over the last year, it's that when you have a feeling about something it's usually on the money. I trust your judgment, sweetheart, and if this is what you and PJ truly want, you have my full support."

"Thanks, Mom. It's a big step, but we're ready."

"This certainly is a new beginning. And now that I think about it, I'll be a grandmother."

"You sound excited," Alexandria said with surprise.

"I can't believe I'm saying this, but I kind of am," Victoria said with a light laugh.

Alexandria was glad that her mother actually sounded excited about the trip, and in particular, the news she'd just delivered. She'd initially thought she'd have to spend hours convincing Victoria about her and PJ adopting Gary, let alone going to Nedine. But the fact that her mother was accepting of both was further confirmation that grandma Allene was right and that a visit to Nedine was just what their family needed.

"This is actually happening at just the right time," Victoria said. "Sometimes inspiration comes in unexpected ways."

"Yes, and as a matter of fact, I was looking on the Nedine website last night and the town is celebrating a big flower festival that weekend."

"Oh, yes! It's an annual event that's really grown over the years. I remember Mom, Daddy, and Uncle Maxx going back for it, and they always said they had a ball."

"It seems to be a pretty big deal because there's a ton of activities planned, and they're expecting a large turnout of people from both in and out of town."

"It's a good thing we won't have to worry about trying to find hotel rooms because small towns fill up fast. We can stay at the family homestead. It's the house Daddy grew up in, and it's beautiful. You've never been, but it's a grand old place with six bedrooms and four and a half bathrooms. I'll call Percy at the property management company and make arrangements to have it spruced up before we arrive."

"That sounds perfect." Now Alexandria was just as excited as her mother.

"Okay, I'll call your dad now, and then I'll see if Christian can make the trip."

"I have a feeling that Christian needs to go more than any of us."

Victoria breathed a deep sigh into the phone. "Unfortunately you're right. I'd hoped he would change his ways and do what's right, especially given the fact that he's about to start grad school this fall. I can't believe he's willing to throw it all away over a temporary high."

"Who knows? Maybe he'll get some kind of revelation from being around good energy."

"From your lips to God's ears."

Alexandria nodded. "He hears everything we say and watches what we do."

"Yes, that's how God works."

"This is going to be a great trip, Mom. You'll see."

After Alexandria hung up the phone she felt a sense of relief and hope. She was relieved because now that her mother had bought in to the trip, she knew the rest of the family would follow, and she felt hope for the new and unlimited possibilities that lay ahead for her and her family, which was going to soon expand. "Everything is going to work out. It has to," she said aloud.

She walked over to the window and smiled as she looked up at the sky. A big gray cloud that had been looming all morning suddenly burst open, producing a hard rain. The unexpected downpour sent an immediate chill through Alexandria's body. In that instant, all the happy optimism she'd just felt was gone, replaced with the uncomfortable knowledge that something bad, and maybe even dangerous, was lurking, waiting to happen.

Alexandria watched the rain puddle on the ground several stories below as lightning flashed and thunder rumbled in the sky. She knew this wasn't a quick passing storm, and that the rain would continue every day for the next two weeks until she and her family arrived in Nedine. "Grandma Allene, please guide me, and watch over us all."

Chapter 10
Victoria

Victoria sat behind her desk and said a quick prayer of thanks as she watched the rain fall outside her office window. She'd just made three important phone calls, each ending in the result she'd wanted. Ted, Christian, and her uncle Maxx had all agreed to travel to Nedine next weekend. She'd simply explained to them that Alexandria had requested it on behalf of Grandma Allene, which was all that needed to be said to make her case. Although, clearly, no one in the family understood the extent of Alexandria's gift, including herself, they all knew it was real, and if going to Nedine was what Alexandria said they needed to do, they were going to be there.

When Alexandria had first told Victoria that Grandma Allene had contacted her and wanted the family to return to Nedine, Victoria had been cautious and a little afraid. She immediately associated a visit from Grandma Allene with trouble—a sign that something bad was on the way. But the more Victoria talked about the trip, the more it made her think about her current situation, and how a visit to her parents' beloved hometown might just be the answer to her problems.

Ever since her ill-fated attempt to clear the air with Ted and jumpstart the passion in her marriage last night, Victoria had been feeling at a loss about what was really going on with her husband, and more importantly, what she could do about it. But when Alexandria had told her that Grandma Allene had said traveling to Nedine would allow them to bury the past so new beginnings could start, she'd known that was a good sign.

In addition to what she felt the visit would offer her daughter, which was an opportunity to gain closure by releasing the last of her fears and pay final respects to her grandparents and their parents before them, Victoria's gut told her that Grandma Allene's words about burying the past and beginning anew held a special meaning for her life, too. Parker was the past, and what she planned to reignite with Ted represented a new chapter in their marriage as they entered the golden years of their lives.

She and Ted hadn't taken a vacation or even a quick weekend getaway together since she could remember, which was very unlike them. She knew they needed to escape from what had slowly become a dangerously mundane routine. "We need to find our way back to each other," Victoria whispered to herself.

Once they were away from the stress and hectic grind of their everyday lives, the peaceful quiet of Nedine she hoped that being in the house her grandfather had built, which was full of love, would reignite the spark that had always kept her and Ted's marriage going.

Every time Victoria thought about the huge wedge she'd put in their relationship by nearly sleeping with Parker, all she could do was shake her head. She hadn't made many mistakes in their marriage, and she'd worked hard to be a good wife, but her transgression with Parker and the way it had all unfolded still haunted her today. And what was worst of all, Ted couldn't seem to let it go.

There were days when Victoria wished she'd never walked into The Cheesecake Factory all those years ago and spotted Parker, instantly falling for him. "If I'd only stayed home and made a sandwich," she said, thinking about that night. But what was done was done, and she knew there was no way to change the hands of time. All she could do was deal with what was in front of her and move forward the best way she knew how.

As she thought about dealing with tough situations, her mind fell on Tyler. She'd wanted to meet him for coffee this morning, but his schedule was tight so they'd decided to have an early lunch. Victoria hadn't liked the tired sound in his voice and she'd known the problems in his home were taking a toll.

"Everybody's going through something," Victoria said as she rose from behind her desk, grabbed her handbag and umbrella, and left to meet Tyler. She hoped that just as she was going to fix the problems in her marriage, that Tyler could repair the trouble in his home.

Victoria ate her soup and salad as Tyler stared at his untouched cheeseburger and French fries. Seeing him face-to-face made her even more concerned.

Tyler had always possessed a calm, carefree, and relaxed attitude that complemented his youthful good looks and spirit. As the years passed and his hair had started to gray, he had begun to look more distinguished, which had elevated him from cute to handsome. But over the last twelve months, Victoria had noticed that he'd begun to develop more lines across his forehead, and his eyes often looked heavy with worry.

As she studied Tyler's face more closely, she had no doubt that the idea of his sixteen-year-old son becoming a father had aged him a few more years, practically overnight. For a man who'd always had a healthy appetite, and would eat anything that was put in front of him, the fact that he hadn't taken a bite of his food was further proof to Victoria that her best friend was in bad shape.

Victoria took a sip of her sparkling water and then cleared her throat. "I can't pretend to know exactly how you feel right now. But I'm here to listen and help you in any way I can."

"I don't know where I went wrong," Tyler began. "I run one of the most successful at-risk youth programs in the state, and arguably the region. My curriculum modules for YFI are taught at nonprofits across the country. I lecture to groups at national conventions, and I give individual counseling to some of the roughest knuckleheads you can imagine. I can help prevent young men in the street from becoming teen fathers, but I can't keep my own son from going out and making babies up and down the East Coast."

Victoria stopped eating her salad in mid-bite. "What do you mean, making babies up and down the East Coast? Does Chase have more than one girl pregnant?"

Tyler slowly nodded his head.

Now Victoria's food sat untouched just like Tyler's. She wiped her mouth with her napkin. "Samantha doesn't know about this, does she?"

"Hell no! You know my wife. She'd hit the damn roof and show out so bad I'd have to give her a sedative."

"How many girls has Chase gotten pregnant?"

"Three."

"Lord have mercy, Jesus in heaven."

"Well, let me clarify that. He got one girl pregnant last year, but she had a miscarriage. Then a few months later the other one had an abortion and told him about it after the fact. But this one's different. This girl is four months pregnant and her father called me the night after Chase broke the news to us because he wants to have a family meeting. I can't say that I blame him."

Victoria shook her head. "How did you manage to keep Samantha from finding out about the others?"

"Chase confides in me more than he does his mother because he knows Sam's liable to say or do anything. Plus, I had a man-to-man talk with him when he started puberty. I told him that no matter how bad a situation gets or what kind of trouble he finds himself in, he better come to me and tell me because I'll kick his ass if I have to find out about it in the street."

Victoria let out a deep breath but didn't say anything.

"Hey, don't knock it."

"I'm not—I'm just thinking about what you said. It's tough to raise kids."

"Who you tellin'. But I will say this, I've spared Sam from a lot of Chase's fuck-ups, and honestly, if she knew about half of them she would've probably escalated an already bad situation to another level. I love my wife, and I have to give her credit because she's really grown and matured over the years. But I'm also a realist, and trust me, I know how Sam is."

"You're managing this situation the best way you know how."

He nodded. "I'm just a man trying to keep my family together, but it doesn't look like I'm doing a good job of it right now."

Victoria reached across the table and touched Tyler's hand. "You're doing all you can. Is it okay if I give you a piece of unsolicited advice?"

"Saying no has never stopped you," he said with a smile.

"Take it from a person who's messed up in the past by withholding vital information from their spouse. No matter how much you think it will hurt Samantha, or how much you think she might hurt Chase, or make a situation worse, from now on you have to tell her about what's going on in your son's life. She's his mother, he's her baby, and she deserves to know. You two are a united front, but you'll fall and crumble if you don't stand together on everything, especially when it comes to your children."

Tyler rubbed the stubble growing on his chin. "You're right." He nodded. "From this point forward I'm gonna tell Sam everything, no matter what."

"Good, that way you two can work things out together and you won't have the burden of carrying Chase's problems by yourself."

"True."

Victoria looked at his plate. "Tyler, I know you're struggling with this, but you've got to pull yourself together. You won't be any good to your family if you're not good to yourself, so please eat."

Reluctantly, Tyler stuffed a few French fries into his mouth. "I'm gonna tell you something that I really hate to admit, and I've never shared with another living soul."

"Okay." Victoria braced herself because after his confession about Chase's multiple pregnancy scares she couldn't imagine what he was going to reveal next.

"I love Chase with all my heart. He's funny, smart, and he's a generally good-natured kid when he's not getting into trouble." Tyler paused and then looked at Victoria with what appeared to be defeat. "But he's bad as hell and at the rate he's going, I think prison is in his future. I work with that population, I see it every day, and my son has all the signs."

Victoria thought the same thing about her son, too, but she didn't know what to say so she just listened.

"From the time he was a little kid, he's been out of control, always breaking rules and getting into unnecessary trouble by doing stupid shit. I remember when he was seven years old I enrolled him in Cub Scouts because I thought it would help him build character and learn about teamwork. How about my son was sneaking *Playboy* magazines into the scout meetings."

"Stop lyin'! At seven?"

"Yes. And when the troop leader told me about it, I confronted Chase and asked him where the hell did he get the magazines from, because I know they didn't come from our house. You wanna know what he told me?"

"I'm afraid to ask."

"He said, 'Don't worry about it, Dad. I got connections and I can hook you up, if you want me too.' "

"Good Lord."

"See, it's shit like that, that a seven-year-old shouldn't know anything about, that lets you know he's been a handful out the gate. You would think he was being raised in a brothel. And let's not even talk about the fact that he's been slipping out of the house and going to parties since he was ten."

Over the years Victoria had heard Samantha constantly voice her frustration with Chase, likening him to one of *Bébé's Kids* on steroids. But Victoria had never heard Tyler talk about his son with such disappointment and despair, and it made her heart ache for her best friend because she understood the anguish and stress a wayward child could cause.

She'd observed on her own what a little terror Chase could be when he was just a small child. There had been several occasions when Tyler and Samantha had asked her to babysit, and she remembered literally counting down the minutes until they came to pick him up. He'd been the kind of child who was always into something he had no business having an interest in. "Grown-folks business" as her mother used to call it. One time, Ted had outright threatened Chase.

CJ, on the other hand, had been a complete joy to be around, never once giving his parents or anyone else a moment of trouble. He'd always been a level-headed, mature, and responsible young man, and he'd tried unsuccessfully to help steer his younger brother in the right direction.

"Sometimes I just don't' get it," Tyler said wearily. "We raised CJ and Chase under the same roof, never showing favoritism or differential treatment between the two. We let them know that we loved them equally. We gave both of them the same advantages, the same lectures about right and wrong, and the same unconditional love and support. CJ may not be my biological child, but he's my blood in every way, and he makes me proud to hold my head up and call him my son. But Chase . . ." Tyler sighed. "He has my direct DNA, from the shape of my head down to my body build. But we couldn't be more different, and he makes me want to hit the damn bottle."

"I know what you mean. Look at my two. They're a prime example of everything you just said. Alexandria is one of the most honest, sincere, and naturally kind people you ever want to meet, and she always tries to do the right thing. But Christian," she said, taking a deep breath, "you can't trust anything that comes out of his mouth. If his lips are moving that means he's lying."

"You said it, not me."

"Yes, I did. And I'll tell you something else since we're baring our souls about our children." Victoria leaned forward and exhaled. "I think Christian's getting deeper and deeper into drugs."

Tyler shook his head. "Damn. I hate to hear that. I knew he had some problems but I thought he'd gotten his act together. Isn't he going to Columbia this fall?"

"Yes, he is. And it's a miracle that he's been able to maintain such a great academic record, given the fact that he drank, smoked, snorted, and partied his way through Morehouse," Victoria said with frustration. "And let's not talk about the women. I firmly believe he's one screw away from a paternity suit."

"I tried talking to him a few months ago around spring break, and he assured me that he'd cut back on his drinking and he'd left the drugs alone."

Victoria rolled her eyes. "He lied."

"I know. I could tell when I looked into his eyes."

"Even though Chase makes you want to drink, count your blessings because sometimes I want to do bodily harm to Christian."

"Well, when you put it like that, I guess I should be thankful. And I've got to agree with you, Christian's always been a piece of work."

"That's putting it mildly and you know it. Christian's been in more trouble than I can name and the sad thing about it is that half of the mayhem he causes goes under the radar from Ted and me because he hides things so well. I'm afraid that either the drugs, wild women, or both are going to be his downfall. He's too slick for his own good.

Physically, Christian was strikingly handsome with the perfect combination of Victoria's and Ted's features. He'd taken her smooth chocolate-brown skin, grabbed Ted's deep, ocean-blue eyes, and picked up his height and lean body shape from both of them, sculpting him into the kind of man who commanded attention whenever he walked into a room. But sadly, he took advantage of his assets in all the wrong ways, especially when it came to women.

Every time Victoria thought about Christian, and the kind of lifestyle he was leading, her mind worried with thoughts of what would happen to him. But she would never give up hope that her son could turn things around, and it was something she'd been praying for ever since he was seven years old and had come home with a note in his book bag, explaining that he'd been sniffing glue and stealing cigarettes out of his teacher's desk drawer.

Tyler pushed his plate of cold, uneaten food to the side. "We're a fine pair—two only children who each have a child that's a damn mess."

"It could be worse."

Tyler shook his head. "Please don't say that. I can't take any more right now."

"Okay, I won't go down that road."

"Besides, I haven't told you the clincher."

Victoria put her hand to her temple. "Is Chase's girl-friend having twins?"

"You're right, that would be worse. But no, she's not having twins."

"Whew!"

"Technically, she's not his girlfriend, and she doesn't even live in Atlanta. She's in D.C."

Victoria blinked. "Samantha mentioned that when we talked briefly yesterday, but she said it was compli-cated."

"I'll say. Nothing about my son is ever easy."

Victoria looked perplexed. "How did he manage this?"

"A couple months ago, when we went up to D.C. during spring break to visit Sam's family, Chase hooked up with this little girl, and the rest is history. And to be honest, I don't even know when it could've happened because we thought we'd kept such a close eye on him. But apparently not."

"Tyler, I don't mean to complicate things, but how does Chase know this baby is his? He was up there for a few days, but who knows what that girl was doing prior to or after his visit. Young girls can lay a trap just like grown women can."

"Now you're thinking on my level. I've already made up my mind that as soon as the baby is born we're gonna do a paternity test. Unfortunately, as you know, I have some experience in this area."

Ironically, that was how Tyler had found out that CJ wasn't his biological child. At that time when he and Samantha had been dating, she had still been going through her wild, rebellious stage, and had put herself in a position that caused her and Tyler's breakup once CJ was born and the test results had come in. Fortunately, they were an example of a love that was meant to be because five years later they'd walked back into each other's lives and had been together ever since.

Victoria nodded her head. "That's a good idea. You've got five months to go before you'll have your answer, and I'm going to pray for all of you, Tyler."

"Be sure to get on both knees when you do, and cross all your fingers and toes while you're at it."

"It's gonna be all right." Victoria looked at her watch. "Sorry to cut it short, but I have to get back to the office for a meeting, and then I need to go home early so I can bake your wife a chocolate cocoa cake."

Tyler placed his credit card on the table to pay for their meal. "Thanks, Victoria. I appreciate you doing this for Sam. You've always been a great friend, and I don't know what I'd do without you."

"You know I'll do whatever I can to help both of you. Just say the word."

Tyler's eyes suddenly lit up. "Why didn't I think of it before now?" he said with excitement. "Ask Alexandria if I can bring Chase by her place so she can tell us whether he's the father or not?"

"Listen to you! My daughter's not a circus performer with a crystal ball."

"But she's got skills, Victoria. Talk to her and see if she'll agree to do it."

Victoria shook her head. She didn't want to speak for Alexandria, but she knew her daughter would be uncomfortable with the situation. Alexandria was still learning how to control her gift, measure her abilities, and ration her powers. She'd told Victoria on more than one occasion that she had no interest in interfering with the natural progression of life and events unless someone's health or safety was at serious risk.

"She's your goddaughter," Victoria said. "If you want her help, you're more than welcome to call her with your psychic hotline request."

"That's cold."

"And true."

"I guess on second thought it's not such a good idea. I don't want to put any stress in her life just when she's finally happy and about to jump that broom."

"One thing I've learned is that everything eventually comes out. Time will reveal the truth and you'll know if Chase is the father."

As Victoria drove back to her office, she thought about her lunch conversation with Tyler. She knew that whether they liked it or not, both their youngest children were headed down some rocky roads, and one didn't have to possess the gift of prophecy to see that.

Chapter 11
Allene

Allene smiled as she breathed in the warm, sweet-smelling air. She loved summer nights, and this evening in particular was especially beautiful. After a day of dark clouds and thunderstorms, a rainbow had spread across the city, and now that nighttime had come, a bright moon was hanging in the big black sky, keeping company with the stars.

This was the kind of night Allene used to enjoy in a different lifetime, when she lived in her tiny house up the road. Isaiah had fussed and wanted to build her a large stucco and brick ranch-style home that he thought would be more fitting, but Allene wouldn't hear of it. "I just need a lil peace of somethin' where I can grow vegetables out back, flowers in the front, and lay my head down at night," she'd told him. Isaiah had grumbled, but he'd also respected his mother's wishes when he'd purchased her modest two-bedroom home and handed her the keys.

Allene loved that little house. She'd sit on her front

porch, enjoying her own company and the peace she felt from a life well lived. Now, as she sat in her rocking chair on her son's front porch, she wished that Isaiah, Henrietta, John, Elizabeth, and all the other family members whom she'd loved could enjoy this night with her.

"I sure do miss y'all something awful," Allene said aloud. "Things just ain't the same without the ones you love."

Allene was grateful that she had a new generation of relatives whom she could see in the here and now. She smiled when she thought about how good it would be to have her family under one roof, back at the house her son had built with so much love. She'd always valued the power of family and the fact that it created bonds that could get you through joys and sorrows. Family was strong and resilient, and stood the test of time. Allene knew it was imperative that she do everything she could to hold hers together, especially now that lives were at stake.

Family was just as important to Alexandria, and Allene knew that the young woman was equally committed to making sure theirs thrived for generations to come. "You're doin' good, baby girl. I know you're worried 'cause you feel what's comin', but it's gonna be all right." As Allene whispered those words into the calm night air, she knew Alexandria could hear her, and that it would give her peace as a storm raged several hundred miles away in Atlanta.

Allene had focused her mind, concentrated, and sought out anyone who would be able to assist her in helping Alexandria. She had been pleasantly surprised when she'd stumbled upon Anita Brown, a sixty-year-old nurse who worked at PJ's hospital. Ms. Brown didn't have the advanced abilities that she or Alexandria possessed, but the woman was pure of heart, and she could sense good or evil, which was most important to Allene, and was necessary to protect Alexandria as she and PJ began their family.

Allene was relieved that Alexandria's mind was more at ease knowing that she didn't have to worry about Gary while she and PJ were away next weekend. Now she was free to focus on the conflict that was sure to arise once everyone gathered at the family homestead.

As Allene slowly rocked back and forth in her comfortable old rocking chair, a chill grabbed her that nearly took her breath away. She'd felt it before, though she hadn't wanted to give it much credence—because she knew that sometimes things had a way of working themselves out—but now it let her know that not every situation would be wrapped in a neat bow, no matter how much she hoped it would. Secrets were going to be revealed and one unfortunate person would not survive the weekend.

"Lord, give them all the strength to do what needs to be done." Allene slowly rose to her feet, opened the front door, and went upstairs so she could rest up for the events that were about to take place.

Chapter 12
Samantha

Samantha had taken the day off so she could pack and prepare for her family's trip to Nedine tomorrow. Even though they would only be there for the weekend, she wanted a little extra time to relax and unwind before getting on the road first thing in the morning. Her shoulders had been tense and her nerves had been on edge ever since last week when Chase had told her and Tyler about LaMonica's pregnancy.

Samantha was wrought with worry every time she thought about her teenage son becoming a father. The staggering reality was stressful enough, and now, the possibility that her carefully guarded secret was in danger of coming to light only added to her fears.

She was grateful for the much-needed and unexpected getaway that couldn't have come at a more perfect time, and she saw this trip as an opportunity to help her solve her family's growing problems. Last week when she'd heard Victoria speak in detail about the purpose behind going to Nedine, after dropping by to deliver her world-famous chocolate cocoa cake, Samantha had known right away that the small Southern town was where she, Tyler, and Chase needed to be as well. She smiled to herself, thinking about how that evening had unfolded.

"At first I was a little nervous with the whole idea," Victoria had said as she handed Samantha a large slice of cake. "But after Alexandria explained that this trip will be a way for us to put the past behind us so we can start new beginnings, I knew I had to go to Nedine, and now I can't wait."

Samantha had never been one to believe in spirits or people who possessed so-called supernatural powers. She'd seen psychics on late-night TV infomercials and hustlers in the streets of D.C. who tried to make a quick buck with tarot cards and mindreading tricks, none of which she'd given a second thought. But the moment she'd met Alexandria, her opinion had changed.

Samantha still remembered the night many years ago when Tyler had brought her over to Victoria's house to share their good news right after they'd gotten engaged. Victoria and Ted had been happy for them and they'd all toasted with champagne, having a joyous time. As she and Tyler were about to leave, an eleven-year-old Alexandria had come up to her and told her something that still haunted her to this day.

With a face and tone more serious than any adult Samantha knew, Alexandria had stared into her eyes and said she was sorry that Samantha's younger sister had died. It had startled Samantha, especially since her only sibling was an estranged brother whom she hadn't heard from in years. A short time later, she'd found out that her best friend, Emily, had been carrying her father's child and had suffered a miscarriage. It had been a baby girl.

From that moment forward, Samantha had been a

true believer. She banked on whatever Alexandria said, so if this trip was supposed to help with burying the past she was all for it.

"It's going to be a great getaway," Victoria had continued. "Nedine is actually celebrating the fiftieth anniversary of its annual Flower Festival next weekend, so there will be lots to do. We're going to stay at my family homestead, which is a treat in itself because the place is like a Southern inn. We're going to have a great time, and most of all, I know this will be a healing experience that we all need."

After cutting her second slice of cake, Samantha was working her fork toward her mouth as she spoke. "Victoria, I have a really huge favor to ask you."

"No, I already made you a cake, I'm not making you my homemade ice cream, too. I have to draw the line somewhere."

"Actually, that does sound good." She smiled between bites. "But that's not what I was going to ask. Would you mind if Tyler, Chase, and I joined you guys on your trip?"

"You want to come to Nedine?" Victoria said with surprise.

"Yes, it sounds like fun. I've never been to South Carolina, and . . ."

"Samantha, I'm not sure that Nedine's your cup of tea. The anchor store at their mall is Target."

Samantha could see the wheels turning inside Victoria's head. One of the things she'd learned about her friend over the years was that Victoria was one of the most analytical people she knew, and the woman asked more questions than a police detective. Samantha could feel Victoria about to launch into an interrogation so she answered before she could be asked. "As you know, Tyler and I are under a tremendous amount of stress with this whole pregnancy thing. Hell, that's why you're over here now with a cake I know I'll finish by breakfast."

"Goodness!"

"Girl, you know I can eat. Anyway, I'm so stressed lately I can barcly think."

"I know. I had lunch with Tyler earlier today and he told me everything."

"Both of us are frustrated and I think it'll be good for us to get away for a few days. We definitely need to put things in our past so we can start new. For us, that means Chase's behavior. With what we're about to go through as a family, we can't move forward if we don't put some things behind us." Samantha was sincere, but she was also hiding the fact that she hoped she could bury her long-held secret once and for all.

Victoria nodded. "I completely understand. I want the same thing." She paused and cleared her throat. "I'm hoping Ted and I can put the mistake I made with Parker in our past where it belongs."

Samantha could hear the strain in Victoria's voice at the mention of Parker's name. Samantha loved Parker, but she knew how he was. He could be relentless when he wanted something, and he'd always had his sights set on Victoria. He'd dated a number of women over the years, and to everyone's surprise and chagrin, he'd been with his current bitch of a girlfriend for quite some time. But he would never make a commitment, and Samantha knew it was because his heart had never gotten what it truly wanted. She understood that feeling because she'd been the same way until she'd reunited with Tyler. "I'm gonna pray for you on that one," she said.

"Thanks, I need it."

"I know it's going to be awkward for you and Ted having Parker as an in-law, but trust me, my cousin is going to behave himself. PJ is his world, and he loves that boy way too much to cause any trouble."

Victoria nodded. "Honestly, I'm more worried about Ted than Parker. We had a conversation last night and even after all these years he's still suspicious when it comes to Parker and me. Can you believe that?"

Samantha wanted to say she didn't blame him, because again, she knew how her cousin was. But at the moment she needed to refocus on the trip to Nedine. "Like I said, I'll pray for you, my friend. Now . . . what do you think about us tagging along? After listening to what you've said, I really believe this is exactly what we need."

Victoria smiled. "Alexandria said this trip was for our family, and you guys are definitely a part of it. Sure, come on and join us. The more the merrier."

Now it was midafternoon and Samantha was relaxed in her cute, hot-pink loungewear tank top and shorts as she sat on her bed with pillows propped behind her back and her laptop perched across her thighs. She stared at the illuminated screen and let out a deep sigh. She was more than ready for her getaway because at the moment she was annoyed to the point of feeling pissed.

"Shit!" Samantha hissed as she looked at the Facebook friend request that had popped up in her notifications last week. For the past seven days she'd been debating whether to click CONFIRM, click NOT NOW, or simply pretend that her past hadn't come back to haunt her.

But time had taught her that you couldn't outrun trouble if it was waiting to find you. She let out a deep breath as she thought about how complicated and downright contradictory life could be, especially hers.

She prided herself on being an open, up-front person. She wasn't the type to beat around the bush and she always told the truth, even when it was difficult to say. That was why being in the situation she now found herself in was so frustrating. She knew that sometimes not only could the truth hurt, it could devastate the people you loved, and when it came to her family she was willing to do whatever it took to protect them—in this case, from the truth.

"This bastard has some nerve," she seethed as she continued to look at her computer screen. Even with the disguised name he was hiding behind, which had pissed her off just reading it, and the profile picture he was using of a lady holding a sword in one hand while balancing a scale in the other, representing the universal symbol for justice, Samantha knew exactly who had sent her the request. It made her sick, mad, and a little afraid all at once.

"If that asshole thinks I'm gonna play his game, he's got another thing coming," Samantha whispered aloud. "He's the one who should be sitting in bed, worried about the truth coming out, not me."

She'd been plagued with anxiety ever since last week when she'd realized that LaMonica's father was David Carpenter, and now she was unsettled by the fact that he was contacting her through Facebook. She wanted to snap her fingers and make him go away, but she knew that was impossible. At the very least, if his daughter was indeed carrying Chase's baby, David would once again be entwined in her life, much like Parker was in Victoria's.

Samantha had been nervous when Tyler had told her that he and David had spoken by phone and that David had suggested they have a conference call last weekend to discuss their children's predicament. She'd been on pins and needles all last Saturday, waiting for David to call Tyler's cell, but he never did. Tyler had been pissed that the man hadn't followed through as he'd said he would, but his negligence had felt like a wave of relief over Samantha's burdened mind.

Now, sitting on her bed, worried out of her mind, the longer she stared at David's friend request, the angrier she got. "He's still a punk," she said aloud. "He'll dodge my husband, but his sneaky ass will send me a friend request. He's still the same fucking snake I remember. Well, I'm gonna get to the bottom of this shit right now."

Samantha took a deep breath and clicked CONFIRM.

She immediately went on his page and started looking around for information. She was disappointed that it took all of two minutes to search through his photos, timeline, about section, and his events. David hadn't provided much beyond his stock photo profile picture and his phony name, TicTacToe. Every time Samantha saw that name, she wanted to scream. He'd used it on purpose to make sure she knew it was him.

She was about to check out Chase's page to see if he'd posted any crazy or inappropriate messages since last night, when the alert sound dinged, notifying her that she had a message waiting in her inbox. Her heart started pounding when she saw that it was from TicTacToe. She clicked on the message, opened it, and started reading.

Sam,

It's been a long time. I know when you saw my screen name you knew it was me. Who would've thought we'd be reunited after all these years, especially under these circumstances? I won't burden you with small talk. You know I was never good at that. So here's the deal. My daughter and your son have made a terrible mistake. LaMonica waited until it was too late for her

mother and me to do anything about this preg-
nancy, because apparently she wants this baby.
So here we are. If you're anything like I remem-
ber, you're just as disappointed about this as I
am. I'm reaching out to you to make sure we still
have an understanding. As long as you're quiet,
I'll be quiet. Don't do something that we'll both
regret.

TicTacToe

Samantha hadn't realized she'd been holding her
breath until she finished reading his message and gasped
for air. "I know his ass didn't just threaten me?!" she
yelled directly at the screen.

She was livid. Her first thought was to go down to
the kitchen drawer where Tyler had written David's cell
phone number on a sticky note, dial him up, and curse
him out. But after taking a few deep breaths, which Tyler
had taught her to do over the years as a way to help center
her temper and calm her emotions, she decided against
taking that action. "I can't let that bastard get to me."

She put her laptop to the side, got out of bed, and
walked downstairs. If it weren't for the fact that it had
been raining day and night for two weeks straight, she
would have laced up her running shoes and gone outside
to clear her head. But she didn't do rain, and she didn't
want to ruin her hairdo after having had it styled early
this morning, so instead she headed to the kitchen to pour
herself a glass of wine.

This time, instead of bringing the bottle upstairs and
drinking the whole thing as she'd done last week, she
poured a modest glass and stood at the sink as she drank.
She was sorry that she'd ever started down a road of deceit. It was long, rough, and bumpy, and she'd never thought

she'd still be on the journey all these years later. She thought back to when her secret had started and why, and it made her feel like crying.

Looking back on things, Samantha knew she should've let the truth come out a long time ago. It would've been painful, but she was also sure that time would've healed the wound. Now, twenty-seven years later, everyone's lives had changed in such complex ways that the truth held more hurtful consequences today than if she'd just come clean from the very beginning.

As she sipped the last of her wine, she thought about the secret that David was keeping, too. She used to believe that his dirt was far worse than hers. But then she realized that after everything was said and done, they were neck and neck. Her secret required lies, pretense, and deceit, just like his. "How did I get myself into this mess?" she said aloud. She gulped down the last of the wine in her glass. "It's time for me to take some action."

Samantha charged back upstairs, reclaimed her spot on her bed, and started typing away on her laptop.

> *Hello Asshole,*
>   *I'm not good at small talk either, so I'll get right down to business. We've never had an understanding. What we have is secrets. Motherfucker, don't you ever threaten me again. If you do, your punk ass will be the one who'll regret it.*

Samantha pressed reply and then jumped when her cell phone rang. She looked at the name on her screen and saw that it was Tyler.

"Hey, baby," she said, trying to sound as though everything were fine.

"What's wrong?"

"Nothing. Why?"

"You sound funny. Like when you're upset. What happened?"

"Tyler, I'm fine."

"You sure?"

"Yes, I was trying to pack and get a few things ready for our trip tomorrow." She hated lying to her husband, so she threw in a sliver of truth for good measure. "I guess I'm still a little stressed about this situation with Chase. It's all I can think about these days."

"Me too. But like you were saying the other day, maybe this weekend will help ease some of our worries."

Samantha sighed. "I pray it will."

"We've gotta have faith, Sam. Besides, I've never known Alexandria to be wrong about anything with her visions."

"You're right about that." She had to agree with Tyler. Alexandria's prediction was the only reason she was going to Nedine in the first place, and she knew her family's future was resting on the hope that Alexandria's words would ring true. "Are you still coming home early?" she asked.

"Yeah, that's why I'm calling. I'm gonna pick up Chase from Brad's so you won't have to, and then we'll stop by Spring Garden and get takeout for dinner before we head home. Just sit back, relax, and ease your pretty mind."

Samantha smiled. "A man who'll take care of my child, bring me food, *and* ease my mind . . . baby, you're a keeper."

Tyler laughed. "I better be because you're not getting rid of me. Even if you tried."

After they ended their conversation, Samantha walked back over to her laptop to see if TicTacToe had left her another message. She was glad to see that he hadn't. But her relief was only temporary because two seconds later she heard the familiar ding that let her know she had another message waiting. When she looked, sure enough it was David.

Sam,

I see you haven't changed after all these years, or maybe you have and you just reserved those words in your previous message especially for me. You need to know that I don't make threats. I give warnings, and that was yours. Don't push me. All it takes is one stamped envelope to the law offices of Bailey, Bernstein, and Baldwin.

TicTacToe

The calmness that Samantha had managed to muster after hearing Tyler's protective, caring voice was now gone. She reread David's message two times and felt the rock that had been in her stomach last week return. "This is what I get for lying down with a dog," she sighed. "Fleas and even ticks all over me."

Samantha shook her head and closed her eyes as her mind took her back to the past.

The second Samantha laid eyes on David Carpenter, she knew she had to have him. His handsome face, tall athletic body, and smooth caramel-colored skin had drawn her in. They were both in their junior year of college, she at Spelman, he at Georgetown, when they'd met. She was home in D.C. on Christmas break and spotted David at a mutual friend's holiday party. Samantha immediately got the 411 on him.

She found out that David was a good ol' boy from

Tennessee, a dean's list student, a track star, and the president of the Black Student Alliance. His look definitely fit her MO, but his seemingly clean-cut image didn't. Samantha liked men with an edge who'd been around the block a few times. But when she found out about the other side of David, her interest was piqued. Her girlfriend, who was throwing the party, told her the real deal.

"Stay away from David Carpenter unless you want some drama," Samantha's friend had warned. "He's a really nice guy. Smart, funny, and will probably go places in life. But when it comes to women, he's one of the biggest whores on campus. He's been dating the same girl, Millie, since freshman year, and that relationship is a joke because every weekend he's in some other girl's bed. And Millie . . . let's just say she's a few screws shy of coming undone. If you know what's good for you, you'll keep your distance from the both of them."

That night at the party, Samantha found out that David's girlfriend was indeed a little unstable. Millie busted in, created a loud scene, started a fistfight with a girl whom David had been talking to, and then stormed out, practically dragging him with her, but not before David slipped Samantha his number. She and David hooked up a few nights later. Over the next three weeks of Samantha's holiday break, David carried on with her behind his girlfriend's back, as well as with another woman who found Samantha's number in David's address book, called her, and threatened her life. The adrenaline rush of drama mixed with a hint of danger made Samantha want David even more. Their love making was hot and steamy, bordering on hedonistic.

Samantha loved his duality. He was a clean cut, athletic honor student whose favorite board game was Tic Tac Toe, yet he kept whips, chains, and feathers under his bed for sexual pleasure. Samantha thought she'd found the perfect man, but she soon discovered there was a darker side to her new found prince charming than she'd ever imagined.

One night Samantha had snuck David into her house while her parents were out at her father's holiday office party. While Samantha was down the hall taking a long shower, David used the opportunity to go through her things. When she came back into her bedroom with a towel wrapped around her body, she had no idea that the sexy, good-looking man standing in front of her had just discovered the secret she'd been keeping that could tear her family apart.

It wasn't until the explosive evening of their break-up a few nights later that Samantha found out how ruth-less he really was. She went over to his apartment and accidentally stumbled upon a shocking discovery that made her nearly lose her breath. While she was in the middle of cursing him out, David raised his hand and said, "You're gonna walk out that door, you're gonna keep your mouth shut, and this is why." He proceeded to tell her what he'd read in her journal when she had been in the shower a few nights before, and when he was fin-ished, Samantha was left silent, doing just as David had said, walking out the door with her mouth shut.

"Getting mixed up with David Carpenter should've taught me a lesson a long time ago," But that incident hadn't stopped her. She'd spent the next ten years mask-ing her pain and heartache by making one mistake after another, until Tyler had reentered her life and helped her find the strength to change.

As she stared at David's cryptic message, she thought about the truth. She knew that once Edward Baldwin, Esq. found out that he wasn't her biological father, it would crush him. But what would hurt even more, and cause tidal waves within their family was the other part of the truth—that Samantha was the product of an affair that her mother had with her own sister's husband.

Samantha shook her head again as she thought about the sobering fact that Parker was her brother, not her cousin. "I definitely need to bury the past so that hopefully a good and new beginning can come out of all this hurt," Samantha said, trying to stop her voice from shaking. She zipped her suitcase and made up her mind right then and there that she was going to expose the truth, even if it was at a cost to the people she loved. She moved her fingers toward her computer keys and started typing.

> *I'm not putting up with your bullshit, and I won't be warned, threatened, or whatever the hell else you try to pull. You're fucking with the wrong one this time. I'm not that scared co-ed you remember who was afraid of the truth. This is a new day, so hear me clear. Do what you feel you have to because that's exactly what I'm gonna do, you dick sucking punk. That's right, I said it, and if you keep fucking with me, I'll say it to your wife.*

Samantha hit reply and waited for David's response. When thirty minutes went by with no reply message, she knew she'd gotten her point across. But she also knew this meant she'd have to be confronted with her past very soon.

Chapter 13
Alexandria

Alexandria and PJ were patiently sitting at their gate waiting for an announcement to see if they'd be heading to Nedine by air, or if they'd be forced to make the nearly seven-hour drive by car. Heavy rain and thunderstorms had grounded over half the flights out of Hartsfield-Jackson International Airport for the last two weeks. It was 7:00 AM, and the Delta terminal was full of disgruntled passengers whose travel plans had been foiled by the unrelenting weather.

"We might have to either drive, or fly out of a different airport," PJ said. "The weather's bad and I just don't trust it. We need to be prepared if they cancel this flight because that's a very real possibility."

Alexandria shook her head without the slightest worry. "We'll make our flight. Trust me."

Sure enough, their plane took off on time despite the bumpy start caused by the steady rain and winds. Once they were in the air, gray turned to yellow, allowing the sun to be their guide as they soared through the sky, headed for a weekend that held both promise and danger.

Alexandria was too wired to sleep on the flight, so she listened to the soft hum of PJ's breathing as he rested his head on her shoulder while he dozed. He'd pulled two all-nighters in a row at the hospital, and Alexandria was amazed that he still had energy to travel. She was thankful for PJ's kind spirit and genuine goodness, and she was determined to do whatever was necessary to make sure she kept him safe this weekend.

Ever since that morning two weeks ago when Alexandria had called her mother to set plans in motion for a family trip to Nedine, she had known there would be trouble. The first sign had been the rain and thunderstorms that had started almost immediately and hadn't let up since. Even though Grandma Allene had taught her that rain was a good sign and a healing force that could change whatever was wrong, washing it away to help make the way to a path for new growth, Alexandria knew that wasn't the case this time. Deception, love, and secrets came at a heavy price, and unfortunately she knew this weekend someone was going to have to pay the cost.

Before Alexandria had time to think about what type of misfortune might ensue, or whom it would befall, the captain's voice boomed through the cabin, alerting everyone that they needed to prepare for landing. Alexandria felt a smidgen of relief when she looked out the window and saw that the sun was still shining. It made her hopeful that maybe things would turn out better than the pit of her stomach was telling her they would.

"We made it," PJ said as he awoke. "I needed that nap. Now I feel like a new man."

"I'm glad you were able to rest because we have a

busy weekend ahead of us. Between family visits and the festivities going on for the Flower Festival, we're going to hit the ground running."

PJ smiled. "All right, I'm ready."

Twenty minutes later, Alexandria and PJ were in their rental car headed for Nedine. Even though Alexandria knew this weekend was going to prove to be extremely challenging, she felt more and more at ease with each mile they traveled, and she knew it was because she would finally be able to see her grandma Allene. She couldn't wait to sit at the old woman's feet, where she knew she would surely learn, grow, and feel the presence of love. She and Grandma Allene shared a special connection through their gift, and it made Alexandria feel less alone in a world that didn't always understand her.

Although she knew her abilities were a blessing, being able to see and do unexplainable things could also present enormous strains that the rest of her family couldn't possibly understand. But Alexandria found comfort in the fact that Grandma Allene did.

She couldn't wait to talk to Allene about all sorts of things that she couldn't readily discuss with others, not even PJ. And she was also looking forward to sharing the exciting news that the process for PJ and her to adopt Gary was already moving forward. Alexandria was grateful that Allene had sent someone to watch over Gary and to protect her soon-to-be husband as well. She'd learned that danger lurked everywhere, especially when you least expected it.

Danger aside, Alexandria knew that her grandma Allene would be just as overjoyed as her mother was about the prospect of adding another generation to their family.

Initially, Victoria had been cautious upon hearing the news last week, which Alexandria understood was reasonable, especially seeing that she was about to embark upon several life-changing events in a short period of time. She'd recently moved in with PJ, she was quitting her unfulfilling but stable and good-paying job to pursue her passion as a writer and spoken-word artist, she was getting married in two weeks, and soon, she would be a new mother to a small child with health challenges.

When Alexandria and PJ had taken Victoria and Ted by the hospital to meet Gary two months ago, and her parents had seen the love and devotion they had for Gary, and that he had for them, all Victoria could do was smile. And now that Alexandria and PJ were going to adopt the little boy, all her mother could do was offer her blessings, and let Alexandria know she was ready for grandmother duties.

Gary was sweet, smart, and thoughtful. Not once had she ever heard him complain or whine, even when he had to suffer through long, painful tests and treatments. He always said thank you to the nurses and doctors, showing courtesy that didn't come from examples learned at home, but rather from the person he'd been born to be. Alexandria loved him with all her heart. She and PJ had scheduled appointments upon their return to meet with the proper authorities and caseworkers at the hospital, as well as with social and child protective services. They had a mountain of paperwork in front of them, but the reward of having a child they could nurture and love was a blessing they were looking forward to just as much as becoming husband and wife.

"We're almost there," PJ said as he steered the car onto an upcoming exit ramp. "I can't believe we've been driving for an hour. It only seems like it's been a few minutes."

Alexandria smiled as she looked out the window. "Yes, our time on the road sped by pretty fast."

"Sure did, and I'm surprised. Usually when I drive

for long stretches without seeing tall buildings or anything other than trees, it feels like it takes forever to get to where I'm going."

Alexandria nodded, knowing that once they reached Nedine it would feel as if time were gliding by on roller skates. They were going to experience a lot of challenges that would test them this weekend, and the next seventy-two hours were going to prove to be crucial in their lives, and in the lives of those they loved most. Alexandria didn't want to reveal too much because she didn't want PJ to worry, and because she didn't fully know all the details herself. But there were a few things she was very clear about, and she knew she needed to prepare him before they arrived in town.

"Your father's going to be here this weekend," she said, trying to sound calm.

"What?!"

"He's arriving late tonight and he'll be staying at a bed-and-breakfast inn, not too far from where we'll be at my family's homestead."

"Ali, you've got to be kidding me. Why is my dad coming to Nedine, and how long have you known about this?"

"Honey, I decided not to tell you until we got here because I didn't want you to worry or get upset, like you are now."

"I'm not worried or upset—I'm confused and irritated."

"I don't want you to be that either, and again, that's why I decided not to tell you until now."

PJ furrowed his brow. "I can't believe you kept something like this from me. We said we'd never keep things from each other."

"I know, and I'm sorry, but you've been working

long hours and I didn't think you needed the stress. Besides, I only realized he was coming a few days ago when I was buying tickets online for some of the Flower Festival events," Alexandria said, trying to gage PJ's mood. "I was calculating how many tickets I needed to purchase when a vision popped into my head that included your father. That's when I knew he'd be here."

PJ took a deep breath, glancing over at Alexandria as he spoke. "I told him about this trip last week, but he never mentioned any interest in coming. And I specifically told him that this was a family thing . . . your family's thing."

Alexandria hesitated for a moment, but she knew she had to tell PJ the full truth. "When I saw the vision that your dad was coming, I also saw that he was worried about you being in Nedine. Just like most members of my family, your dad is aware of my gift. He knows we're coming here specifically to deal with family issues, and since you'll soon be a member of my family, he feels he needs to protect you."

"Protect me from what?" PJ asked, keeping his eyes on the road.

"I don't know. But don't worry. I'm going to make sure nothing happens to you this weekend. I don't like using my gift to change the outcome of events, because as my grandma Allene always says, everything turns out the way it's supposed to. But if I feel that you're in danger of any kind, I'll do whatever it takes to keep you safe."

Alexandria saw the tight strain on PJ's face and she felt terrible. She'd done exactly what she hadn't wanted to do, which was to cause him stress. But she knew it was better to forewarn him, at least about his father, anyway. "Honey, please don't be upset. This visit is about my family. My blood family. I say that because I'm almost certain that if anything unfortunate happens to anyone, it will be to someone who's connected to me by blood."

PJ shook his head. "Sometimes this prophecy stuff is too unreal."

"I know, and I wish you weren't in the middle of this awkward situation with your dad coming. But I had to let you know so it won't be a total surprise when you see him tonight."

"This is crazy."

"Just try to act surprised and happy . . . okay?"

"You know I'm not good at pretending, Ali. Besides, regardless of the fact that my dad feels a need to protect me, I'm not at all comfortable with him being in such close proximity to your mom and dad for an entire weekend."

"I know, and neither am I."

"Our fathers hate each other's guts."

Now it was Alexandria's turn to furrow her brow. "No, they don't. Why would you say that?"

"C'mon, Ali, you know it's true and so does everyone else."

"No, it's not. They don't like each other, which is very evident. But they certainly don't hate each other."

PJ drove in silence and Alexandria could see a look on his face that said she may have the gift, but this was one thing she clearly couldn't see. She had to admit that perhaps he was right. She could see things for others, but she'd always had difficulty foretelling her own circumstances. She hoped that Ted and Parker would be civil toward each other and, most of all, that her mother wouldn't be at the center of any drama between the two headstrong men.

PJ reached for Alexandria's hand. "I can't control what your father might do, or mine, but I can definitely talk to my dad when I see him tonight. I love and admire him, but I also know he has a strong personality and he's not afraid of confrontation."

Alexandria nodded. What PJ had just said was true, and not only was Parker unafraid of confrontation, at times he seemed to actually welcome it. She'd seen that side of his personality the night they'd first met when he'd attended one of her spoken-word performances. Parker had openly flirted with her mother and had made bold statements, almost daring Victoria to respond. Right then Alexandria had known that he was the type of man who didn't mind pushing boundaries, or risking things to get what he wanted.

Alexandria hated to even think about the different scenes that might play out between Parker and her father if they came into contact with one another, so for now she blocked out all hints of trouble from her mind and smiled when she saw the large green sign that said WELCOME TO NEDINE.

Chapter 14
Victoria

The last two weeks had been so hectic that Victoria could barely keep up with the fast pace. Ever since she'd talked to Alexandria about the trip to Nedine, she'd been busy making plans for their family's grand weekend.

She'd immediately created a to-do list, and her first order of business had been to coordinate with Percy Jones. Percy was a trusted and longtime family friend. His father, the late Maurice Jones, whom everyone had called Slim, had been one of John Small's best friends. Slim had been a busboy and cook at a local nightclub, and he'd gotten his start in the real estate and property management business after John loaned him the money to make his start. "I owe Slim my life," Victoria's father had once told her. "That man saved me from a world of trouble many, many years ago, and I'll never forget what he did for me."

After Slim retired, he'd passed his business on to his son, who was every bit as kind and loyal as his father was. For as long as Victoria could remember, Jones Management had been taking care of the Small family homestead, as well as the family's rental properties and other real estate holdings in Nedine and the surrounding county. She was glad she could count on Percy to take care of things.

She'd instructed Percy to arrange for a cleaning service to come out and dust, polish, and scrub the place from top to bottom, supplying each bedroom in the large house with fresh towels, linens, and an array of high-end toiletries. Since she knew she wouldn't have time to go by a grocery store, her next order of business had been a call to Peapod. She'd ordered a mountain of food to be delivered the morning of their arrival, that Percy would personally ensure was stocked in the refrigerator and cupboards. She then called Cora's Bakery and Flower Shop to order fresh arrangements for the entryway, kitchen, dining room, and each bedroom in the house, along with two mouthwatering cakes and one pie to satisfy everyone's sweet tooth.

Victoria had spent the next week making sure all the events she'd scheduled for her company, Divine Occasions, went off without a hitch, while eagerly anticipating her family's trip to Nedine. Before she knew it, the weekend was upon her and even though she was exhausted, her hope of great things to come gave her the energy to keep going.

Now as she sat in the back-row seat nestled next to Ted inside Tyler's roomy SUV, she was praying her plans over the next seventy-two hours would include an evening of passionate lovemaking and emotional reconnection with her husband.

"How much longer till we get there?" Chase asked without bothering to look up from the game he was playing on his phone.

"We've got another hour or so," Tyler answered from behind the wheel.

"Seems like we've been driving forever, Dad."

"I need to make another stop," Maxx said.

Victoria had been afraid that her ninety-six-year-old uncle Maxx would have considerable trouble traveling in a vehicle for several hours, but so far, with the exception of his frequent requests for bathroom breaks—because he refused to wear Depends—Maxx was as lively, alert, and eager as any of them.

"All right, Uncle Maxx," Tyler said, "we'll stop at the next exit."

Victoria leaned over against Ted and whispered into his ear. "You okay?"

Ted had been unusually quiet during most of the drive and Victoria didn't know whether he was tired, frustrated, or just plain disinterested. His behavior was puzzling and she wanted to find out what was bothering him.

When she'd told him about the trip and that it would be a good opportunity for them to bond and have fun since they hadn't been on a vacation in quite some time, he'd nodded with mild enthusiasm. As they had drawn closer and closer to the weekend, Victoria had noticed that he'd seemed to become more despondent by the minute. This morning, when Tyler had come by their house to pick them up, Ted had acted as though he didn't want to go, but knew he had to out of obligation to their daughter.

"I'm fine," Ted responded.

"You sure? You've barely said two words since we got the road."

"I'm just taking in the view as we drive and thinking about a lot of things."

"Like what?"

Victoria watched closely as her husband's forehead wrinkled with a look of frustration.

"Just a lot of things." Ted looked in front of them at Tyler, Samantha, Chase, and Uncle Maxx, then let out a deep breath. "Let's talk privately once we get settled in."

Victoria nodded and didn't say another word to him until they rolled up on the sign written in big, bold calligraphy that said, THE SMALL PROPERTY.

Victoria felt an overwhelming sense of nostalgia mixed with love, gratitude, and pride when she looked upon the house that her grandfather had built. She was still in awe that the son of a sharecropper had been able to amass a small fortune and build such a grand house during a time when black folks didn't even have the right to vote. That alone was a testament of the type of strength and determination that ran in her blood.

Victoria remembered hearing stories about Isaiah Small when she was growing up. Although Isaiah had lacked formal education, her father had said that Isaiah was one of the smartest men he'd ever known. "Your grandfather taught me more about business than Wharton ever did," he'd told Victoria, referring to the business school he'd attended, and where she'd followed in his footsteps, obtaining her MBA.

Victoria was proud of the fact that she was born of people who possessed prodigious will and impenetrable determination. That same moxie had helped her start her own event planning and catering business almost three decades ago, and what was now pushing Alexandria to break out on her own and pursue her artistic dreams.

"Wow!" Samantha said with excitement as she got out of the SUV and wiped her sweaty brow from the summer heat. "Victoria, this place is fabulous. It looks like one of those Southern luxury estates you see in the magazines. Girl, we're gonna have a good time this weekend for sure!"

Victoria nodded. "That's the plan."

"This old house is just like I remember it," Maxx said as he looked at Victoria. "Your daddy and I used to spend many a day hangin' out by the pool out back. Yes, sir, we had some real good times. Ain't a day goes by that I don't miss him and your mama."

"I know. Me too." Victoria felt a rush of sadness, but it quickly dissipated when she heard the sound of her daughter's voice.

"You made it!" Alexandria screamed with excitement as she ran out to the front porch with PJ right beside her.

"Yes, we're finally here," Victoria said as she gave her daughter and future son-in-law a warm hug.

"PJ and I already settled into our rooms, thanks to you, Mom."

Victoria had instructed the cleaning service to leave envelopes on the foyer table with each person's name written on the outside, and a greeting accompanied with their room assignment on the inside. She'd planned this weekend with the same meticulous care she used when orchestrating events for Divine Occasions.

"I hope I got a room with a view," Chase said with a smile and a wink as he dragged his roller bag up the steps.

Samantha cut him a look. "Don't be so concerned about what you can get. You need to thank your Aunt Victoria and Uncle Ted for inviting us on this trip."

"Your mother's right," Tyler chimed in. "You need to thank them."

"Thanks, Aunt Victoria and Uncle Ted," Chase said.

Victoria nodded and smiled, always amazed at how a sixteen-year-old boy could sound and look the way Chase did. She was sure that his Barry White–sounding voice was one of the reasons that girls couldn't resist him. Added to that, he was well-built with a handsome face and a smile like his father's that could charm the skirt off a woman.

"You're more than welcome, sweetie," Victoria told him. "Now why don't we all find our rooms, unpack our things, relax a bit, and then meet back down here so we can go to the town square for the evening festivities."

Once Victoria and Ted put away their things, they walked onto the balcony off the side of their master suite, which overlooked a large pool surrounded by a beautiful garden tucked in between peach, apple, and pear trees. The air was sweltering outside, but the gorgeous view made the heat tolerable.

"This was my grandparents' bedroom," Victoria said. She pointed her hand in the direction to their left. "My grandma Henrietta planted those fruit trees over there. She spent the summer harvesting them to make preserves for the winter months. Daddy said there was nothing like eating his mother's homemade buttermilk biscuits topped with sweet fruit preserves. She was an excellent cook, and legend has it that she served better meals than any of the restaurants in town."

Ted smiled. "You definitely get it honey. Everything you cook is delicious."

This was the first time all day that Ted had seemed excited about anything. Even though his lighter mood had been brought on by the thought of a good meal, Victoria was glad that he seemed a little more at ease. She didn't want to dampen the mood, but she knew they needed to talk about whatever was going on with him, and she decided that now, standing close together amidst nature's heat and beauty, was as good a time as any.

"Ted, you've been distant from me for a while. I

thought the idea of us spending time together, connecting as a couple and as a family, would make you happy. But instead you seem irritated and preoccupied. You've been practically moping around for the last two weeks and you acted as though you were being held against your will on the drive here. I don't want any secrets or walls of silence between us, so please tell me what's going on."

Ted sighed and looked out at the beautiful garden and trees down below. "Like I said earlier, I have a lot on my mind and I have to make a really tough decision that I know is going to drive a wedge in the middle of our family.

"I've decided that when I retire in two years I'm not going to let Christian run ViaTech, or even hold an executive position. I don't want him involved in any managerial aspects of the company."

Victoria stared at her husband in silence. Although this was a major decision and would most definitely cause some hard feelings between Ted and their son, his news didn't surprise her, and in fact, she would have been shocked if Ted's future business plans included Christian at all.

A part of Victoria felt sorry for her son. Running ViaTech one day had been Christian's dream since he was a boy, and it was one of the primary reasons he was entering Columbia University's MBA program. Victoria knew her son believed that by virtue of birth, it was all but written in stone that Ted would pass the business along to him when he retired. But now his dream would become a nightmare once he learned of his father's plans.

Victoria noticed a faraway look in Ted's eyes but couldn't place the emotion on his face. She knew that what he'd just told her was part of the reason he seemed bothered and distant, but she also felt there was something else he wasn't telling her, and that piece of information was the real reason he'd been off kilter for months.

"Your father was lucky," Ted continued, breaking Victoria from her thoughts. "Even though you never wanted to run Queens Bank, and he didn't have a son to pass it onto, your cousin Jeremy, albeit an asshole, stepped up and is leading the company with as much vigor and integrity as your dad did. And now, Jeremy's grooming his oldest son to take the helm in a few years, and judging from what I've seen, the young man is going to do a fine job." Ted paused and tensed his face into a look of disappointment. "But I can't say that about Christian. I love our son, V. But the honest, gut-wrenching truth is that I can't and don't trust him, and I'm certainly not going to let him get a hold of ViaTech so he can run everything I've worked hard to build into the ground."

Victoria swallowed hard. "I can't say that I'm shocked, or that I object to anything you've just said. I've lain awake so many nights praying he'll leave the drugs alone and hoping he'll give up the alcohol and wild women. But he hasn't, and until he does, neither you nor I can entrust anything to him."

Ted let out a deep sigh and shook his head. "You can say that again. If he wasn't my son I'd have him arrested."

Victoria saw the vein in Ted's right temple pop up, and she knew that only happened when he was seriously pissed. She braced herself for what she knew was going to be a bad revelation. "What in the world did he do now?"

"A couple of weeks ago I found out that Christian forged my name on some financial documents and received a rather substantial loan."

"Are you kidding me?"

"I wish I was, but you know I don't kid around when it comes to money."

"If you found out about this a couple of weeks ago, why are you just now telling me?" Victoria instantly thought about how Tyler had confessed that he'd been keeping secrets about Chase from Samantha. Little did she know that Ted had been doing the very same thing in their marriage. Her mind quickly raced with thoughts of what else he was keeping from her.

"It took a while to confirm it. I had to do an investigation without getting a lot of people involved, otherwise Christian might be under indictment right now."

"Oh my, Lord," Victoria whispered, shaking her head.

"When I confirmed what he'd done, I was so angry I needed time to sort out my feelings and figure out the best way to deal with him before I mentioned it to you. Our son reminds me a lot of my brother Charlie. Only I'll give Christian credit in that he's much smarter and far more cunning than Charlie could ever hope to be," Ted said in frustration.

"What kind of child basically steals from his parents? And what in the world would make him think that he could get away with doing such a thing?"

Ted looked out the window in silence, and then back at Victoria. He let out a deep breath and slowly spoke his next words. "A drug addict will do anything, V."

There. He'd said it. Victoria knew their son drank and partied too much, and yes, he used a fair amount of drugs as well. But until this moment she'd never thought of Christian as an addict. At that moment all the worries she had about her marriage took a backseat to the problem facing her son. Her expression went from disappointment, to worry, to fear.

Ted took her hand in his. "We have to face reality. Christian looks good, dresses and presents himself well, and by the grace of God, he manages to maintain his grades, stay in school, and carry on a normal looking life. But he's a functioning addict, and if he doesn't get help he's going to end up like the guys in the street who's addiction is obvious. I've seen a fast decline in him over the last six months, and I intend to talk to him about it this weekend."

Victoria knew that every word coming out of Ted's mouth was the truth. "It must be bad if he's stealing from you."

"I was so mad I could've wrung his neck with my bare hands. If it wasn't for the fact that he's my son I would've pressed charges. He has no idea that I know what he did, but he will when I see him."

"I knew Christian had his issues, but . . ."

Ted gently placed his hand on Victoria's shoulder. "This is the reason I've been stressed and preoccupied. I didn't want to burden you with it, especially with you planning Alexandria's wedding, coordinating the breast cancer walk, and all the other things you have on your plate."

"But Ted, he's our son. You could've told me. What he did wasn't only illegal—it was immoral . . . to betray your family. We need to get him some help."

Ted wrapped his arms around Victoria, drawing her in close to his body. They held each other in the warm summer heat, connecting in a way that Victoria hadn't experienced with him in a very long time. "I love you, Ted," she said.

"I love you, too, V." Ted kissed her softly, squeezing her around her waist until a wide smile came to her face. They stood in each other's arms for a few minutes, enjoying a silent embrace.

But as much as Victoria loved sharing this tender moment with Ted, something didn't feel right about it. A mixture of sadness, happiness, and confusion settled in her stomach. She was sad because she knew her son was headed down a very dangerous road that was paved with disaster. She felt happy because Ted was holding her the way he used to, and it felt good to her senses. But she was also confused because while she enjoyed being in his arms, his explanation about why he'd been distant from her didn't ring completely true.

Victoria knew that the weight of Christian's drug use and the crime he'd committed as a result was heavy on Ted's mind, but she didn't feel it was the reason he'd lost his interest in making love to her. She'd been married to him long enough to know when things were awry, and right now, she knew that something wasn't right, and she was determined to find out what was really going on before the weekend ended.

Chapter 15
Allene

To say that Allene was overjoyed to see Alexandria was an understatement. She was sitting in her rocking chair on the front porch when Alexandria and PJ arrived. Seeing her great-great-granddaughter in visions was one thing, but being face-to-face with her in the living, breathing flesh was a completely different experience.

Allene could clearly see a lot of herself in the young woman. Other than the fact that Alexandria's complexion was light caramel color and Allene's was a deep onyx hue, they both possessed the same impressive height, distinctively squared shoulders, thick hair, and keen facial features that nearly everyone in the Small family had inherited from Susan Jessup, the beautiful young slave girl with the gift of prophecy who was the backbone of their very existence.

As Alexandria walked up the steps to the large wrap-around porch, she paused and looked directly at the rocking chair where Allene was sitting.

"Is everything all right?" PJ asked.

Alexandria smiled wide. "Yes, everything is just fine. That's my grandma Allene's rocking chair, and before her, it belonged to her grandmother, and her mother, a woman named Susan Jessup," she said, pointing to where Allene was presently sitting.

"Is she here? I mean, right now?"

Alexandria nodded. "She most certainly is. But she's going to give us time to settle in. She and I will talk later tonight, when we'll be able to communicate more freely and without time constraints. We have a lot to discuss."

"That's right, baby girl." Allene spoke in words that only Alexandria could hear. "You and PJ go on in and get prepared for everybody that's gonna be comin' shortly. Believe me, you're gonna need your rest for when your brother gets here."

Alexandria sighed, knowing Allene was right. She looked down at her feet with deep concentration, and then back up toward her grandma Allene's empty rocking chair. "All right, Grandma. I can't wait to see you tonight."

Allene smiled with satisfaction and gratitude. It made her feel good to know that Alexandria had been listening to, and learning from, everything that Allene was teaching her. She was picking up on all the little signs, being careful to pay attention so she could make the best decisions possible and use her gift for good. Allene had been proud of her son, Isaiah, and his son, John for all their accomplishments. They'd been the lights of her life. But the love and pride she felt for Alexandria couldn't be put into words.

Not only did Allene feel a special bond to Alexandria because of the gift they shared, her heart swelled with emotion every time she thought about how kind, loving, and selfless Alexandria was. She was about to be a new bride to a surgeon with a demanding schedule, and a new mother to a child who had health challenges and might be plagued by physical illness for the foreseeable future. But even in the face of this, she didn't think twice about accepting the demands both would place on her as she also worked to carve out a new career path of her own. Alexandria wanted to do these things because she knew that her role as wife and mother would benefit two very special people whom she loved.

PJ had always longed to experience the genuine love of a woman, which was something he'd never felt from his own mother, who had never wanted children and had only gotten pregnant to trap Parker into marrying her—which hadn't worked. Alexandria had come into PJ's life and healed his wound, showing him that not only was he worthy of receiving unconditional love from a woman, he deserved it. She was also going to fill a huge void in young Gary's life when, in a few months, she became the mother he'd never had but had always wanted. Alexandria was going to nurture him, protect him, and care for him as if she'd birthed him herself. This was the power of love and family that Allene valued and held close, and she was glad that Alexandria did as well.

Allene watched Alexandria as she walked over to the large gold-colored flowerpot where Victoria had instructed Percy Jones to leave the house key.

She bent down and picked up the key. "I feel blessed to be at the home my great-grandfather built."

"It's quite a house and an impressive legacy that he left," PJ said.

"Yes, it is. My grandpa Isaiah was a strong man, and I know I'll gain a lot just by virtue of being here this weekend. This house holds so much more than just furniture and shelter. I believe it's going to provide healing."

Allene knew that Alexandria's words were true, but she still said a quick prayer of protection to cover her, and their entire family, for the time they'd be here.

After Alexandria and PJ settled in upstairs, Allene watched with delight as Victoria and her small entourage arrived. They all looked a little road worn from their drive. They'd left at sunup, and then traveled seven hours on the highway to reach Nedine. But now that they were safe at the family homestead, Allene knew they would be all right. She decided to take a quick nap so she'd be alert for tonight's activities. But her rest was interrupted when she felt a strong force jolt her from her sleep.

"Have mercy!" She opened her eyes and saw that it was Christian. She knew instantly that he had liquor on his breath, drugs in his system, and trouble brewing all around him.

Chapter 16
Allene

Allene watched closely as Christian made his grand entrance. She shook her head at his extravagance. He couldn't get a basic rental car like Alexandria and PJ had gotten. His vehicle was a sporty, black two-seater with a drop top. "Everything he does is over the top."

Christian turned his coffee cup up to his lips, which was filled with Hennessy, and drank it down as if it was water. He was grinning from ear to ear as he got out of the car, stumbling slightly while throwing his overnight bag on his shoulder.

"Man, it's hot as hell out here," Christian mumbled with irritation. He stopped a few yards short of the porch where Allene was sitting in her rocking chair, and took in a full view of the house. "Damn! This place is nice." He removed his designer sunglasses for a closer inspection, then walked around to the backyard and surveyed the grounds. "Mom said this place was a showstopper, but I never imagined it would be like this," Christian said in a whisper as he walked back around to the front of the house. "When one plan ends, a new one begins. I can rake in a pretty penny with this place. It'll make a great bed-and-breakfast, and I'll make a killing."

Allene sucked in a deep breath of the stiflingly hot summer air. She didn't like inserting herself into situations unless there was a dire need, because doing so could sometimes produce negative and unintended consequences, and she preferred to let things happen naturally. But right then and there she decided that this was one situation she was going to step into. There was no way in this world or the one beyond that she was going to sit back and let Christian get his hands on any part of their family homestead, or the surrounding land and rental properties.

"Isaiah worked hard and even risked his life so he could build this house for his family," Allene said with conviction. She'd never forget the night that the Klan had tried to burn it down. The white-hooded racists would have succeeded in their mission of hate had Allene not stirred up the fear of heaven and hell inside each of them who'd gathered to do her family harm. It was one of the times that she'd known interference was necessary. And just as she'd interceded in that situation, she was prepared to do the same where Christian was concerned, if she had to.

Allene slowly rose from her rocking chair and followed Christian as he walked into the house. He stood in the elegant foyer, inspecting the natural wood details, expensive marble and high-end antiques that decorated the home's entrance. "I'm here," he announced loudly, as if he were royalty waiting to be greeted.

Alexandria and PJ came out from the den in the back to greet him and immediately, they could see that not only had Christian been drinking, he was high on top of that. It amazed Allene how he could look so clean-cut and presentable when most addicts literally wore their addiction on their face and body. But Christian was a different breed. He was like a white collar criminal, and they always knew how to set themselves apart.

Allene watched as Alexandria glanced from her brother over to PJ and let out a sigh. She knew just as everyone else did that PJ didn't care for Christian. From the moment he'd met Christian last year, his future brother-in-law had rubbed him the wrong way.

Christian's first mistake with PJ had come when Christian invited him to an Atlanta Hawks game. But instead of cheering on the home team in courtside seats as Christian had said they'd do, he'd taken PJ to a strip club, where he'd proceeded to get drunk. When he refused to leave PJ had to call a cab and ended up watching the game from the seat of his couch. Christian's second misstep came when he'd had the nerve to ask PJ to write him prescriptions for Oxycontin, Valium, and Percocet, and then acted as if he was offended when PJ refused his bold request.

Allene watched as Alexandria approached her brother with caution, but PJ stepped up to him, displaying what Allene thought was a good amount of civility when he gave Christian a firm handshake accompanied by a smile. "What's up, man? How've you been?"

Christian flashed his brilliant white teeth and spoke with slurred words. "Lovin' life, man. It's all good."

Alexandria rolled her eyes and couldn't hold back. "Christian, I can't believe you came here drunk. Did you drive?" she asked incredulously.

"First off, I'm not drunk, and if I was it's really none of your business. And second, yes, I drove and my rental car is parked out front."

"I can't believe you."

"Believe what?"

"You smell like alcohol."

Christian let out a frustrated sigh, "There you go."

PJ looked on in silence while Alexandria crossed her arms and shook her head. "You're drunk," she said. "I can smell liquor on your breath, and I can look into your eyes and tell you're high."

Allene knew that last week Christian had scouted out where he could find drugs in Nedine. As soon as he got off the plane and picked up his rental car, he'd headed straight to a part of town known as The Bottom, a notorious hangout for unsavory characters. He'd met with his connection to get his supply of cocaine for the weekend and he'd snorted two lines on his way to the house, followed up by the cognac he'd picked up at the ABC store in town. As Allene reflected on what she'd seen, she knew that Alexandria was looking into his recent past as well as what he'd done in the present.

Christian crossed his arms just as Alexandria had done and looked at her with the same scrutiny she'd leveled on him. "Why're you monitoring me? I'm a grown ass man and if I want to sip a little drink to start my weekend off right, it's nobody's business but mine."

"See, that's where you're wrong. The minute you walked into this house you made it PJ's and my business, Mom and Dad's business, and everyone else who'll be under this roof this weekend."

"Oh, so now I'm fuckin' up everyone's weekend just because I want to enjoy myself. Man, that's some bullshit."

"Hey man, watch your tone," PJ piped in. "Your sister's trying to help you."

Christian glanced at PJ, looking as if he wanted to say something, but knowing he better tread lightly. He cleared his throat and smiled. "I don't need any help. I'm fine."

Alexandria shook her head. "You don't even realize what you're doing, Christian. Just because you're educated and you're able to dress yourself up that doesn't mean you don't have a problem."

"Right now you're my only problem."

"No, your problem is that Vodka and Hennessy you drink and the cocaine you snort."

"I don't have to listen to this self-righteous shit. Fuck you!" Christian spat out.

"Lord Jesus, help 'em," Allene whispered as she watched on.

"You must be out of your mind!" PJ shouted. He was an easygoing man, but when it came to Alexandria, he didn't play around. "Apologize to Ali, right now," he said in a threatening voice.

Alexandria put her hand on PJ's arm. "Calm down, honey."

"You better listen to your little wifey," Christian said in an equally threatening tone.

PJ narrowed his eyes on Christian and looked as though he was ready to take him down. "Apologize," he demanded.

Christian widened his legs to balance himself, clearly feeling his high. "Man, I know you not tryin' to flex."

"Boys flex, men step straight to you," PJ said as he took a step toward Christian. "You will not disrespect your sister. Period. And I'll be damned if I'm gonna stand by and watch it."

"Man, fuck you, too!"

Allene could see anger rising up in Alexandria. She closed her eyes and sent her a gentle message, warning her not to engage Christian any further because of what would surely happen if she did—a physical confrontation between her fiancé and her brother. But Alexandria was too far gone. She was so angry that she lost control, allowing her mind to get to a state that Allene couldn't penetrate.

"Oh no!" Allene said. "She's gon' tell what she knows." Allene knew what was coming when she saw Alexandria take a deep breath, briefly close her eyes, and then aim them like bullets on Christian. She'd read his thoughts and knew the sneaky plan he'd laid.

"You low down, dirty dog," Alexandria hissed. "You pretended like you wanted to come here this weekend for our family's sake, but the *only* reason you're here in Nedine, standing in the house that our great-grandfather built, is because you have plans to swindle it right out from under Mom's nose."

Christian raised his hand and tried to interrupt her, but Alexandria kept going.

"I know about the misleading documents you're going to ask her to sign that will cause her to lose everything while you take control of it all . . . and I also know about the other low-down, despicable crime you've already committed. You think you're slick, but you're not. I even know about the professor you're screwing so she'll give you an A in your summer class."

Lord, she done gon' and exposed everything! Allene thought.

Christian's face went blank. He knew his sister had an amazing gift, one which he still didn't fully understand, and the fact that she'd looked into his life more closely than he'd imagined made him visibly frightened.

By this time, Tyler, Samantha, and Uncle Maxx heard the commotion and were coming out to the foyer to see what was going on. Allene was glad that Chase was still up in his room listening to music, unaffected by the drama unfolding around him.

It was only a matter of seconds before Victoria and Ted entered.

"What's going on down here?" Ted asked as he descended the stairs with Victoria hot on his heels. Ted looked from Alexandria to PJ, and finally to Christian. "I said, what's going on down here?"

No one said a word, but it was clear that tempers were high. Then, without warning, Christian burst into a big smile as if someone had just handed him a winning Lotto ticket. "Hi, Mom and Dad!" He greeted them as if all were well and he hadn't just been fussing and cussing like he was in a bar. "Great to see you. I just got here and everyone came out to welcome me. Now we're one big happy family."

"You're sick," PJ said under his breath as he shook his head.

"And twisted," Samantha threw in.

The room fell silent as Ted and Victoria looked from person to person, with no one saying a word.

"Something is wrong because we heard raised voices down here and now everyone is quiet," Victoria said, looking between Alexandria and Christian. "What in the world is going on?"

PJ looked straight ahead while Alexandria and Christian remained silent.

"Well?" Victoria stood with her hand on her right hip, this time aiming her question at Tyler, Samantha, and Uncle Maxx.

Allene could see that no one wanted any part of the family feud. Samantha craned her neck and looked at Christian with disgust. She was getting ready to open her mouth when Tyler touched her arm.

"Sam, this isn't your business to tell," Tyler cautioned in a low voice.

"It's not my business, but she's my friend."

Over the past year, Allene had grown to love Tyler and his family as if they were her own. Tyler was the voice of calm reason to Samantha's well-intentioned but often confrontational manner. Allene knew that Samantha meant well, but Tyler was right, and she needed to stay out of the fray.

Victoria's eyes grew wide. "Samantha, what are you talking about?"

Tyler cleared his throat. "Victoria, you and your son need to talk."

"About what?" Victoria asked as she looked at Christian.

The disappointment and concern on Victoria's face made Allene want to reach out and hug her. No matter what the situation, no mother wanted to see her child unhappy, unsafe, or unloved. Christian had always been loved, but his reckless behavior invited a mountain of unhappiness and danger into his life. Victoria narrowed her eyes on her son. "What have you done now?"

"Mom, I just got here and I haven't even unpacked. Why don't we save it for later, when I'm more rested?"

Uncle Maxx exhaled deeply and looked around the room. "I'ma tell y'all right now. I'm too old to be goin' through any bullshit. If Mr. Isaiah was alive, God rest his soul, he wouldn't tolerate family actin' a damn fool up and under his roof." Allene nodded her head in agreement as Maxx continued. "This is a time for celebration, not raisin' hell. Respect this house and respect your family," he said, throwing a hard look at Christian.

"Well said, Uncle Maxx." Christian stared back at his great-uncle as if he hadn't done a thing. He picked up the envelope with his name written on it from the foyer table. "I'll be heading up to my room now. See you all in a bit."

Christian boldly walked up the stairs as everyone stood in silence and looked on with a mixture of frustration and worry. Allene could see that no one wanted to get into it with Christian so early in the trip, but she also knew that things would reach a confrontational head tomorrow, and she was glad because the boy was in need of an intervention.

"I noticed that the bar in the den is fully stocked," Samantha said, "I'm about to mix some drinks. Anyone want to join me?"

"You my kinda woman," Uncle Maxx said with a flirty wink.

They all followed Samantha and Uncle Maxx back to the den so they could decompress after the tense moment that Christian had created.

"That boy's gonna make somebody hurt him bad," Allene said as she walked back out to the porch and sat down in her rocking chair. She looked up at the sunny sky, just as she'd done so many days in the past, and nodded her head at what she'd just heard. Alexandria had used her powers to whisper into Allene's ear. "I'm sorry for my outburst, Grandma Allene. I'm going to listen to you the next time. This won't happen again."

"It's all right, baby girl," Allene answered back. "Sometimes you got to tell the truth and shame the devil."

Chapter 17
Alexandria

Alexandria had known that this weekend was going to be filled with challenges, but she hadn't bargained on an immediate confrontation with her brother. She'd hoped that by some miracle, Christian would've shown up sober, calm, and ready to change his life. But when she saw what kind of shape he was in, and then read his mind and discovered the underhanded things he'd done to their father, and was planning to do to their mother, she lost it. She knew she was going to have to exercise better control of her gift, not just with him, but with a few others this weekend as well.

After the intense scene that Christian had caused, everyone calmed themselves with Samantha's delicious but potent mixed drinks, before gathering outside to relax by the pool. A few hours later, they changed clothes and then piled into their vehicles and headed downtown to enjoy Nedine's grand festival activities.

The night air was hot, humid, and sticky, but it didn't

stop the residents of the small town and neighboring hamlets from coming out to celebrate in the droves. Alexandria was hoping the good time would rub off on PJ because she'd never seen him so upset.

Other than her father, PJ was one of the most even-tempered, easygoing people Alexandria knew, and like Ted, he didn't let stressful situations or people get the better of him. But she knew that when her brother was drunk and high, he could make the devil curse, and this afternoon he'd pushed PJ's buttons.

Alexandria wanted PJ to enjoy this weekend and she knew she needed to say something to lift his mood. She spoke to him in a soft, gentle tone. "Honey, I know you were upset today, but please let it go. I'm not thinking about my brother, and you shouldn't either. Don't let him spoil our weekend."

"I don't like the way he disrespected you, Ali, and I'm not going to stand by and let any man, family or otherwise, talk out of order to you. You're going to be my wife, and I'm not going to tolerate the kind of nonsense that Christian pulled this afternoon. And then trying to swindle your mom? What kind of person is he?"

"The kind we have to pray for. He's an addict," she whispered in a sad voice. "This isn't my brother, this is the drugs inside him."

"Baby, I don't mean to sound insensitive, but I know how this goes. Yes, he's an addict, but he also knows what he's doing, and he's taking advantage of everyone's patience with him. But trust me, this isn't the time to be understanding or sympathetic. He's in trouble and he needs tough love before it's too late."

"I'm hoping this weekend will help him. Maybe this will be the start of Christian's new beginning."

Alexandria wrapped her arms around PJ, causing him to soften in her embrace. "Thank you for standing up for me today, and for caring enough about my brother to see that he needs help. Did I tell you today that I love you?"

"Yes, you did. But you can tell me again."

"I love you, Dr. Parker Brightwood, II, and I know that I'm the luckiest woman alive to have you in my life. Now let's forget about everything that happened this afternoon and enjoy this beautiful night of celebration."

They strolled hand in hand, taking in the smells, sights, and sounds of Nedine. Food carts lined the main street, supplying everything from cotton candy and funnel cakes to barbecue and collard greens. Vendors were selling paintings and jewelry, artists were drawing caricature portraits for the adults and painting faces for the children, and musicians were performing in a variety of genres from bluegrass to soul. But the most dynamic part of all was the array of flowers displayed throughout downtown. The sight and mixture of tulips, wildflowers, roses, azaleas, and chrysanthemums was beautiful and the smell was intoxicating.

Alexandria was glad to see that her parents were laughing and having fun, looking like a happy-go-lucky couple in love. Tyler and Samantha were checking out the African art display in the middle of the town square, Chase was rocking to the beat with a group of teenagers and young adults gathered in front of the stage where a hip-hop group was performing, and Uncle Maxx was sitting on a bench reminiscing with some of the town's older residents whom he hadn't seen since he was home for John Small's burial service six years ago.

Everyone seemed to be enjoying themselves, including Christian, who was engaged in what looked like an intense and flirtatious conversation with an attractive young woman sporting an Angela Davis–like afro. Alexandria couldn't put her finger on it, but the more she looked at the two, the stranger she felt. She didn't know if it was her brother's dangerous and unpredictable energy she sensed, the woman's, or both combined, but there was an aura hanging over them that she didn't like. "Don't let him stress you," Alexandria said to herself.

She erased the thought of Christian and his new girl-toy from her mind as she and PJ continued to stroll through the lively crowds. They slowed down when they came up to a small coffee bistro nestled in between a clothing store and a gift shop. Alexandria could feel the vibes coming from the building just by standing outside, and when she looked through the large glass windows and doors, people were packed inside, lining the walls.

"I wonder what's going on in there?" Alexandria asked.

"Let's go inside and take a look."

They walked hand in hand inside the quaint coffee shop, inhaling the flavorful aroma of arabica, robusta, and liberica coffee beans. Every chair was taken, and some patrons were even sitting on the floor. To the side, beautiful pink colored roses and yellow daisies lined a large counter that was filled with cups, condiments, and paper products. When Alexandria heard melodic words being spun to the rhythm of an a cappella delivery, she instantly knew why the small coffee shop was so crowded. It was spoken-word night.

"Ali, you should see if they'll let you perform," PJ said.

Alexandria looked around the room of relaxed Southern hipsters and searched for the person who she thought was in charge of the lineup. "I wonder if they have a set program or if it's open mic night?"

"There's only one way to find out."

"Okay, I'll go up front and see if I can talk to someone."

Alexandria walked up to the front of the room and quickly found the owner. A tall, heavyset pale looking woman with long blond hair, and the thickest Southern accent Victoria had ever heard, stretched out her hand an introduced herself. "I'm Penny Simms, the owner, and this here is the Coffee House. Welcome."

"It's nice to meet you, Penny. My name is Alexandria."

Alexandria felt as though she was under inspection as Penny eyed her up and down, from her fuchsia-colored backless halter top, to the skinny jeans that hugged her thick thighs and sultry curves, to the jewel-toned sandals that adorned her feet. "You ain't from 'round here, are ya?" Penny asked.

"No, ma'am. I'm from Atlanta, and my family and I are in town for the Flower Festival," Alexandria told her.

Penny smiled, revealing small pink gums and teeth so large they didn't look real. Alexandria thought she looked like a cartoon that had come to life. But there was no doubt that Penny was real, and she read Alexandria's mind. "We're havin' open mic tonight. You wanna perform?"

"Yes, how did you know?"

"You look like one of them artist types, all flowery and pretty and such. I just kinda figured that's why you wanted to speak to me."

"I'm a regular at a club called The Lazy Day in downtown Atlanta, and I'd love to perform for your audience here."

"All righty." Penny smiled and then paused. "What'cha gonna speak about? World peace or somethin'? From the way you look, maybe somethin' about fashion or a nice love poem? I only ask 'cause it seems like this is a hard crowd to please tonight."

Alexandria looked around the room and saw why

Penny had made that statement. There was an eclectic mix of bohemians, hipsters, local good ol' boys and girls, and sophisticated urbanites who were obviously only in town for the Flower Festival. Alexandria knew from experience that diverse crowds were the hardest because everyone's tastes were so different. But they were also the perfect crowd for testing out new material, which she planned to do tonight.

She thought about which new piece she should perform, and she knew she needed to pick a universal theme that everyone could relate to. It came to her. "I'll perform a piece about love."

"Everybody needs a little love," Penny said with a wink. "I'll go up and introduce you now."

Alexandria stood to the side with anticipation as she looked out into the crowd. She always felt a rush of nervous energy when she was about to go onstage and tonight was no different. When she heard her name, followed by mild applause at best, she took a deep breath and walked up to the microphone across the room. She smiled when she saw PJ giving her a thumbs-up sign from where he was standing against the wall.

"Good evening," Alexandria began. "How y'all doing?"

That question usually warmed up the crowd, as it forced a response that led to engagement, which then spurred interaction. But in this case most of the patrons simply sipped their iced lattes and looked on with bored expressions. She knew she was going to have to connect with the audience on a personal level, draw them in slowly, and then give it to them hard.

"I'm visiting Nedine with my family, and we're here not just because of the Flower Festival, but because this is where our roots were planted. My mother's father lived here, and his father before him. So I come to Nedine standing on the life and legacy of family and love. And that's what I'm going to speak about tonight. Love."

The crowd seemed to perk up a bit, and a few even put their drinks down to listen.

"Love is just like the flowers this town is celebrating. It starts out as a small seed, and it takes time, patience, and careful attention to make it bloom. It's a process. The soil has to be cultivated, the temperature has to be right, and the conditions need to be stable so the stem can take root and grow into this," Alexandria said, pointing to the large vase of colorful flowers sitting on the table beside her. "A beautiful example of love in bloom. Tonight I'm going to talk about how love feels, what it can do, and the beauty it can bring to life.

When she saw the crowd nodding she knew she had their attention. She looked out at PJ again, who was nodding his head and smiling. She took a deep breath and closed her eyes, then opened them as she began.

"This piece is titled, 'You Make Me . . .'

You make me . . . Dream—while I'm still awake, eyes wide open and aware, fully engaged, helping me walk through life without doubt or fear

You make me . . . Feel—alive with passion, touching me the way I like, igniting a fire that only you can create, paying careful attention to my wants, making sure you give me what I need

You make me . . . Smile—like a schoolgirl when you call my name, hold my hand, drape your coat around my shoulders, and tell me, 'baby, it'll be all right'

You make me . . . Tremble—when you rest your hand upon the small of my back, whisper in my ear, slide your tongue across my lips, and kiss me like I'm the only woman you'll ever touch or feel

You make me . . . Want—to be a better person when you challenge me to be my best, call me out when I'm wrong, acknowledge me when I'm right, and encourage me in every small thing I do

You make me . . . Proud—when you protect your family, show kindness to strangers, share your humanity with the world, and kneel beside me, head bowed in reverent prayer

You make me . . . Believe—in fairy tales, and unicorns, and happy endings filled with a pot of gold at the end of a glorious rainbow you make when you smile and your sunshine clears away my tears

You make me . . . Hope—with the innocence of a child, fighting like a warrior, standing in faith like a tree anchored in what is real, meaningful, and true

You make me . . . Know—that I can do anything, be anything, and have every single thing I've ever hoped for or dared to dream of

You make me . . . feel loved, worthy, wonderful, beautiful, and free . . . You make me know that I am simply . . . Loved.

"Thank you," Alexandria said as she bowed to applause. She stepped away from the microphone and walked back to where Penny was standing as the crowd continued to clap with approval.

"That was fantastic, young lady! You really brought this crowd to life," Penny said with a smile as she displayed what looked like a hundred teeth.

"Thank you, Penny. I'm glad you enjoyed my performance."

PJ walked up to her and put his arms around her trim waist, giving her a big hug. "You were great. I loved it."

"It was about you, and the way you make me feel. You're a part of me, and your love is embedded in everything I do."

They walked out of the Coffee House just as they'd come in, hand in hand, enjoying the energy and festivities of the night. As they walked back into the main hub of the festival, they could see that the crowd had grown even larger.

"This afternoon got off to a rocky start, but this evening has been great," Alexandria said.

"Yeah, I'm having a really good time."

As soon as PJ declared his happy mood, his phone started buzzing. He sighed as he looked down and read his incoming text out loud. Right then, Alexandria knew that things were about to take another turn.

"I'm here, at the corner of Second Street and Main," PJ said, reciting the text his father had just sent him.

Alexandria was glad that PJ had acted surprised when his father had called him earlier this afternoon and told him that he was in Nedine. Parker had explained that he'd decided to come at the last minute, partly because he was curious to get a look at the town where his future daughter-in-law's roots had been planted, and also because his fatherly instincts told him he needed to be there. "When you're a parent, you'll understand where I'm coming from," Parker had told him.

Alexandria wished that the circumstances of Parker's relationship with her parents were different, because if they were, his presence here wouldn't be an issue. But as things stood, it was a huge issue, and an adversarial one at that. It was a conundrum she was afraid may not ever change.

Over the last year she'd grown to love Parker like a second father, and just as he'd accepted her unique gift, she'd accepted his unique ways. Unlike PJ, who affectionately called her parents Mom and Pops, Parker preferred to be addressed as Parker—which was actually for the best, as Ted would've had a problem with a fatherly title. And there were other things about Parker that she'd discovered and found quite interesting.

She'd come to learn that he was a little arrogant, a bit of a snob, and he had little patience for people or things who didn't understand the world as he did. But she also knew and admired the fact that he was fiercely loyal, loved his family, and was a man of his word. Parker was an authentic straight shooter who didn't pretend. Alexandria appreciated that last quality just as much as she did the fact that he'd raised PJ to be the kind of man she found so easy to love.

She'd believed Parker when he'd told PJ that he wasn't there to cause trouble, and that he would stay out of the way of their family's activities unless invited. After PJ had told him about her conversation with her grandmother, and the purpose of the trip, Parker's main priority was to make sure PJ was safe, and he was willing to put himself in harm's way to ensure that nothing bad happened to his only child. But Alexandria also knew that although Parker's main concern was for his son, he still had feelings for her mother, and she was afraid of where that could lead.

Alexandria watched as PJ texted his father back. "I told him to give us ten minutes and we'll walk over to where he is. But I can't lie, I'm not comfortable with the fact that he's here."

"He probably isn't either, but there's nothing we can do about that now."

"When I talked to him this afternoon, he told me that he couldn't explain it, but he felt like he needed to be here this weekend. He said his gut told him to come so he had to listen."

Alexandria nodded. "I believe him, and I completely understand that feeling. Grandma Allene always says that your gut is God talking to you, and when He speaks, you have to listen. I can't blame him for wanting to protect you. You're his child. I'd go to the end of the earth and back to protect Gary."

"Me too."

PJ looked across the street at Victoria and Ted, who were laughing like little kids as Ted played the balloon and dart game, trying to win a prize for his wife. "We need to tell your parents that my dad is here."

"Yes, I suppose you're right. It wouldn't be good if they accidentally ran into each other, so it's best my mom and dad know."

Alexandria put on a smile as they walked toward her parents. Although Victoria and Ted were only a few yards away, the distance seemed as though it were a mile. Alexandria was in no hurry to approach them, though, because she knew that once she did their entire mood and evening would change.

"Hey, you two!" Victoria said with excitement. "Look

what your father just won for me." She held a huge teddy bear that had a big red bow tied around its neck in front of her. "Isn't this the cutest thing!"

Ted smiled. "Anything for you, my love."

Victoria gave him a soft kiss on his lips as she held her bear tightly. "This is the best night I've had in a long time." She smiled wide as she looked at Alexandria and PJ. "I hope you two lovebirds are having as good a time as we are. I'm so glad we all came here to Nedine. This is just what our family needed."

Alexandria felt PJ's hand tighten around hers as he cleared his throat. "I wanted to come over and let you know that my dad is in town."

Victoria looked at PJ as if he'd just asked her to solve a complex math equation, and Ted's expression was equally as puzzling.

"What?" Victoria asked.

Ted dug his hands into the pockets of his well-tailored khakis and stared at Victoria. "You invited him here?"

"Hell no!" Victoria immediately spat out. "Why would I do a stupid thing like that?"

Alexandria knew her mother was upset because she apparently hadn't taken the time to think about what had come out of her mouth, or how bad it would sound, before it had slipped out. Parker's presence made both her parents uneasy, for different reasons, but it ended in the same result—tension.

Alexandria wished she could turn back the hands of time. If she could, she would have never gone to visit her Grandpa John and Nana Elizabeth the summer that Victoria had narrowly escaped having an affair with Parker. She knew that her mere presence would have kept her mother from any free-time mischief. But hindsight was something she knew she shouldn't entertain because, as her grandma Allene had always told her, intervening in things could end up making a bad situation even worse.

"If you didn't ask him to come, why is he here?" Ted asked, looking at Victoria with suspicion

PJ spoke up. "Last week, I told my dad that Ali and I were coming here to Nedine, for a family trip before the wedding. When he asked me why we'd decided to plan a trip on such short notice, just two weeks before the wedding, I told him what Grandma Allene had told Ali."

"Uh-huh," Ted said in an even voice.

"I think the unique circumstances of this visit made him feel a little uncomfortable and overprotective. That's why he wanted to come here."

Victoria bit her bottom lip and listened, still looking confused and now slightly agitated. Alexandria could tell that her father was doing a remarkably good job of maintaining his composure, even though the vein in his right temple had popped up and was waving hello.

"He's not here to cause trouble," PJ continued. "He said he's not going to come around unless he's invited. He just wants to make sure that I'm okay."

Victoria shook her head. "You're a grown man. Why does he feel the need to come look after you like you're a child?"

Alexandria could see that Parker's arrival in town was more upsetting to her parents, especially her mother, than she'd thought. She knew she had to step in. "Mom, if someone like me told you that Christian or me, or anyone you love, was going on a trip because a nearly two-hundred-year-old ghost told them to, wouldn't you be concerned about our safety?"

Victoria turned her head to the side and looked off into the distance as she mumbled to herself.

"Where is he?" Ted asked.

"He's up the street on the corner of Second and Main . . . waiting for us . . . Ali and me."

Ted took a deep breath and squared his shoulders. "Then I guess you better not keep your father waiting."

Alexandria wanted to say something that would ease the tension, but she knew there were no words that could bring back the happy feeling her parents had experienced just moments ago. "We're going to go now," she said quietly. "If you're in bed when we get back, we'll see you bright and early for breakfast in the morning."

Victoria looked as if she'd gone from exuberant to exhausted in a matter of minutes. "Okay," she responded, trying to pull herself together. "Be safe and we'll see you later."

Ted nodded, told them to enjoy the rest of their evening, and then stood stiffly next to Victoria as if someone had just erected a concrete wall between them. Alexandria hated seeing her parents like this, and she wished there were something she could do that would bring them back to where they were.

As she and PJ walked away, she felt sad and disappointed for the second time today. *First the outburst with Christian and now this,* she thought to herself. She hoped that once she and PJ met up with his father that the evening would get better and they could all share a few laughs. But as they approached Parker, standing on the sidewalk up the street, she knew her night was going to take another nosedive when she saw her brother standing beside him with a wild look in his eyes and a grin on his face.

Chapter 18
Samantha

If anyone had told Samantha that she would practically beg to go on a weekend getaway to a town with a total population equivalent to her local mall, she wouldn't have believed them, and if someone had told her that she'd actually be having fun, she'd have laughed right in that person's face. But here she was, smack dab in the middle of Nedine, South Carolina, having the time of her life.

Her day had started early. Samantha had never been a morning person, and rising before dawn had always been a challenge. But this morning it was Samantha who had risen and dressed before Tyler or Chance had even gotten into the shower. She had been more than ready to begin their weekend, hoping that Alexandria's words and the next three days would bring about a great change for the better. "I can't believe you're dressed and ready before I am," Tyler had said as he walked out of the shower with a towel wrapped around his waist.

Samantha looked at the tiny droplets of water that

clung to her husband's skin, and smiled. After seventeen years of marriage, she loved that Tyler still made her temperature rise below her waist. "I'm ready because I'm excited," she said with a mischievous grin that let Tyler know what she wanted.

"Sam, we've got to hit the road, and we've got to pick up Victoria and Ted, plus drive out to Dunwoody and get Uncle Maxx before we even get on the highway."

Samantha pulled off her shorts and T-shirt as she watched Tyler shake his head and smile. She walked up to him and unfastened his towel, letting it drop to the floor. "This'll be a good pick-me-up for the road."

"Mmmm," Tyler moaned as she kissed his neck and flicked his skin with her tongue.

"Ten minutes won't put us too far behind, and it'll give me just enough of what I need," she purred.

Tyler embraced her, kissing her softly until they both fell against their queen-size bed. "Just ten minutes, huh?" Tyler said in between heavy panting. "You know I like to take my time."

When he slowly eased himself inside Samantha, she let out a soft moan that rose up from the back of her throat. She relaxed her body as Tyler gently kissed her skin and made love to her slowly, taking his time as he'd said he would. His deep, penetrating thrusts filled her with the kind of pleasure that made her thighs tremble. His rhythm and skill was so precise and knowing that it didn't take long for her to reach an orgasm that shook her body into a wave of ecstasy.

Samantha loved that Tyler's mission was to always please her, and she was glad to say that every time they made love he achieved his goal. She moaned softly as he continued to stroke her, increasing his pace. Once he reached his breaking point and found the gratifying place she'd just discovered, they lay wrapped in each other's arms for a few minutes before they had hurriedly pulled on their clothes and packed their SUV.

The tension, headache, and stress Samantha had felt over the last two weeks melted away as they hit the road and headed to Nedine.

Now as Samantha stood in the middle of downtown Nedine, looking at African art with Tyler, she couldn't remember the last time she'd had this much fun.

"This is unique and well-crafted," Tyler said as he picked up a large wooden mask. "It would look great in my office. How much?" he asked the vendor.

"A hundred dollars," the man said.

Samantha reached inside her handbag, opened her wallet, and was ready to give the man her money.

"Not so fast," Tyler whispered. "We can negotiate a better price."

Samantha turned to face her husband. "I know that. But I think this beautiful mask is worth it, and I know you certainly are, so I don't mind paying full price."

All Tyler could do was smile and accept his wife's gracious gift. "Thanks, Sam."

After the vendor wrapped the mask and handed it to Tyler in a large bag, they walked up and down the crowded street, taking in the sights and sounds of the night. Samantha was surprised by the amount of people who had come out to celebrate the Flower Festival, and even though the crowd wasn't as diverse as she'd hoped, she was glad there were a few black vendors, like the one she'd just patronized, and one or two others sprinkled throughout the area.

She and Tyler hadn't eaten since lunchtime, so they walked over to the barbecue stand for a taste of Southern comfort food. After they made their selection—hickory-smoked barbecue chicken, baked beans, coleslaw, collard greens, and cornbread—they found a place to sit that was close to the music stage, allowing them to keep an eye on Chase. Samantha watched as her son danced to the rhymes the hip-hop group was performing.

As Samantha studied Chase, she paid close attention to the girls around him. They stared and flirted boldly. And to Samantha's surprise, even some of the twenty-something young women were checking him out. She secretly wished that Chase weren't so handsome, tall, and charismatic, and she definitely didn't want his voice to be as deep and seductive as it was. She knew this was the reason his cell phone battery was always low. Girls texted and called him nonstop.

"Damn, this food is good," Tyler said as he bit into his chicken, pulling Samantha from her thoughts.

"It sure is. I so wish I could cook like this."

"Me too." He laughed. "You can't boil water, but it's all good, baby."

Samantha shook her head and laughed. Among the many things she loved about Tyler was that he was honest to a fault. If there was one thing she knew she could count on, it was that her husband would always be truthful with her no matter what the situation. Tyler had suffered many losses in his life, from losing his parents when he was a young boy, to becoming a widower when his first wife and college sweetheart died of a rare kidney disease. And when he hadn't thought his heart could ache any more, he'd had to bury his aunt Beatrice, who had raised him and had been the only real family he'd had left. In spite of his struggles, Tyler's spirit and positive energy had kept him going, even when he hadn't wanted to.

"I'm glad you asked Victoria to let us tag along," Tyler said "This town is pretty cool. This is what you call a down-home Southern good time."

Samantha smiled. "It sure is."

"Chase seems to be having a good time, too." Tyler

nodded in the direction of their son, who was talking to a young woman who looked to be a few years older than him.

"He better not have too much of a good time. That's what's got him in trouble right now."

"Having a good time isn't his problem—it's the decisions he makes while he's having fun that worry me. I'm gonna have a straight-up man-to-man with him tomorrow. No holding back."

"Good, and I pray he listens to you this time." Samantha had finished her food while Tyler was still working on his plate. She drank her sweet tea, which tasted like a dessert, and watched as her son laughed and flirted just a few yards away. "I made a lot of mistakes when I was his age, and even as a young woman, and I don't want Chase to follow down the same path."

Tyler nodded. "He's a good kid. We're gonna get through this."

"I hope so."

"After we get back home, I'm calling David Carpenter to arrange a trip up to D.C."

Samantha nearly choked on her tea. Just the mere mention of the man's name made the contents in her stomach rumble with anxiety. She'd been checking her phone every few hours to see if she'd received another inbox message from David, but thankfully he hadn't contacted her since yesterday. She was hoping she wouldn't hear from him this weekend, much less have to meet with him as Tyler was suggesting. But she knew she'd eventually have to. The more she thought about the situation the more tense her body felt, and she knew she needed to step away and calm herself. "I need to go to the restroom," she told Tyler. "I'll be right back."

Samantha walked in the opposite direction toward the public rest-rooms and lingered around the food stands as she took a few deep breaths. She reached inside her bag to check her phone again, and sure enough, David had sent her another message. She braced herself as she read.

> *Since you want to play hard-ball that's fine with me. If you decide you want to relive the past just remember it's the word of a woman with a very checkered past, against the word of a family man and respected business owner. With those odds I'll take my chances.*

Samantha was furious and she knew she needed to end her back and forth with David. She searched her phone's contact list where she'd stored his number yesterday and dialed him. He picked up the phone on the first ring.

"Hello."

His voice was still slow and easy with a down-home Tennessee drawl that used to drive Samantha wild. But she knew what kind of snake he was and it made her blood pressure rise. "Who the fuck do you think you are, threatening me?" Samantha asked.

"That's no way to greet an old friend," David answered with sarcasm. "But then again, we were never friends, were we?"

"Cut the bullshit, David. Why are you acting like an asshole? There's no reason to threaten me."

"Like I said, it wasn't a threat, it was a warning. Honestly, I was hoping I'd never lay eyes on you again, but now that this disaster has happened with my daughter and your son, here we are."

"Yeah, motherfucker, I feel the same way. But you don't see me contacting you with crazy bullshit . . ."

"Hold up," David interrupted. "You need to stop with the motherfuckers. I haven't called you out of your name and I damn sure don't want you calling me out of mine."

"I don't give a shit what you want and I can say whatever the hell I want to, bitch!"

David let out a snide chuckle. "Now it all makes sense."

"What?"

"With a mother like you, it's no wonder your son has no morals. I'm sure that after following your example he had no problem taking advantage of my daughter."

Samantha was so livid she felt like screaming. She let out a deep breath before she unleashed her next words. "You have some nerve. First of all, you don't know shit about how I parent my child and you have no room to judge. You don't hear me saying that with a booty busting father like you, it's no wonder your daughter spread her legs like you spread your ass! You act like your past isn't littered with dirt."

"Fuck you!" David said in an angry voice.

Samantha knew she'd hit a nerve but she didn't care. She wanted to put an end to what David was trying to start. "Why did you contact me and threaten me?"

"Because I know you're a loose cannon and you're angry about our children's situation. I am, too, but I know how to control myself and I know what's at stake."

"Motherfucker, you don't know shit about who I am or what I feel. I know that my son's future is at stake and stands to be ruined by a baby that might not even be his."

David drew in a deep, frustrated breath. "There you go again. I told you about your disrespectful language, so you need to stop. And furthermore, if my daughter says your son is the father, he is."

"And I told you that I'll say whatever the hell I want to," Samantha shot back, ignoring his last comment.

"Now tell me why you even contacted me in the first place."

"Because I want to make sure that our understanding is still intact."

Samantha wanted to jump through the phone and wring his neck. "Seriously . . . are you kidding me? It was you who threatened me from the very beginning, back then and now. I didn't say a word about what I saw your trifling ass do with those men. After I took a STD test and it came back negative, I didn't give a damn then and I still don't today. That's Millie's problem, not mine."

"Leave my wife out of it."

"And you leave my father out of it."

David chuckled. "Your father, that's a good one."

Samantha had had enough. "Okay, so this is what's gonna happen. I'm burying the past so I can start new beginnings, and in order to do that I need to bring the truth to light—my truth. You continue to keep your secret, but I'm gonna tell mine."

There was a moment of silence on the phone before David spoke up. "So what you're saying is that you're not going to tell what you saw?"

"No, I'm not. Contrary to what you think, I've grown and evolved. It's up to you to tell your wife that twenty-plus years ago you were in a threesome with two other men, doing shit I couldn't dream up even if I tried. The fact that you like sucking dick, taking it in the ass, and using kitchen gadgets to get off, is on you. So don't send me any more messages, you bitch ass punk."

"You expect me to believe that you're going to expose your secret, yet keep mine? You must think I'm a fool."

"No, I think you're a troublemaker with no conscious," Samantha quickly replied.

"Speak for yourself. I'm not the one living a double life."

"Oh, but you are. You're no different from me because you're pretending to be someone you're not."

He'd just confirmed that he was still on the down low, living a double life while deceiving his family. Samantha knew he couldn't be reasoned with so she didn't try. "Like I said from the beginning. Do what you feel you have to."

"Oh, don't worry, I will."

Her head was beginning to hurt. She was tired of going round and round with David and she was ready to end the conversation. "I'm going to clean the skeletons out of my closet. What you do with the bones in yours is your business." She hung up the phone, dropped it back down in her purse, and headed back to the table where Tyler was sitting.

She walked up to him and gave him a kiss. As Samantha looked into Tyler's loving and trusting eyes, then over to her son, who was now making his way toward them, she knew it was time. She was going to tell Tyler the truth tonight so she could start a fresh new beginning.

Samantha and Tyler settled into their room after they said good night to Uncle Maxx and then to Chase. They would've wished Victoria and Ted a good night, too, if it hadn't been for the fact that the two had retreated to their room as soon as they'd returned to the house. The loving couple had been in a sour mood ever since they'd found out that Parker was in town.

Samantha had wanted to give Victoria a few words of encouragement on their drive back to the house, but she'd decided to table that talk for another time when she had seen how preoccupied her friend's mind seemed to be. She understood exactly how Victoria felt. As soon as life seemed to be back on track, something would come along and knock everything over again.

"Life is so unpredictable," Tyler said as he climbed into bed beside Samantha.

"Yes, it is. You never know what's waiting around the corner."

"Who'd of thought that Parker would show up here in Nedine? He should've kept his troublemaking ass back in D.C., where he belongs. Now Victoria's upset, Ted's upset, and even PJ's not too happy about him being here."

Samantha could see that Tyler was going to go on a mini-rant about Parker, whom he'd never cared for, so she decided to stop him before he went too far. "Let's just hope things work out for everyone," she said.

Tyler looked at her closely. "Are you okay?"

"Why? Do I look like something's wrong?"

"Yes, you do. Ever since we finished eating tonight you've had a strange look on your face. I thought it may have been the food, but it's something else."

Samantha nodded. "You're right, Tyler. I've had a lot on my mind the last two weeks . . . and it's not just about Chase and LaMonica."

"Baby, what's wrong?" Tyler asked with concern.

Samantha's mind went back to the night that had changed her life forever.

She'd been a student at Spelman when she'd gotten pregnant by LaDondre Johnson, a roughneck poster child for bad behavior. Samantha had fallen hard and fast, and so had LaDondre. They had even talked about a future to-gether, which had included a walk down the aisle. But their good times had come to a quick end when she had gone to the local clinic and confirmed what a drug store pregnancy test had told her. She was two months pregnant.

Samantha immediately called LaDondre to tell him the news, but he didn't return her call. After a few days had passed with no word from him, she went by his apartment one night, irritated and ready for a confrontation. When the door opened, she was greeted by his brother, who informed her that LaDondre had been arrested and that neither she, nor anyone else, would be seeing him for quite some time.

After Emily helped nurse her back to health from the abortion, Samantha felt like she needed to get away so she could deal with her hurt and loss. She drove back to D.C. in the middle of the night, longing for the comfort of her familiar bed and the encouraging words of support, wisdom, and love she knew her father would provide. When she got home, the house was dark and her father's car was gone. She wanted to kick herself when she realized that she'd forgotten that Ed had told her he'd be out of town that weekend on business. She immediately felt worse when she thought about the fact that she'd be home all weekend in the company of her mother.

Brenda had never been a loving mother to Samantha, or to her older brother, Jeffery. She was absorbed in her own world, which centered around her wants and needs instead of those of her children and husband. Jeffery had been conceived in order for Brenda to trap Ed into marrying her, and Samantha would soon discover that her arrival into the world was the consequence of a very tangled family web.

When Samantha entered the dark, quiet house in the middle of the night she was careful to be extra quiet because she didn't want to wake her mother, lest a nasty conversation ensue. As she crept up the stairs with her weekend bag slung over her shoulder, she saw light coming from her parents' bedroom and heard her mother's voice engaged in a phone conversation. Samantha thought this was highly unusual because her mother always went to bed early. As she rounded the corner and headed down the long hallway toward her bedroom, she came to an abrupt stop when she heard her name.

"I told you, Fred," Brenda practically yelled into the phone. "Neither Dorothy nor Ed, nor anyone else, will ever find out that Samantha is your child. It's going to my grave with me, and the only way the truth will come to light is if you open your big mouth, which I suggest you keep closed. Now I want you to stop this foolishness right now because it won't do anyone any good."

Samantha stood against the wall, out of sight, and continued to listen. After ten minutes of a life-changing conversation, all she could do was stand frozen in place like a hollow statue. The man who'd cut her umbilical cord, raised her with love, and been her champion all her life wasn't really her father, but the uncle she'd always been fond of and admired was. Brenda had slept with her sister's husband and Samantha was the result. The only reason Brenda and Fred were even having the conversation was because Samantha was about celebrate her twentieth milestone birthday in the coming summer and Fred's guilty conscience was getting the better of him.

Samantha stood in the hallway well after her mother hung up the phone, turned off her bedroom light, and fell fast asleep. Finally, after what seemed like an eternity, she walked down to her room. She slept for a few hours, then rose with the sun and headed back down the highway to Atlanta. When Brenda finally stirred from beneath her sheets at her usual noontime hour, she had no idea that Samantha had ever been in the house.

Samantha's emotions went from disbelief to anger, to sadness, and finally to tears during her twelve-hour drive back to school. But the long trip gave her a lot of time to think. She loved her father more than anything, and she knew this revelation would devastate him. Not only was she not his biological child, he'd been betrayed by his wife, and his brother-in-law, with whom he golfed, played cards, and had grown up with, because the two men also happened to be first cousins.

All her life, Ed had been Samantha's biggest cheerleader. He loved her and believed in her when no one else did. He was her hero and she didn't want to see him hurt. She decided to keep what she knew to herself, and like her mother, she'd planned to take what she knew to her grave. But a year later, a soul-baring journal and the treachery of David Carpenter disrupted those plans.

"Sam, what's wrong," Tyler asked again. "Talk to me."

Samantha sat up in bed and took a deep breath. "I wanted to come here this weekend because I've been carrying a terrible secret for a long time, and now I need to let it out so I can bury my guilt and move on without any burdens."

Tyler sat up beside her and listened as Samantha told him everything from beginning to end.

Tyler shook his head as Samantha finished her confession. "I'll never forget the night before Thanksgiving, the year before we got married, when you told me that Emily and your dad were having an affair. I thought that was the wildest, most surprising shit I'd ever heard. But this right here?"

"Um, hold on. I'm not finished."

"There's more, Tyler said with raised brows.

Samantha nodded and proceeded to tell him about David. She explained how they'd met and the holiday tryst they'd shared many years ago. She also told him how David had invaded her privacy and discovered her secret, as well as how she'd accidentally stumbled upon his. When she ended her story this time, Tyler looked as though he'd just watched a movie with no ending. He was left with a blank stare.

"I don't even know what to say," Tyler mouthed in bewilderment. "This is some truly messed up shit, Sam. How in the hell?"

"I know."

"Of all the people Chase could go out and screw . . ."

Samantha lowered her head. "Baby, I'm sorry."

"Why? You've done nothing to be sorry about. David's triflin' ass needs to be sorry." Tyler reached over to the nightstand and grabbed his phone.

"What're you doing?"

"I'm callin' that punk ass motherfucker. Nobody threatens my wife and gets away with it! His ass is mine . . . well, you know what I mean."

"No, don't say anything to him," Samantha said. She took the phone out of Tyler's hand. "Let him squirm in the dirt he's done. The truth will eventually come out. Let's focus on getting our family straight right now, and that means dealing with this situation about my father along with what Chase is about to face.

They sat in silence for several minutes before Tyler spoke again. "Okay, you're right. Let's deal with our family for right now. But I'm telling you, if David calls you again with any nonsense I'm flying to D.C. and I'm gonna kick his ass. Plain and simple."

"Okay. We have to deal with him eventually because of the baby, so let's cross that bridge when we get to it."

Tyler let out a deep breath.

"I know. It's pretty fucked up."

"It sure is. First the news about your family, and now this." Tyler paused. "And speaking of your family, I knew your mother was a trip, but screwing her own sister's husband? That's just foul. And it's sad because they're so tight."

"They used to be, but they're not close anymore, and it's not because of the secret. Uncle Fred's been dead for ten years now, and Aunt Dorothy still doesn't know the truth. Uncle Fred went to his grave with it, and you know my mother will, too. She'll tell somebody else's business in a heartbeat, but she won't dare breathe a word about her own shit."

"Then what happened to drive a wedge between them?"

"The same thing that always happens with my mother. Aunt Dorothy finally got tired of putting up with Mother's crap. Now don't be fooled, Aunt Dorothy is a bitch for real, too. But my mother's on a whole other level. From what I understand from Parker, Aunt Dorothy told Mother off a few years ago and they haven't really spoken since. Hell, I haven't spoken to her in almost a year . . . and do you think she's picked up the phone to check on me or her grandchildren?"

"I didn't want to say anything because I know you and your mom have always had issues, but I was wondering why she hasn't been in touch."

"It's like she doesn't even exist. The boys don't even ask about her. They figure they have Daddy and Emily, so it's cool. Plus you know CJ's always loved Emily."

Tyler repositioned himself on his pillow. "I'm still trying to take this all in."

"It's a lot to process."

"Yeah, it is. And I can't believe that Parker is really your brother."

"I know," Samantha said.

Over the years she'd thought about what Parker's reaction might be if he found out. Would he be mad at her for keeping the truth from him? Would he embrace her as the sister he'd never had? Would he have mixed feelings? She knew they'd always been close, but she also knew that, like herself, when it came to family, Parker was very loyal and fiercely protective, so she hoped he'd look at the secret she'd kept as something that was for the family's greater good.

"Is that why you've always loved him and been so close to him?"

"No, actually. Parker and I have been each other's favorite cousins since forever. I didn't find out he was my brother until I was in college. By then we were pretty much like siblings, especially since he doesn't have any sisters and my brother is practically a ghost."

"I hope to meet Jeffery one day."

"Don't hold your breath." Samantha knew that many things were possible, but Jeffery ever coming back to the States and wanting to reunite with the family wasn't one of them. He'd always been an intensely private and deeply tortured soul. Their mother had manipulated, intimidated, and mistreated him so much that his fragile psyche had nearly broken into a million pieces once he'd come out of the closet and she'd completely rejected him. Paris, with his lover, was where he wanted to be, and as long as he was happy and safe, Samantha was okay with it.

"So are you gonna tell your dad?" Tyler asked.

She nodded. "I have to. I've waited too long already."

Tyler held his head down in silence.

"What're you thinking?"

"How I'd react and feel if someone told me that Chase wasn't mine, and that his biological father was a relative, and someone I had considered to be one of my closest friends. That's rough."

"Why do you think I've kept this secret in the first place? I would've loved to burn Mother's low-down, hypocritical ass, but I never would because it would've meant hurting Daddy. But now I realize that the truth has to come out. I can't carry this weight anymore. Uncle Fred was my biological father, but that won't change the fact that Edward Curtis Baldwin will always be my daddy."

Tyler took Samantha's hand in his. "Whenever you decide to tell him, I'll be with you every step of the way."

Samantha was a self-proclaimed tough chick, a bad-ass who rarely showed signs of emotional weakness. But as her husband wrapped her in his arms and rocked her back and forth, she cried just like she had the night before Thanksgiving, all those years ago.

Chapter 19
Victoria

Victoria felt as though she'd been walking on eggshells for the past two hours.

The drama from earlier that afternoon, combined with the stress of her evening, had begun to create nervous knots in her stomach. Ever since PJ and Alexandria had delivered the news that Parker was in town, the light-hearted fun that she and Ted had been having had quickly deflated, and left both of them feeling as if they were in a fog.

They had stood beside each other not saying a word for what seemed like hours, but had really only been five minutes. Victoria knew her husband was mad, and so was she. She had wanted to talk to Ted and explain things, but she'd known that a downtown street full of strangers wasn't the time or place to clear the air between them. So instead of trying to talk it out, she'd decided to follow Ted's quiet lead and wait until they were back at the house to discuss things.

After an hour of the two of them walking through the crowds, filling their time with festival distractions while they waited for the rest of their group to wind things down, Victoria and Ted had piled into Tyler's SUV and headed back to the house. She had known everyone had noticed the shift between her and Ted, so she'd told Samantha the reason for Ted's frosty mood. She knew Samantha had wanted to give her words of encouragement, and she appreciated that her friend was thoughtful enough to save it for another time.

The ride back to the house was only ten miles, but it might as well have been a hundred because Victoria had felt as though she were in solitary confinement as she sat next to Ted, neither of them saying a word.

Now, she and Ted were in their bedroom, busying themselves with more quiet distractions, not saying a word to each other just as they'd done for the past two hours. When Ted took a shower, Victoria polished her nails. When she showered, he read through the paperwork he'd brought along in his briefcase. Finally, when they were in bed, Victoria was the first to speak. "I know you're angry and so am I. But it's not fair for you to continue to blame and mistrust me for a mistake I made so long ago."

"I'm not blaming you for anything, and I already told you that I trust you," Ted said as he removed his reading glasses and put his papers on the nightstand.

"You don't act like it. I was just as surprised as you were to learn that Parker is in Nedine, but your first reaction was to think that I invited him. If that doesn't speak to mistrust, I don't know what does."

Ted looked straight ahead but said nothing.

"Am I wrong? You did think I'd invited him, right?"

"I don't know, V. I guess on some level I do feel . . ." He breathed out, letting his words trail off.

"Feel what?"

Ted was silent.

"You can't continue to block me out and I won't sit by and be ignored. I've been patient and I've tried to be understanding. I even agreed not to be alone in the same room with Parker, all so you can feel more secure."

"It's not about me being insecure. It's about maintaining boundaries."

Victoria shook her head. "You actually think that I'd cross the line and cheat on you?"

Ted still remained silent as a wave of hurt rushed over Victoria.

"I can't believe that after all these years and all we've gone through, that you have such little faith in me."

"V, it's not that simple."

"I don't even know how you can form your mouth to say that."

"Because it's the truth."

"You haven't made love to me in over six months, yet when you tell me that there's no other woman I'm supposed to believe you."

Ted looked at her incredulously. "What does that have to do with the conversation we're having now?"

Victoria didn't say a word. She stood and reached for her silk bathrobe that was draped over the sitting bench at the foot of the bed.

"Where are you going?" Ted asked.

"I need some air. Besides, I'm sure you don't want to lie down next to someone you can't trust."

Victoria slipped on her furry slippers and didn't look back as she walked out the door.

Chapter 20
Alexandria

Alexandria was determined not to let Christian rattle her nerves or further upset PJ, as he'd done this afternoon. She knew it was time to intervene because she could see certain danger on the horizon, but she also understood he needed to accept that he had a problem before anyone could help him. But an uneasy feeling came over when she saw her brother standing next to Parker, looking as though he was on a mission to stir up more trouble.

It pained Alexandria when she thought about the person her brother had become.

She remembered how excited she had been when a vision had come to her, letting her know that she was going to have a little brother. She'd seen him in her mind as clear as day, and she'd proudly drawn a picture of him at school so she could show it off to everyone. A year later, when Christian was born, she'd eagerly gone to the hospital with her father to see her new brother. But as soon as she'd laid eyes on him she'd known something was wrong. Even though she had been just a young girl, not equipped to understand certain things about relationships, life, or the unique gift she possessed, she had known right away that Christian would eventually lead a life filled with trouble.

At the time, she hadn't said a word about what she felt because at six years old she hadn't really been sure how or why she knew the things she knew, plus she'd seen the perplexed look that would show up on people's faces whenever she spoke about the interesting things she saw, felt, and heard in her head. So she'd kept quiet and watched as her brother slowly grew from a rambunctious child to a rebellious teenager into the slick young man he was today. He wasn't a bad person, but his addiction was turning him into someone she barely recognized.

Now as she and PJ approached Parker and Christian standing on the corner at the end of the street, she tried to remain calm. She whispered into PJ's ear. "No matter what my brother says or does, please don't let him get to you."

PJ didn't respond. He simply looked straight ahead, focused on what was in front of him.

"Good to see you two," Parker said as he greeted them both with a hug.

When Parker held Alexandria in his embrace, she smiled because of what she felt, which was pure love. Parker loved her as though she was his own daughter, and that gave her a sense of comfort.

She looked into his eyes and she could see that Parker's primary concern was for PJ, but he also wanted to see her mother as well. The hard fact that he still loved Victoria after all these years was one of his biggest frustrations. Holding on to the memory of their love wasn't the way he wanted to continue to live his life, and he saw this weekend as a way to test his theory that Victoria still had feelings for him, too.

As they stood making small talk, Alexandria could tell that Parker had had his fill of Christian and was ready to leave him standing on the corner by himself. It was clear to her that Parker knew exactly what was going on with her brother, and he didn't want any parts of dealing with him.

"Have you two eaten?" Parker asked, looking only at PJ and Alexandria. "I got a really great recommendation about a restaurant that's not too far from here."

"Sounds good to me," PJ said. "Is that okay with you, Ali?"

"Sure. A nice meal after this long day sounds wonderful."

They were talking among themselves in a way that let Christian know he wasn't invited. But just as Alexandria had known he would, her brother inserted himself into their plans.

"That does sound good," Christian said. He scratched his head and looked from side to side as if someone was calling his name.

Alexandria knew that he was experiencing paranoia brought on by whatever drug he'd taken tonight. She saw that PJ and Parker could see the same thing, too.

"Should we follow you, Mr. Brightwood?" Christian asked as he wiped his nose, "Or should we all ride together to the restaurant and then come back here and pick up our vehicles after dinner?"

Alexandria wanted to laugh when Parker looked at Christian as if he'd just asked for directions to the moon. Just as Christian could often be blunt and brash, so could Parker, and now, this was one of those times when Alexandria was glad that her future father-in-law could be a bit of an asshole.

Parker turned to Christian. "The invitation was extended to PJ and Alexandria." His tone was so flat and so matter of fact that there was no question that Parker didn't want Christian anywhere around.

Instead of leaving well enough alone, Christian's high gave him a sense of invincibility to push on. But as Alexandria well knew, his efforts were going to be a waste of time.

Christian's eyes widened. "Are you saying you don't want me to go?"

"Yes, that's exactly what I'm saying," Parker responded without blinking an eye.

"Do you have a problem with me or something?"

"Son, I have a problem with the fact that you're obviously under the influence of some kind of controlled substance. I don't know what it is, but I'm a trained health professional and I can see what's going on with you," Parker said matter-of-factly.

"So they got you in on this shit, too," Christian said, darting his eyes between Alexandria and PJ. "This is some bullshit."

Parker shook his head. "I don't need anyone to show me what's in front of my eyes. And as a black man visiting a strange southern town, I don't want any trouble. Like I said, the invitation was extended to PJ and Alexandria.

"We'll see you back at the house," Alexandria said to her brother.

Christian shrugged and grinned like it was no big deal. "Cool. I hope you all enjoy your dinner."

Alexandria quickly read his mind and knew his real thoughts were that he hoped they choked on their meal or got food poisoning bad enough to warrant a hospital stay. But she put her brother out of her mind so she could enjoy the rest of her evening with PJ and his father.

Chapter 21
Victoria

Victoria was upset and frustrated after her conversation with Ted. They'd had their disagreements in the past but they'd always been able to talk about whatever was bothering them and then work it out. This was the first time in their marriage that she could remember where Ted couldn't or wouldn't talk to her. She knew that the quickest way to end a marriage was to create distance, and because mistrust was already an issue, she feared they were headed for trouble.

Victoria shook her head when she thought about the way Ted was acting toward her. As long as Parker had been out of their lives, things had been fine. But from the moment her old lover had reentered the scene, Ted's entire demeanor and mood were always on edge.

She was tired but she needed to clear her head so she walked outside into the humid night. "It's so peaceful out here. This is exactly what I need," Victoria said aloud as she breathed in the scent of sweet smelling magnolias and honeysuckles all around her. "I'll take a walk to clear my nerves."

She loosened her bathrobe, enjoying the way the humid air felt against her skin. She looked up at the moon shining bright in the sky, illuminating the tall trees and beautifully landscaped road leading to the Small Property. She let out a long sigh as she passed Tyler's SUV and Alexandria and PJ's rental car in the driveway, and thought about her marriage. "I'm so tired of having to repent for the past. Didn't Grandma Allene say that is where we bury it?" Victoria said aloud. "Hell, I'm ready to cremate it."

As she approached the edge of the long driveway heading out toward the long road leading away from the property, she was startled by two bright headlights coming her way. "Who in the world could this be, coming up here this time of night?"

Victoria looked around; knowing everyone in the house was probably asleep. She felt a twinge of uneasiness being out in the dark by herself. Even though this was Nedine, and her family's property was secluded, crime could happen anywhere. She tightened her robe around her waist and straightened her back, bracing herself as the car came to a stop beside her.

She peered into the late model sedan and frowned when she saw Parker's eyes staring back at her. "What in the world are you doing here?" she asked, tightening her robe even more securely around her body.

Parker smiled and stepped out of his rental car. "You're going to have to stop wowing me with your Southern hospitality." He leaned against the car and looked up at the sky. "It's a beautiful night, isn't it?"

Even though she didn't want to, Victoria couldn't help but admire how handsome and sexy Parker was. She appraised the way his lightweight cotton shirt hung perfectly across his broad chest. When he tucked his hands into his tan linen pants she could see that they fit him as though they'd been specially made for his body. His curly salt and pepper hair and bright smile complimented his golden colored skin and deep brown eyes that were staring directly into hers.

Victoria hated to admit that Parker's stare excited her, but it did. She looked over her shoulder back toward the house, hoping everyone had indeed drifted off to sleep, especially Ted.

"You have a curfew or something?" Parker teased. "And by the way, why are you out here walking around in your robe—which is beautiful, I might add—all by yourself, this late at night?"

Victoria crossed her arms at her chest. "You're on my property and you have the nerve to ask me what I'm doing out here? The question is what are *you* doing here?"

"PJ left his cell phone in my car, so I found your address and drove over here to give it to him."

"Oh, okay. Give it to me and I'll make sure he gets it."

She watched Parker's every move as he leaned into the car and picked up his son's phone from the passenger's seat and handed it to her.

"I'll make sure he gets it," Victoria said. She was about to turn and walk away when Parker asked her a simple question that stopped her in her tracks.

"Are you happy, Victoria?"

She cleared her throat. "Why are you asking me that question?"

"It's been a long time, but some things never change. I can look into your eyes and tell when you're happy and when you're not, and right now you don't look happy to me. Is something troubling you?"

Victoria didn't like the direction this conversation was going, or the way it was making her feel, like she'd done something she wasn't supposed to. She remembered she'd promised Ted that she wouldn't be alone with Parker, and here she was, standing in front of him, dressed only in a night gown and silk robe, in the middle of the night, with no one else around. She knew she had to get back to the house. "I appreciate your concern, but I'm doing just fine."

Victoria turned and started walking toward the house and before she realized it, Parker was walking right beside her. "Please get in your car and drive away," she said as he walked beside her, step for step.

"I'm escorting you to the door like any gentleman would do for a lady," Parker responded.

Victoria sped up her pace until they were at the front door. "Thanks for bringing over PJ's phone. Have a good night."

Parker purposely eased in close to her, smiling with confidence. "I don't get any thanks for walking you to your door?"

"I asked you not to."

He chuckled. "Fair enough"

"You really need to leave."

"Why were you out there walking by yourself in the middle of the night?"

Victoria let out a sigh. "That's none of your business. But if you must know, I just wanted to enjoy the night air."

She could tell by the way Parker was looking at her that he didn't believe her. But she had no intentions of telling him that she and Ted were at odds over their lack of intimacy in the bedroom.

"I know something's bothering you," he said. "I can see it on your face."

"It's nothing I can't handle."

He took a deep breath and rubbed his hand over his smooth chin. "I saw your son tonight, and he was clearly under the influence of more than just alcohol. He's using."

Victoria was silent.

"I can tell when someone has a problem, and Victoria, Christian has one. He was so high I didn't want him going to dinner with PJ, Alexandria, and me tonight because I could see he was in a state that might have caused trouble."

Victoria shook her head and looked down. "I know. Christian is an addict, and he's in trouble, Parker."

"I'm very sorry to hear that."

"I've exhausted myself trying to talk to him, discipline him, and get him help. His substance abuse is at a point where neither I, nor anyone else in our family can do anything for him. He needs rehab."

"I'm going to put in a few calls to some colleagues so we can find a good treatment center for him."

"We?"

"Yes, Victoria." Parker's tone became soft and full of genuine care and concern. "Your family is my family. We're in this together."

Victoria could feel his sincerity and also his passion. "I fear something bad is going to happen to him. I'm at the end of my rope and there's not much more I can do."

"You're a great mother with a loving spirit, and I know you've given both Alexandria and Christian the best of you. So don't beat yourself up about the choices your son has made. When he's ready to change and get some help he knows you'll be there for him."

Victoria's eyes softened at his words. "Thanks for saying that. I needed to hear something good right now."

Parker smiled. "You know I only speak the truth."

She smiled back. "Well . . . most of the time."

"What's that supposed to mean?"

His tone was playful and seductive, and Victoria knew she had to quickly disengage him. She was about to open the door when she felt Parker step up to her and give her a warm embrace. "You didn't answer my question, but I'll let it go for now," he whispered softly into her ear.

Victoria's head rested against his chest and she could smell the sensual scent of his cologne. He tightened his grip around her, forcing her body to cling against his. His strong arms felt good and she closed her eyes briefly, wishing Ted would hold her the way Parker was doing now.

"Victoria, if you ever need anything, I want you to know that I'm here for you, and I always will be," Parker whispered gently.

"Thank you," she whispered back, knowing she needed to push him away, but being in his arms felt good, so good that she had to suppress the moan fighting to release itself from her throat. She knew she had to stop the moment before things spiraled out of control. *Ted needs to hold me like this,* she thought. Just as she was about to release herself from Parker's grip, Ted appeared in the doorway behind her.

"Take your hands off my wife." Ted's eyes were aimed on Parker with an intensity that made Victoria's heart beat with fear.

Victoria backed away from Parker as if a bomb was strapped to him. She looked at Ted and could see that he was beyond pissed. He was angry.

"Good evening," Parker said, leveling a sly smile and hardened eyes on Ted.

Victoria thought they looked like two old bulldogs about to square off. This moment took her back to a night many years ago, before she and Ted were married, when

Parker had shown up on her doorstep unannounced, and he and Ted had nearly come to blows. She'd had to threaten to call the police in order to get Parker to leave.

Now, standing on the front porch of her family's homestead, she was sorry she hadn't turned around when she first saw Parker down the road.

Ted stood erect and his eyes looked as though they could slice a diamond in half as he continued to stare at Parker. "What are you doing here?"

"I came to bring something to my son."

"PJ left his cell phone in Parker's car," Victoria said as she nervously held the phone up as proof, "so he brought it over to him."

Victoria wished she could turn back the clock twenty minutes because if she could she would have never walked outside after her discussion with Ted. She could only imagine what must be going through her husband's mind right now. There she was, in her silk bathrobe, hugged up with the man they'd just had an argument about.

"You need to leave. Right now," Ted said in a stern voice.

Parker smiled again, but this time only at Victoria. "I meant what I said, so please don't forget. Good night, Victoria."

"What did you say to her?" Ted nearly growled.

Parker shook his head. "I'm trying not to get pissed off, but I don't like your tone so you better back up."

"I don't give a damn about what you like or don't like. She's my wife, and when it comes to her and my family I won't be told what I can or can't do."

Victoria could see that the situation was one comment away from someone ending up in the hospital. She didn't want that to happen, nor did she want to wake up everyone in the house. "Parker, can you please leave," she said. "We've all had a long day and I personally can't take any more drama. Just go."

Parker didn't take his eyes off Ted as he spoke. "I don't want to cause you any problems, so I'll leave."

Victoria didn't wait for Parker to get off the porch before she went back into the house. She followed Ted in complete silence as they walked up the stairs, and when they reached their bedroom, Victoria knew it was going to be a very rough night ahead.

Chapter 22
Alexandria

After a long day that had ended with a good meal, Alexandria and PJ were preparing for bed.

She wanted to call Gary, whom she'd been thinking about ever since she and PJ had spoken to him earlier that afternoon. She looked at her watch and knew he was already asleep, so she planned to call Ms. Brown and check on him first thing tomorrow morning.

"How do you feel?" PJ asked, letting a yawn escape his mouth.

"I feel good, and I had a great time with you and your father tonight."

"Yeah, and I feel bad about saying I didn't want him here. I don't like the circumstances, of course, but I'm glad he came to Nedine, and that he cares enough about me to want to make sure I'm safe."

Alexandria smiled. "That's love."

"Sure is." PJ nodded and let out another yawn, stretching his arms as he lay back onto the soft comfort of the bed.

"You tired?" she asked.

"Exhausted. After the week I had at work and all the activities we did today, I'm beat. As a matter of fact, once I take a shower I think it's gonna be a wrap."

"I'll be right behind you. But first I need to go talk with Grandma Allene. She's downstairs, waiting for me."

PJ looked at her with wonderment. "Sometimes I wish I had your gift, or at least some parts of it. If I did, I'd talk to my grandpa Fred. I really miss him."

Alexandria could see a glimmer of sadness in PJ's eyes. He'd developed severe asthma when he was six years old, sending him in and out of hospitals for several years. During those times, Parker would visit him in between his rounds, but it was Parker's father, Fred Brightwood, who had stayed at the hospital with PJ each day. Alexandria wished he could talk with his grandpa Fred, too. But she knew that wasn't going to happen.

"Honey, your grandpa is with you every day. Even though you can't talk with him, his spirit is close by, and always will be, until you two meet again."

PJ hesitated, then gave Alexandria a curious look. "When will that be? When will I see him again?"

She knew he was really asking her when his time was going to expire on this earth. It was a question that Alexandria didn't want to know the answer to, and had purposefully put out of her mind. The only reason she knew when she was going to pass on was because it had been revealed to her during a conversation with Allene, and even then, she was sorry that she knew. But she couldn't bring herself to speculate about PJ because the burden of knowing would be too great. She'd decided that she was going to live every day with him as though it was their last together, and in doing that, she would enjoy the journey instead of being attached to its outcome.

Alexandria walked over to the edge of the bed, where

PJ was sitting. She took his hand in hers and gave it a gentle squeeze. "I honestly don't know, and I have no desire to learn the answer to that question. Life is a gift and we need to enjoy each day that we're blessed to have instead of thinking about the next."

"You're right." PJ leaned in and gave her a gentle kiss. "Now go and talk with Grandma Allene. I'll try to wait up for you, but I might be asleep when you get back."

"Don't wait up. Get some rest because we've got a busy day tomorrow. I think I'm going to be on the front porch with my grandma for a long time."

Alexandria gave PJ a good-night kiss and then rose from the bed. She walked out into the hallway and was headed downstairs when she saw her mother and father slip into their room. Both their faces looked worried, and Alexandria instantly knew that Parker was the cause. In a flash she felt the negative energy of his visit that had ended just moments ago. She was tempted to close her eyes and watch the vision come to her so she could see what happened, but she decided against it. She knew that at the moment she had to concentrate and prepare for her first live, face-to-face meeting with her grandma Allene.

Chapter 23
Allene

Allene could only shake her head in amazement as she thought about the scene she'd just witnessed on the front porch. Victoria, Ted, and Parker had been caught in a love triangle for nearly thirty years. Even though time had moved along, the pain of betrayal between Ted and Victoria hadn't. And now Parker's presence in Nedine along with his unexpected appearance here tonight had added more tension to an already heated situation.

Allene knew she couldn't get involved and that the three of them needed to work out their long-standing problems on their own. "Lord ha' mercy. Look over all three of 'em, 'cause they need it," Allene said with a sigh. She also knew that Alexandria was aware of the situation and that she, too, had come to the same understanding.

She stretched her long legs as she pivoted back and forth in her rocking chair. She rubbed her wrinkled fingers back and forth along the top of the armrest and smiled.

"This old chair's been through a lot, and seen a lot, too. Just like me and the ones before me."

From Allene's great-grandmother, Susan Jessup, down to Allene, four generations of women had sat and rocked in that chair. They'd cried, laughed, raised their families, buried loved ones, celebrated, mourned, and then found joy again. They were women of strong will, body, and mind, and they held themselves and their families together knowing that love was the greatest blessing they could pass on to the next generation.

"I love nights like this," Allene said. "Makes me think about the old days when I'd sit on my little front porch and count my blessin's." She looked up at the diamond-like stars in the sky, and took a deep breath to absorb everything around her. The night air was hot and sticky, but the peaceful sounds of crickets chirping in the distance and the gentle rustle the leaves made as they swayed on the trees gave her a sense of calm, which was what she needed considering all that was about to happen.

She looked over to her right when she heard the front door open and saw Alexandria walk onto the porch. Allene had yet to make herself visible in the flesh, but she knew that the girl was aware of her presence. She watched Alexandria as the beautiful young woman stood still, looking at the rocking chair that Allene was occupying. She walked to the side of the porch and sat down just a foot away from Allene's chair.

"I'm glad I'm here, Grandma Allene," Alexandria said as a shade of sadness covered her voice. "But I'm so worried and confused. I'm not sure of what to do or when to use my gift. Sometimes I think I have it figured out, but then on days like today . . . well, I know for sure that I don't. I feel like I'm running in a maze.

"Sometimes I want to look into the future and know

everything that's going to happen to me and the people I love. Then I remember what you've told me about how interfering isn't always good. I know you're right, but there've been times when I wish I'd said something, but didn't. Then there've been times when I've been sorry that I opened my mouth at all, or I wish I'd tried to prevent something from happening that I saw coming. I just don't know, Grandma."

Allene took a deep breath and closed her eyes. When she opened them again, she could see Alexandria's smile widen across her face.

Happy tears spilled from Alexandria's eyes as she covered her mouth with both her hands. "I can see you!" she said in an excited whisper. "I've waited so long to see you up close, face-to-face, in the flesh, and not in some distant vision. This feels like a dream, but I know it's not."

Allene smiled back at her. "No, baby girl. This ain't a dream. I'm here and this is real."

Alexandria tilted her head to the side, looking as though she'd just stumbled upon a unicorn. Allene had to laugh at her great-great-granddaughter's expression as the girl continued to stare at her in awe.

"Grandma, you're taller than I thought. I mean, even though you're sitting down, I can see that you're taller than I am."

Allene nodded. "Nearly six foot in my bare feet. Back in my day, I was considered somethin' of a giant, especially for a woman. It was a good and bad thing. But then again, I was never one to pay much mind to what folks thought. I had too much livin' to do to worry about that."

"My mom said that everyone on her paternal side of the family was tall, men and women alike."

"That's true."

"And you're beautiful, too. Your skin looks smooth,

like I remember Grandpa John's used to be. You sure don't look ninety-eight," Alexandria said, then paused. "But you're much older than that now, right?"

"I'll always be ninety-eight in my mind. But you're right. If you count up all the time I been around, shoot, I'm older than some of those trees you see out in this here yard." Allene pointed her long fingers toward the majestic pines that lined the property's entrance.

"I've never seen trees and flowers more beautiful than the ones here in Nedine."

Allene nodded. "Nature is the oldest form of life. God made the earth, sun, moon, and stars before he made us. We're connected to the ground and the sky. It's a part of who we are, and that's why I love everything that blooms from the ground, like those magnolias you see and smell. And I always look up to show thanks to the stars shinin' in the sky. Always remember to take time to appreciate nature. Honor and respect it 'cause it was here before us and it'll be here long after we pass on."

"I'll remember that." Alexandria looked up at the night sky as she breathed in the sweet air. "I knew I'd learn so much from you. I'm thankful you're here, and that I'm with you." She opened her arms and moved toward Allene, but then she stopped when she saw the look on Allene's face. "I can't hug you, can I?"

"I'm 'fraid not. We can't mix our worlds through touch. The best I can do is sit here on this porch and look at you, like I'm doin' right now."

Alexandria looked disappointed. "I understand."

"Bein' in your time is a blessin' for me. It took a lot for me to get here. I'll never forget when my great-grandma came to me in the livin' world. It was the first time I saw her outside of a vision or dream, and it was also the last time I saw her while I was alive."

Alexandria's eyes grew wide. "This isn't going to be the last time I see you in my world, is it?"

"No, baby girl. I'ma be around for a good while."

Allene's answer gave them both a measure of comfort. They shared a few silent moments before Allene spoke. "Let's talk," she said in a concerned voice. "What's this about you feelin' worried and confused?"

"I've been making a lot of mistakes. I know this weekend is important for our family, and I'm struggling between wanting to know what's going to happen, and allowing life to play out as it's supposed to."

"Join the club. It takes time."

Alexandria nodded. "Sometimes I feel like my time is running out and if I don't make a decision about a situation something bad will happen.

"You just gotta do like I do and trust your gut."

"But you're wise, and you know so much more than I do."

Allene shook her head. "I don't know everything and I never will. All anyone can do, whether they have the gift or not, is pray and try to make the best decisions they can."

Alexandria looked down toward her feet. "I'm sorry that I didn't listen to you this afternoon when you were trying to warn me about confronting Christian. I lost control and I feel really bad about what I said."

Allene shook her head as she let out a deep sigh. "You sure did tell him off."

"Even though Christian deserved a good cussing out and a few other things, I should've taken your advice and been quiet. But instead I exposed his plan to steal property from Mom, and I almost told about how he forged Daddy's name in order to steal money. Those things are between him and my parents, and it wasn't my business to tell."

"Well, when it comes to family, it is your business. I just didn't want you to work yourself up to a point where you looked too far into the future. But you did right by exposin' what he was fixin' to do to your mama. This house been in our family a long time, and it's gonna stay that way thanks to you."

"Yeah, I guess me opening my mouth about that was a good thing. But I know Daddy wants to deal with Christian in his own way, and I almost ruined things."

"There ain't no need in beatin' yourself up over somethin' that's already happened, 'specially since you can't change it. The good thing is that you understand what you did and what you need to do the next time, 'cause there will be a next time, trust me. That brother of yours . . . Lord ha' mercy."

"I love him and I'm so worried about him. I know we have to deal with his addiction head-on."

Allene nodded. "You're right."

"But I'll tell you this. Christian can change his ways if he wants to."

"That's the key. If he wants to. He's been partying and dabbling in drugs for so long that he thinks what he's doing is normal. He's in denial, and honestly, I guess I've been, too. I knew he had a problem, but until this weekend I never saw him as an addict."

Allene shook her head. "That boy knows right from wrong, and he knows he's goin' around doin' wrong, he just don't care is all. He's gonna have to lose somethin' he cares about for him to change. It might take a real long time, or it might take just one day, but before he closes his eyes on this side of life, a change in him is gonna come, and when it does you'll have a different brother."

"Thank goodness there's hope for him."

"There's always hope. Don't never give up on anything or anyone."

"My mom says the same thing."

"She's right."

Alexandria exhaled and looked up at the moonlit sky again. "I have so much to learn."

"You know more than you think, baby girl. You just gotta be patient. Take your time and do the best you can with what you have and what you know."

"That's just it. I don't know what I should act on or what I should block out. Sometimes I feel like I'm going crazy."

Allene wished she could take Alexandria through a crash course in prophecy, but she knew that was impossible from her own experience. It had taken her years to fully embrace her gift, let alone figure out how to use it. But she was glad that although Alexandria was experiencing worries and frustration, the girl's abilities were growing, even if she didn't realize it. Allene knew that once Alexandria fully matured into who she was destined to be, she would use what she'd learned to help others in need. The thought made Allene proud.

"Grandma, please tell me what to do about this weekend."

"What do you mean?"

Alexandria paused, and Allene could see the doubt and questions in her eyes. "Tomorrow morning when everything starts happening, how will I know when to act and when to just stay still?"

"That's a hard one, and there ain't no easy answer. There's gonna be times when you might have to do both. The only way to know which road to travel is to look at what's in front of you, listen to your gut and trust it. Your gut is God, and He won't never lead you wrong."

"Just a little while ago, PJ asked me how long he was going to live. I've never wanted to know that answer, mostly because of the worry it might bring, and the fact that if I know when, where, and how, I will most definitely try to prevent it."

"Which might cause even more problems."

"I know."

"What did you tell him?"

"I said we should just enjoy each day as it comes," Alexandria said with a heavy weight in her words. "I know you're right, and I believe in what I said. But sometimes a small part of me wants to know, not just about him, but about Mom and Dad, and Gary, too."

"I sure do understand that longin' to know. But please don't walk that road."

"It's hard not to when you want to protect the people you love."

Allene felt Alexandria's pain because she'd experienced the same thing. Wanting, but then not wanting to know, about deaths, births, fortunes, losses, loves, and broken hearts had caused her many sleepless nights. That was the primary reason why she had refused to live in the very house on which porch she now sat. Allene had loved her family more than she could put into words, and she had known that if she lived under the same roof with Isaiah and Henrietta, she'd be tempted to peer into the future to see what it held for them.

She remembered the day Isaiah had come to her, knowing he was sick, wanting her to confirm whether the cancer growing inside his body was fatal, or if there was something that could be done. She'd stood in the middle of her living room, looked into Isaiah's eyes, and known right away that his disease was too far along, and that any treatment he received would only put a Band-Aid on a wound that couldn't be healed. She listened to her motherly instincts and to what her gut was telling her, and then she stretched her arms to embrace him as she delivered the sad news to her beloved child.

Looking back, Allene was glad she'd told her son what to expect. Isaiah had lived a good life, and he'd still had time to put important things in order to protect and provide for his family. He'd enjoyed three more years of love and laughter with them, and held on just long enough to witness the birth of a granddaughter who would proudly carry on his legacy and one day return to the house he'd built. Allene smiled, knowing that this visit would start Victoria's journey back to Nedine, where she and Ted would settle in for the rest of their days.

Just as Allene had done with Isaiah, and now Victoria, there were plenty of times when she'd looked into the future to see what was going to happen to someone she loved. But the tricky part of venturing down that road was trusting her gift enough to know when her gut was talking, versus her human heart. For that reason, whenever she talked to Alexandria in a vision, she always told her to pray for guidance in all situations.

"Havin' this gift is a blessin'," Allene said, "but as you know, it's also a heavy burden. There's gonna be times when people won't understand you and they might even become afraid of you once they see what you can do. Then you'll have some who want to use you so they can benefit off of what you know."

Alexandria nodded in agreement. "When we were out by the pool this afternoon after Aunt Samantha made all of us drinks, I could tell that Uncle Tyler wanted to ask me whether the baby that girl in D.C. is carrying is Chase's or not. I know that Uncle Tyler's intentions are good, because he wants to help Chase, but he still wanted me to use my gift."

"Tyler's a good man and he's been a good friend to your mama for a long time."

"He's the best. Do you think I should tell him?"

Alexandria asked. "Right after I felt Uncle Tyler's question, I looked over at Chase and knew the answer."

Allene understood that the complications of Tyler's family situation were much greater than a baby, which was going to be born at the end of this year. Hurt and disbelief were going to touch the life of a good man who had done no wrong, and it was going to reopen old wounds between two friends, yet again testing their allegiance to one another. Allene sighed. "What does your gut tell you?"

Alexandria closed her eyes and concentrated for a few moments. "I just saw that there's a lot more to their situation than just the baby they're all worried about."

"Yes, there certainly is."

"My gut tells me that I need to let them know the truth."

"Then listen to what's inside you and do it."

Alexandria smiled. "I will. And another thing I know is that Christian plans to use what he learns in business school to do all kinds of wrong. He wants to use me, so I can help him invest in stocks and manipulate the market. I don't have to ask my gut to know that's wrong and it will never, ever happen."

"Bless his heart. That boy's so slick he could steal shortnin' outta a biscuit."

Alexandria laughed, and then her mood became serious. "I just can't stop thinking about PJ asking me how long he was going to live. I was really tempted to find the answer. I love him so much, Grandma."

Allene could see that Alexandria was feeling sad, and she wanted so badly to hold her in her arms and rock her until her worries went away. But she knew she couldn't do that, so she did the next best thing. "Baby girl, look into my eyes."

Alexandria looked up and when their eyes met, Allene channeled all the energy, warmth, joy, love, and hope she had inside her into Alexandria's spirit. The longer they held each other's stare, the more relaxed Alexandria became, to the point that Allene saw her smile.

After a few minutes, Allene looked away and smiled. She leaned back into her rocking chair feeling happy.

"Grandma, that hug was amazing. I felt all your emotions and so much love. Thank you for being so good to me."

Allene smiled again. "There ain't nothin' I won't do for you. I don't want you to worry yourself to pieces over your gift. The answers ain't gonna come overnight, but as you grow and learn, you'll know exactly what you need to do. Just always remember to trust your gut."

"I'm so glad you're guiding me. I don't know what I'd do without you."

"Like I said, you know more than you think you do. What you told PJ was right on the money. You and him can't live your lives wonderin' 'bout what's gonna happen tomorrow. You need to live in the present. Every second, minute, and hour is a gift, and that's the beauty of life. Enjoy each experience you have and live every day like it's the last one you ever gonna see. Do that and you'll be all right."

"You just made me feel a whole lot better."

Allene and Alexandria sat in comforting love and silence enjoying each other's presence. As the minutes ticked away Alexandria began to grow tired. "Grandma, my eyes are getting heavy."

"Then let's call it a night and we'll talk tomorrow."

"Okay, I love you," Alexandria said, "and I'm so happy we had this time to talk."

Allene smiled. "I love you, too. Oh, and tell PJ that his grandpa Fred misses him, too, and that he's real, real proud of him."

Alexandria's eyes grew wide. "You spoke with PJ's grandfather?"

"Yep."

"That's amazing! I can't wait to tell PJ about this."

"I know it'll make him happy. Now you go on and get some rest."

Allene could see that Alexandria wanted to probe and ask more questions about PJ's grandfather, but she knew it was a conversation best left for another time. She blew a kiss to Allene and then walked back into the house.

Allene relaxed and took a deep breath, once again enjoying the warmth and beauty of the night. But her peaceful moment was interrupted when she heard a car drive up. She looked down the long walkway and saw Christian headed toward the house. He was holding his arm around the small waist of an attractive woman sporting a large afro.

"I can't believe I'm standing on the grounds of the Small property," the young woman said. "And I'm actually going inside the house!"

Allene could see the woman's excitement from where she sat, and she immediately knew that not only was Christian going to cause more drama, but, unbeknownst to him, he was bringing trouble to his family's doorstep.

"Believe it," Christian said with a sly smile. "My great-grandfather had this house custom built."

"Yes, I know. I've lived in Nedine my whole life, and I've heard so many stories about your family and how y'all were the richest black folks around."

"We still are," Christian said with pride. "My family still has vast real estate holdings in this area."

Allene wished Christian would close his mouth and not say another word because he truly didn't know what he was doing at the moment. He'd been snorting more cocaine and drinking tonight, and was liable to give away family secrets if he talked too long.

"Now that's impressive," the woman said. "This place is so beautiful on the outside; I can't wait to see what it looks like inside."

Christian smiled. "Hopefully you'll like what you see enough to spend the night."

Allene wanted to intervene so badly, but as she'd told Alexandria, everything had a way of working itself out the way it was supposed to, including the big mess that Christian was going to find himself stuck in when the sun rose.

Chapter 24
Victoria

Victoria felt sluggish as she gathered mixing bowls, frying pans, cooking utensils, spices, and a countertop full of food she would need to prepare a big breakfast for her family. Even though she was tired after having only two hours of sleep last night, she knew that being in the kitchen, doing something that she could control, would help her feel better because right now she felt powerless to what was going on around her.

She'd thought that once she and Ted returned to their bedroom after Parker had left last night, they would talk and work out their growing problems. But that didn't happen. Ted was furious and couldn't be reasoned with.

"Damn it, V. I trusted you," he'd said.

"As well you should. I haven't done anything wrong. I told you, Parker came here to drop off PJ's cell phone and I happened to be outside to see him. He walked me back up to the house and that was it."

"What did he say to you?"

Victoria blinked twice and bit her bottom lip.

"Please answer me." Ted was breathing so hard Victoria could feel his heated breath. "What is it that he told you not to forget?"

"He said he'll always be there for me. That's it."

"There for you? . . . for what?"

"He knows the problems Christian is going through and he offered to call a few of his colleagues to get recommendations for treatment centers."

"Bullshit. He wants to help with treatment all right . . . special treatment from you."

It was late, Victoria was tired, and she'd had enough. "Oh just stop it! I'm sick of defending myself after all these years. If you think I'd be stupid, uncaring, and flat out disrespectful enough to do something with Parker right here at the house you must not know me at all."

Ted looked away from her. "Right now I don't know what to think."

Neither of them said a word as they climbed into bed and went to sleep.

Now, as she prepared breakfast, Victoria's mind was heavy with worry. "My son is walking a dangerous path and so is my marriage," Victoria said to herself. "As God is my witness, I'm going to find a way to save both of them."

She looked up when she saw Ted enter the room, and she could see that he was just as tired as she was. When their eyes locked they both spoke without saying a word. Ted walked over to where she was standing by the stove.

"I didn't sleep at all," he said.

"I managed to get about two hours."

Ted rubbed the morning stubble coating his chin. "I don't want to start today like we ended last night."

"Me either."

He pulled her into his arms. Just as they'd done last

night, neither of them said a word. But this time it was different because they were connecting on a different level. His hand on the small of her back said, I love you, and his arm that embraced her shoulders whispered I'm sorry.

Victoria looked into his eyes. "I want us to work things out."

"Me too. I love you, V."

"I love you, too. We need to have a serious talk about what's going on with us. I'm confused and I really need some answers."

Ted nodded. "I know. There's a lot I need to share with you, and the one thing I want to assure you of is that I have no intention of leaving you and I don't want you to leave me."

"Leave you?" Victoria said with surprise. "I can honestly say that not once since we said I do have I thought about leaving you. But lately I've felt that you want to leave me. When a man becomes distant and no longer desires his wife . . ."

"V, please don't say that. It's not true."

"Yes it is," she said as she pulled away.

Ted drew her back into his arms and kissed the side of her neck. "Please trust me when I say that I desire you more than you know. This isn't the time to talk about it because you're making breakfast and we have a busy day ahead of us. But we'll talk tonight when we get back, okay?"

Victoria kissed him softly on his lips. "Okay."

"Now let me help you get breakfast going."

Victoria and Ted got busy preparing a small feast for their family, working together in the kitchen side-by-side.

"Daddy really loved this house," Victoria said as she carefully arranged thick slices of hickory-smoked bacon in the frying pan. "I remember the year before he died; we came down here and went over plans with the contractor to update all the bathrooms as well as this kitchen. He told me that some of his best memories were in this house and right here in this kitchen where his mother used to cook all their meals."

Ted nodded as he juiced an orange. "It's a beautiful place and you're lucky to still have possession of the home your father grew up in. He left a great legacy."

"Yes, he did."

"We'd still have my parents' house right now if Charlie hadn't pissed it away, right up from under our noses."

Victoria shook her head. Ted was referring to his older brother, Charlie, who was as unscrupulous as anyone Victoria had ever known. Unlike Ted, and his sister, Lilly, Charlie had always been sneaky, conniving, and a charlatan at heart. He'd stolen money from his own mother before she'd passed away, and then tried to feign sorrow at her funeral.

She sighed, knowing that raising children was a job that never ended. Although hers were grown, she still worried over them just like she had when they were kids. She was proud of Alexandria, and even though Christian had disappointed her in many ways, Victoria still had hope for him. She knew that once he became clean and sober he would do great things in the business world. Thinking about her children, she smiled at Ted. "We haven't gotten up early like this and cooked breakfast since Alexandria and Christian were little."

"No, we haven't. This feels like old times."

"I want the two of us to get back to old times, too," Victoria said.

Ted put the orange he'd been juicing to the side and walked over to Victoria. She let out a small moan as he stood close behind her, wrapped his arms around her waist, and kissed her softly on her neck. "Oh yeah. This is definitely like old times," she purred.

"Y'all need to take that back upstairs," Maxx said with a laugh.

Victoria laughed too. "Good morning, Uncle Maxx. How did you sleep? Was your bed comfortable?"

"Yes, it was. I slept like a baby wit' a full belly. I sure am glad your daddy turned that extra room in the back into a guest bedroom. There's no way I could've made it up those stairs. I got everything I need down here. I even came in here and got a snack last night."

"I'm glad to hear you slept well, and that things were comfortable for you."

"It don't take much to please me, 'specially these days. Every mornin' I open my eyes is a good day."

Ted smiled. "I feel the same way, Uncle Maxx. You want some fresh squeezed orange juice?"

"If you can pull yourself away from my favorite niece long enough, I'd love a glass. Uh, and put a lil shot of somethin' in it."

Victoria had to smile. She adored her uncle Maxx. He'd always been supportive and kind. Even after her mother's family had shunned Elizabeth and basically hadn't had anything more to do with her once she married John, whose complexion had been too dark for their taste, Maxx had never stopped being a loving brother to Elizabeth and best friend to John. Victoria was thankful that Uncle Maxx had lived this long and she knew it would be hard on her once he passed away.

"This is good," Maxx said as he drank from the glass Ted had given him. "Nothin' beats fresh, homemade cookin', and juicin' wit' a lil kick."

Ted nodded and gave him a wink. "Glad you like it."

"Yes indeed. This'll get me goin'. And once I eat some of that delicious food Victoria's cookin', I'll be ready to get out and about. We got a lotta visitin' to do today."

"Are you sure you're up to it?" Victoria asked. "You had a pretty long day yesterday, and today is going to be just as long."

"Don't worry 'bout me. This is why I wanted to come on this trip. Bein' here in Nedine's like breathin' fresh air for me. I haven't felt this good since I was in my seventies."

"And you still look like you're in your seventies."

Uncle Maxx smiled. "I would say it's from good genes and good livin', but that ain't true. Your mama was the only one in our family that didn't show her age, and as far as good livin', well, let's just say I could write a couple books 'bout what not to do in life."

"But you're still here, looking good, and kicking," Victoria said.

"Praise God."

Just then Alexandria and PJ walked into the kitchen. "Mom, that bacon you're cooking drew us out of bed," Alexandria said. She walked over and gave Uncle Maxx a kiss on his cheek and sat on one of the bar stools at the long granite island. "You sure this seat is comfortable enough for you, Uncle Maxx?" she asked. "Maybe you should sit in one of the cushioned chairs at the kitchen table over there."

Victoria loved that her daughter was so thoughtful and always concerned about the comfort, safety, and well-being of others. She'd been that way ever since she was a little girl.

"I'm good right here, sweetheart," Maxx said with a grin. "But thanks for tryin' to look out for an old man."

"Old man." She laughed. "You looked like a school-boy last night. You had people flocking around you at the festival like you were a celebrity."

"Shoot, I guess that's 'cause most everybody proba-bly thought I was dead. All those folks was comin' over just to make sure it was really me."

Victoria shook her head. "Uncle Maxx, you're a mess."

"Well, it's the truth if I ever told it. Everybody, and I mean everybody that I knew from the good ol' days is layin' out in Butler's Cemetery. All those folks I was talk-in' to last night was the sons, daughters, grandchildren, and even great-grands of the folks I grew up with. That's one of the things nobody tells you 'bout livin' a long time."

Maxx shook his head and sighed, pausing for a mo-ment as a sad look came over him. "Everybody you know passes on, and then you look around and it's just you, liv-in' in a new world and a new time that seems to pass you right on by while you standin' still."

"That's what Grandma Allene, says," Alexandria told him and touched his arm. "You've lived a good life, Uncle Maxx, and you've made every day count."

"Thanks, Alex. Your grandma was a good woman. I'll be seein' her real soon."

Victoria started whisking a bowl of eggs as she spoke. "Not too soon. You still have some more living to do."

"I've experienced and seen so much, I feel like I done lived three lifetimes. I love life, but I'm all right wit' leavin, too," Maxx said to Victoria.

Alexandria nodded. "Grandma Allene said she felt the same way when it was her time."

"Can we not talk about death first thing in the morn-ing?" Victoria said. "Nobody's going anywhere. Today is about family, celebration, and new beginnings."

Maxx nodded. "Okay, but I'll tell you one thing about your Grandma Allene, she was a great woman. She was like a grandma to me when I was growin' up, and I remember folks always talkin' 'bout how she had the gift. I witnessed some things she talked about that ended up happenin' so I know it was true. And Alex, you the same way. Been prophesyin' 'bout stuff since you was a little girl. Your grandparents used to talk about it all the time."

Victoria nodded. "Mom used to always say that Alexandria was an old soul, and had been here before. She knew about her gift, even before I did."

"I remember her telling me that," Alexandria said. "And Grandpa John used to just nod and smile. I'm so thankful that I have a family that accepts who I am."

"We got your back," Tyler said as he walked into the room with Samantha and Chase trailing behind him. "Plus you got skills. Can you hook a brotha up and tell me who's gonna win the Super Bowl? I can make a nice spread on the odds."

Victoria shook her head. "You're always joking around."

"I'm serious," Tyler said with a grin. "I'll even give you a cut."

Everyone laughed as they gathered around the kitchen island like one big happy family. Victoria removed a stack of plates from the cabinet in preparation for their breakfast buffet. Bacon, sausage, eggs, home fries, jalapeño cheese grits, buttermilk biscuits, fruit, and Ted's freshly squeezed orange juice.

"Dig in!" Victoria said.

But the happy family breakfast came to a screeching halt when Christian walked into the room. "This is a regular Norman Rockwell scene," he said with a big smile on his face. "Mom, Dad, you guys really outdid yourselves. All this good food *and* fresh squeezed orange juice. Now this is living!"

Victoria had to pause and stop herself from catching an attitude because she couldn't believe what she was seeing. Christian was standing in the kitchen with a young woman whom Victoria had never seen. But what was worse than the fact that he'd apparently invited a complete stranger to spend the night in a house that wasn't even his, was the fact that he was wearing a T-shirt and boxers, not even dressed, and the attractive afro-clad woman had donned nothing more than one of Christian's T-shirts and a huge smile.

Chapter 25
Alexandria

Alexandria knew her brother was a lot of things, but until now, she'd never thought that stupid was one of them. But he'd just proven her wrong because not only had he hooked up with a complete stranger whom he'd met last night; he'd brought the woman to the house. And if that weren't bad enough, he was now parading her in front of the family—both of them half-dressed—like it was no big deal. She knew drugs could make people do things they'd normally never dream of, and this was definitely the case with Christian.

Alexandria took one look at her mother's face and could see that Victoria was livid. And she couldn't say that she blamed her one bit. She knew that her mother wasn't a prude by any measure, and that she was fairly liberal and open minded about most things. But this situation with Christian was about a matter of simple respect, and as her mother had said many times, carrying oneself with pride and protecting your family.

Alexandria knew that her mother had put up with a lot of things from Christian over the years, from him sneaking out the house during his teenage years to hang out in clubs, to him getting in trouble for trying to buy alcohol with a fake ID. But now his life was out of control. This wasn't teenage rebellion; it was him playing Russian roulette with his life.

As she looked around the room, she could see that everyone was visibly upset, except Chase, who was looking at the young woman's shapely thighs, which Christian's shirt barely covered. Alexandria shook her head at the hot-blooded teenager. If the situation in front of them weren't so potentially disastrous, she'd tell Chase and his parents the truth about his possible paternity. But right now she had to focus on the drama her brother had just created.

Alexandria couldn't believe that Christian had the nerve to stand in front of everyone as if what was happening was perfectly okay. Aside from the fact that sleeping with a complete stranger and bringing her into the house was in poor judgment and taste, the woman could be a stark raving lunatic for all he knew. Alexandria was pissed that Christian had taken it upon himself to invite the woman to sleep under the roof of the house their family was sharing, not even thinking or caring that he could possibly put others in danger, all for the sake of his own pleasure.

Between his behavior yesterday afternoon, last night, and now this morning, Alexandria had had enough. She was tired of her brother always causing or being in the middle of trouble, and she was now ready to give him a piece of her mind. "You know you're wrong, don't you?"

Christian reared back his shoulders and stuck out his chest. "I know there is a host of things that I can't do right in your book, so you're gonna have to be a little more specific."

"You're such an ass."

PJ was poised to say something, but Ted stepped in. He folded his arms across his chest and looked at his son. "Since you've put all of us in an uncomfortable situation you're about to get it back in return." He paused and looked at Christian's friend. "Young lady, what is your name?"

Alexandria swallowed hard because she knew her father was getting ready to bring the thunder, lightning, and rain.

"Brandy," the woman said with a chipper smile.

This isn't going to go well . . . at all, Alexandria thought to herself. Whenever the vein in her father's temple pulsated, it was a clear indication that he was pissed, and right now it was pumping. As she looked at the young woman—whose happy expression was oddly inappropriate and much too cheerful, given the uncomfortable stares she was drawing from everyone other than Chase— Alexandria began to get a strange vibe from her, as if she knew this woman. And not just from seeing her standing next to Christian when they'd been at the festival last night. She felt as if she'd met Brandy before. *Our paths have crossed, somewhere, somehow,* Alexandria thought to herself.

Ted cast his eyes back on his son. "You and Brandy need to leave, right now."

Alexandria wasn't surprised when Christian didn't react. Instead, he just stood there as if their father had asked him if he preferred sausage or bacon on his plate. She looked into his thoughts and could see that this morning he'd taken several Valiums, and instead of acting jittery he was now relaxed to the point that he appeared to be floating.

"Why, Dad?" Christian had the nerve to ask.

"Because you've disrespected your great-grandfather's house and everyone in it. I don't know anything about Brandy," Ted said, not even looking at the young woman, "and I suspect you don't either. Yet you chose to bring her under the same roof where your family is sleeping. And now you're standing here in front of us, not even dressed, either one of you, acting like you don't know that what you've done is unacceptable."

"What you did yesterday was foul," Samantha said, "But this right here . . . it's just straight up wrong."

"That's right," Victoria chimed in, taking a step forward, planting herself right beside Ted. She looked at Christian and pointed her finger. "I've tried to be patient with you. I've tried to get you help over the years. I spent yesterday afternoon trying to make sense of the fact that you came here to try and steal this property and a lot more. But I just can't take any more. You know you have a problem but you won't admit to it. Meanwhile, everyone around you suffers, and I for one am tired of it." Alexandria wanted to second that, because, in fact, she knew it to be true. "And you," Victoria continued. "Young lady, how can you even stand here in a room full of strangers wearing practically nothing, and still feel comfortable? I can only assume that it's because you're on drugs too and just as messed up as my son."

"Excuse me?" the woman said, craning her neck as she stared at Victoria. "Bitch, who you think you talkin' to?"

Alexandria felt as though she were having an out-of-body experience. The air in the room was quiet and yet still full of energy; the bad something's-about-to-pop-off-up-in-here kind of energy. Everyone was on alert. Victoria put her hand on her hip and leaned forward, the vein in Ted's temple roared, PJ adopted a defensive stance, Tyler's eyes bulged, Samantha started taking off her earrings, Chase blinked his eyes rapidly, and Uncle Maxx said, "What the hell!"

Alexandria took in the entire scene with lightning-quick speed, which at the same time seemed to play out in slow motion. In that instant, she knew exactly why she felt she knew Brandy. It was because she indeed did.

"Yes, baby girl," Allene said softly as she floated into the room. "She's exactly who you think she is."

Alexandria looked to her right and saw Allene standing close beside her. She was relieved to know that her grandma was in the room to guide her in this situation, because just like yesterday, she was going to need it.

"That's right. I'm here to help you, so don't be afraid," Allene said with a gentle smile.

Instead of talking to the vacant space beside her, which would have added another layer of disruption to the room, Alexandria communicated with Allene through thought. She could feel Allene telling her not to jump into the situation, but instead stay calm and watch it play out.

But this heifer just called my mother a bitch! Alexandria seethed. *And seeing what I just discovered about Brandy, it's going to take Aunt Samantha and the rest of us to handle her.*

"Let him do it," Allene said.

Alexandria wondered who the him was, but a split second later, she found out. She was caught off guard when Christian suddenly showed an outburst of emotion. He turned his body toward Brandy, aimed his eyes on her, and let loose.

"Have you lost your mothafuckin' mind?" His angular nose spread as if he were breathing fire. "No one talks to my mother like that!"

In one quick move, Christian took Brandy by her elbow in an attempt to escort her out of the room. But he soon saw that she wasn't going without a fight.

"Get your mothafuckin' hands off me!" Brandy growled. "I'll say whatever the hell I want to say."

"Not in this house you won't!" Samantha jumped in, taking a step forward. She tossed her earrings on the counter and leaned forward, ready to exchange blows. "I see that you need to learn a few things, and I'm definitely the one who can show you."

Tyler reached for his wife and held her back. "Sam, control yourself."

"Get the hell out!" Christian shouted to Brandy.

"What? I don't believe this!" Brandy yelled back. "You the one who invited me here, and you said this house is practically yours 'cause your mama's gonna sign it over to you this weekend, and when you turn it into a bed-and-breakfast I can run it. Now you gonna turn on me and kick me out?"

Christian's face knotted into a ball of fury. "I should've never brought your low-budget ass to this house to begin with."

Ted raised his hand in the air and boomed, his voice so loud it sounded as though it was bouncing off the walls. "Everyone needs to calm down and be quiet!" He looked directly at Brandy, this time in a no-nonsense, "this is your last warning" kind of way. "You're going to sit on the bench in the foyer while my son gets your clothes from upstairs, and while you're doing that, I'll call a cab so you can leave. Now I don't want to hear another word on the matter. Are we clear?"

Alexandria could see that her father was about to reach his limit, and she knew that Brandy could see it, too. The young siren let out a defeated huff and rolled her eyes. "Yes."

"Good, now before you leave, you owe my wife an apology."

It was clear to see that Brandy didn't want to comply, but she knew from the seriousness of Ted's tone and the stern look in his eyes that she needed to straighten up. She looked at Victoria, then held her head down. "I'm sorry."

Alexandria thought it was the poorest excuse for an apology she'd ever heard, but she also knew that this was a big deal for Brandy, given what her vision a few moments ago had revealed about the woman.

Brandy lifted her head, straightened her shoulders, and glared at Christian. "Go get my things and don't keep me waiting." She turned on her bare feet and started toward the foyer. But after a few steps, she twirled back around and smiled. "Hope y'all have a good day. Enjoy the festival tonight."

The young woman's smile was sinister and her tone was still confrontational. Alexandria exhaled and tried to stay calm. She could feel a million thoughts running through her head at once, and she was trying to keep them all straight. There were so many dynamics she was trying to process. Every person in the room was dealing with an issue and their collective energy was coming at her all at once.

She knew she had to concentrate and let most of what she was feeling fall by the wayside because there was very little she could or should do to change it.

"Listen to your gut," Allene whispered. "Only take on what you know is right."

Alexandria nodded, knowing what she needed to do. "I can never go wrong doing right."

Chapter 26
Allene

Allene shook her head at the big mess brewing in front of her. When she'd seen Brandy last night, strolling up the walkway with a spring in her step and mischief in her eyes, she had known exactly who the young she-devil was, and what she was up to.

Even though Brandy was taller, a little thinner, and slightly darker than her grandmother, Allene could see the resemblance in looks, and unfortunately, this young woman had a far worse temperament. "Umph! She's a lot like her grandmamma," Allene had said. "But this child is sneakier, more connivin', and nothin' but trouble."

It was amazing to her how much Brandy looked like Mary-Marie Jackson.

Mary-Marie was a voluptuous, seductive woman with whom John Small had enjoyed dalliances before he'd started dating Elizabeth. Even though Mary-Marie had been living with her boyfriend for years, each time John came home to visit from New York, the two would enjoy lust-filled nights in his hotel room, fueled by passion and raw attraction. Though that was as far as the feelings went for John, Mary-Marie had seen things differently.

Mary-Marie had wanted John so badly that she'd been willing to have him under any conditions, which was the reason she'd maintained their secret rendezvous every time he came to town. But John had grown tired of sex for sex's sake, and had started aiming his eyes on something more meaningful, which for him meant a future that included a wife and children. Unfortunately for her, Mary-Marie wasn't included in those plans.

When John came home one weekend to help celebrate Maxx's thirty-second birthday, that time proved to be a pivotal turning point in Mary-Marie's life, as well as John's and Maxx's.

Over those three days, Mary-Marie had been confronted with the disappointing and hurtful fact that not only did John not want to be with her, he'd met someone else and had fallen in love. But even with that knowledge, Mary-Marie had still held out hope that they could have a future together, especially after she'd come to John's rescue. She'd used information she had on Madeline King, John's deranged and scheming girlfriend, to help thwart the crazy woman's trap, which could have landed John in a world of trouble.

Even though John had appreciated Mary-Marie's help, he still hadn't wanted to build a future with her because his heart and love lay with another woman. He'd been up-front and honest, not wanting to hurt Mary-Marie, but not wanting to lead her on, either. Still, Mary-Marie had refused to take to heart what John had told her. It wasn't until she'd shown up at his house unannounced, during the middle of his family's Sunday dinner, that she had been forced to accept the situation.

Allene shook her head again when she thought about

what she'd had to do in order to make a believer out of Mary-Marie. "Some women's got to learn the hard way," she said to herself. She'd hated to have to use her gift in the way she had, but she knew that tough times called or rough measures.

But just as Allene's favorite saying went, good things had sprung forth from bad that weekend. John had become reacquainted with Maxx's younger sister, Elizabeth, and had fallen in love at the first sight of her. Their whirlwind courtship had defied conventional wisdom, produced a beautiful daughter, and provided them with over fifty years of married bliss.

For Maxx's part, his weekend had been full of drama, too. He'd been celebrating his birthday in grand style at the nicest nightclub in town when his scorned girlfriend had shown up, toting revenge and a loaded pistol. She'd shot Maxx in his backside, leaving him with a permanent limp that he carried to this day. But that moment had sobered him up, and although he'd run the ladies until his legs got tired, he'd never again lied or misled another woman about his intentions.

Now, in the present, Allene thought about that eventful weekend from long ago, and she couldn't help but feel nostalgic about how life truly did come full circle. Many of the people from the past were still living on in the form of their offspring. But unfortunately, Brandy was the result of a bad seed from the past that had sprouted up in the present.

As Allene watched the young woman swish her shapely hips from side to side, out to the foyer, she noticed that young Chase wasn't the only one who couldn't take his eyes off Brandy. Maxx was looking at her, too.

"Ol' Maxx ain't never gonna change," Allene said. But then she realized that Maxx's glare wasn't rooted in lust or attraction; it was steeped in knowing.

"There's somethin' real familiar 'bout that gal," Maxx said as he stared at the back of Brandy's head while she was leaving the room. He took a moment, rubbed the thin, white strands of hair on his head, and thought it over until it came to him. "I know 'xactly who she reminds me of."

Allene could tell by the disturbance in Maxx's voice and the concerned look in his eyes that he'd made the connection to the past.

"Who does she remind you of?" Alexandria asked.

"Way back in the day before your granddaddy ever started datin' your grandmamma, he used to fool around with this girl named Mary-Marie. She was a nice enough young lady, but she was what y'all would call a stalker today. She was crazy 'bout John."

"Yes, I heard Daddy was quite the ladies' man back then," Victoria said. "And you too, Uncle Maxx."

"We was somethin'," Maxx chuckled. "But the weekend I had my thirty-second birthday party taught both of us a lesson."

"The party where you got shot?" Victoria asked.

"Yep. The very one. John was datin' a crazy woman named Madeline King, and he brought her down wit' him for the weekend. Well, that woman put him through some changes, and even ended up draggin' Slim into it."

Victoria nodded her head. "I remember Daddy telling me about it. And Percy said his father talked about that night until the day he died."

"I bet he did. That crazy woman beat up her own self and then tried to say Slim did it, all so she could get back at John and trap him. I done a lotta livin', and I still ain't met nobody crazy as Madeline King was in all my life."

Ted shook his head. "Sounds like it was one hell of a weekend."

"Yeah, I reckon it was," Maxx said. "But I got to

give Mary-Marie credit. If it wasn't from her, poor Slim and John woulda ended up in a big mess. From what I heard, she had some dirt on Madeline and threatened to tell it if she didn't leave John alone. It musta been real bad because the crazy woman packed her things and left town on a bus before John could even say good-bye. Yep, I'll never forget that weekend long as I live."

Allene nodded her head in agreement with Maxx, thinking he'd never spoken truer words. She'd never forget that weekend either, because it had been the first time she'd seen what the other side of her gift could do if she used it while she was angry—and she'd discovered that firsthand when she'd confronted Mary-Marie on the doorstep of the very house she was standing in right now.

Yes, that weekend had been filled with many challenges, and it was a time when Allene had lost and gained what mattered to her most—her family. It was the last time she had laid eyes on Susan Jessup during her days on earth, and that loss had been hard. But had also been a new beginning because, along with the darker side of what she'd realized her gift could do, she'd tapped into the infinite possibilities and the hope it could bring. She'd been able to look into the future, contact her yet to be born great-great-granddaughter, and communicate with her in another time and place. Allene still didn't understand how she'd been able to do it, or how their times had merged into one, but she was grateful she'd had the experience.

Maxx shook his head. "Even though her grand-mamma was a nice enough woman, I can tell by lookin' at that gal that she nothing but trouble," he said about Brandy. "And outta all the people Christian could take up with, who'da ever thought it would be wit' somebody who look just like the woman his granddaddy used to fool 'round wit'. I mean, she the spittin' image of Mary-Marie."

"I hope Brandy's not a stalker like that woman was," Victoria said.

Maxx shook his head. "Me too, but if that gal's anything like I think she is, Christian's done met his match."

"I don't know what I'm going to do about that son of mine." Victoria let out a loud sigh.

Ted put his hand on her shoulder. "There's nothing you, I, or anyone can do. Christian is a grown man and he's going to have to start taking responsibility and acting like one."

"I don't know about anyone else, but I'm starving," PJ said, looking at the food spread out on the table.

Allene could see that was PJ's way of steering the subject away from Christian. She knew he'd had a hard time not confronting Christian about his rude and disrespectful behavior, and she was glad PJ hadn't punched him liked he'd wanted to.

"I'm with PJ," Ted said in agreement. "Let's rewind to ten minutes ago and start over."

Victoria smiled. "Okay, I'll try this again. . . . Everyone, dig in!"

As the happy group filled their plates with food, Allene noticed that Alexandria was quiet, sitting on her bar stool in deep concentration. Her eyes closed and opened quickly, signaling the telltale signs of what Allene knew was a glimpse into something.

What should I do, Grandma? Alexandria asked.

"You had a vision. You know who she is, and you know what's gonna happen, don't you?"

Yes, and I'm not sure if I should intercede or let things play out. What should I do? she asked again.

Allene sighed. This was part of the blessing and the burden of having the gift. "Baby girl," Allene said, "Don't think too hard on it. Trust in what you feel and know that you have the gift for a reason. Let your gut guide you."

Alexandria nodded her head. "I'll be right back," she said to PJ and the others.

"I thought you were hungry. Where're you going?"

"I've got to take care of something. I'll be back before you butter your biscuit." She gave him a kiss on his cheek and walked out of the kitchen.

Allene smiled to herself. She was happy, nervous, and cautious all at once. Just like that drama-filled weekend Maxx had talked about many, many years ago, she knew this weekend was going to prove just as eventful. And reminiscent of that time, this one would present deep losses as well as joyous gains.

"Yes, Lord," Allene said. "You truly do know what's best."

Allene's vision told her that Sunday was going to be a day of blessings, not just because it was a holy day, but because wrongs would be made right and the past would surely be buried as new beginnings started for everyone.

As Allene floated down the hall, following Alexandria toward the foyer, she knew this was the first step in what was about to unfold.

Chapter 27
Alexandria

Alexandria walked slowly toward the foyer. She could feel Allene close behind her, which gave her both comfort and courage for what she was about to do. She knew she had to proceed with caution, but she also knew she needed to be direct, if not bold, in her approach because of whom she was about to deal with.

As she got closer, she made sure to take in every detail of Brandy's physical appearance and mannerisms, knowing she had to be prepared for anything in case things turned nasty. She carefully observed the dangerous woman's large, neatly coiffed afro, high forehead, clear eyes, and soft yet distinctive facial contours. She examined Brandy as the woman turned her head, shining light on her flawless ebony-colored skin. She stretched her long, well-toned legs, and then crossed them at her ankles, revealing narrow feet adorned with hot-pink-colored toenail polish.

Alexandria could see that Brandy's perfectly erect

posture spoke of her obvious confidence, and the way she sat upright with her shoulders back, indicated that she'd been taught some modicum of comportment. Her tall, almost towering stature dominated the space where she sat, and it let Alexandria know that Brandy was ready for her.

"I know why you're here, and I know what you're up to," Alexandria said as she looked at Brandy with the same kind of intense, no-nonsense stare that her father had just worn only minutes ago.

"First off, you don't know me from Adam." Brandy looked Alexandria up and down, inspecting her head full of thick brown curls, strong shoulders, fitted halter top, and long floral-print skirt that was paired with jewel-toned sandals. "And second, you need to watch how you talk to people. Didn't your mama teach you any manners?"

Oh, this heffa wants a beat down! Alexandria had to calm herself. "You're real lucky, Brandy. You got away with disrespecting my mother and calling her out of her name once, so don't push it. You need to stop while you're ahead." Alexandria placed her right hand on her hip and leaned forward with the look of a pit bull on her face. "And don't ever let me hear you mention my mother for any reason, ever again."

Brandy uncrossed her legs and shifted in place on the antique sitting bench where she was perched. She appeared unfazed, but Alexandria could read her mind and tell that for the first time in a long time, Brandy was a little nervous. "You think you fancy and shit, just 'cause you a lawyer. But like I said, you need a lesson in manners."

Alexandria was slightly taken aback, and wondered how Brandy knew she was an attorney. She tried to access the information from the woman's thoughts, but for some reason she was unable to break through. But she didn't let it throw her off her game because she knew she couldn't let Brandy rattle her.

Alexandria knew that just like Mary-Marie, Brandy had issues. Only unlike her grandmother, whose primary transgression was an obsessive personality and a need to control, Brandy was a different animal altogether. This young woman had done many immoral, unethical, and illegal things, and unfortunately, she wasn't above murder. She was more dangerous than a loaded gun.

But even knowing this, Alexandria was bold and unafraid. She was normally a fairly mild-tempered person, but right now she understood that the situation called for something else entirely. She wondered if her fearlessness came from the fact that she knew her grandma Allene was standing close beside her, or if it was because she was in a new environment, which had given her an edge. She suddenly realized it was neither. She felt empowered because she knew she was doing the right thing. She'd listened to what Allene had told her and trusted her gut.

When Alexandria had first laid eyes on Brandy last night she'd felt a bad vibe permeate the air. But at the time she hadn't been sure if it was really Brandy she was sensing or if it was Christian, who she knew was clearly up to no good. But a few minutes ago when Alexandria had been sitting on the bar stool in the kitchen, feeling the same intense vibe she'd picked up last night, she'd closed her eyes and allowed her gift to guide her, and what she had seen was the reason she was standing in front of Brandy right now, prepared to fight the woman if she had to.

"I want you to forget that you even know this address," Alexandria said through gritted teeth. "Don't ever come back here again, and don't ever think about messing with my family, especially my brother."

Brandy stood and walked to within a few inches of Alexandria. They were the same towering height, so she looked Alexandria directly in the eyes as she spoke. "Is that a threat?"

Alexandria took two steps forward, putting her so close to Brandy that their bodies nearly touched. She narrowed her eyes right back at the brazen woman. "I didn't stutter, did I?"

When Alexandria said those words, Brandy looked as if she'd just seen a ghost. She moved back two paces, nearly stumbling over her own two feet as her eyes bucked wide.

"She knows you have the gift," Allene said. "Her grandmamma used to say those words, and now you just repeated it. "

Alexandria knew that Allene was right. Brandy had grown up hearing her grandmother quote that haunting phrase many times through the years, and much like what had happened to Slim, the experience it came from had been so impactful she'd talked about it until the day she'd died. Alexandria closed her eyes for a quick second to reach back in time and see exactly what it all meant. Her body was jolted with shock when she saw that Allene had threatened Mary-Marie's life using those words.

Mary-Marie had known that Madeline was a dangerous killer. Her cousin, who'd known Madeline, had told Mary-Marie all about the crazy woman's ways, and that she often told her unsuspecting victims, "I didn't stutter, did I?" to let them know she meant business before she set out to either trap or kill them. Those words had been something that Mary-Marie remembered because they sounded playful and chilling at the same time.

When Mary-Marie had come to the house that Sunday afternoon, planning to disrupt John's family dinner by telling Elizabeth that she and John had been having a long-running affair, Allene had known she couldn't let that happen.

John and Elizabeth had to end up together so that Victoria could be born and Alexandria could exist. Allene knew that if Mary-Marie had gotten anywhere near their dinner table that day her family's future would not be possible. So she had risen from the dinner table, gone to the front door where Mary-Marie was trying to get past Henrietta to gain access inside the house, and taken care of business.

Allene had instructed Henrietta to leave her alone with Mary-Marie. Once it was just the two of them, she'd looked into Mary-Marie's eyes and conjured up a vision that unfolded with the young woman as dead as any corpse out in Butler's Cemetery. The vision didn't show how Mary-Marie would meet her fate, but Allene communicated to her that she would surely die if she didn't stay away from John.

"You better leave this property right now," Allene had told her. "And if you know what's good for you, you'll never come back."

"Are you threatenin' my life?" Mary-Marie had asked in an attempt to be bold.

"I didn't stutter, did I?" Allene had said with a steely face.

Alexandria looked over to Allene, who nodded her head. "Baby girl, tough times call for rough measures."

Brandy jumped when she heard the loud beep of a horn coming from outside. The cab that Ted called had arrived just in time. Alexandria let out a sigh of relief, but she knew she had to maintain her position. "Remember, don't ever come to this house again."

"I told you, I don't like threats."

"That's fine. You don't have to like it, but you will respect it."

Alexandria turned her head when she heard Christian

come down the stairs carrying Brandy's things in his hands.

Brandy rushed past Alexandria and met Christian at the foot of the steps. "Give me my things so I can get the hell up outta here," she hissed.

"And don't come back," Christian yelled.

"Your punk ass invited me, remember?" Brandy reached out and snatched her clothes and shoes out of his hand. "You said you wanted to show me a good time and spend your parents' money on me once you got this big ol' house. You're full of shit! Lyin' bitch ass punk! And so is the rest of this crazy family."

Alexandria could see that Christian was so furious he was close to doing something that was going to land him with a charge for aggravated assault. She'd seen it play out in her vision, complete with handcuffs and him sitting in the county jail because her parents refused to post his bail.

Alexandria was going to stand by and let it happen, but in a split second she changed her mind. She didn't know why, but her brother being in jail didn't feel right. He needed to be free to learn his lesson in a different way. She quickly rushed over and caught Christian's hand before it could make contact with Brandy's face.

"There's never an excuse to hit a woman," Alexandria said to her brother. "Let it go."

Brandy stepped away, then turned and ran toward the front door just as the cab driver blew his horn again. "I'm coming, and I can't wait to get the hell outta here!" she said, not bothering to look back as she slammed the door behind her.

Alexandria and Christian stood in the foyer, silent, looking at each other. She didn't have to read his mind because his feelings were written on his face and in the slump of his shoulders. He actually felt remorseful about what he'd done.

"You hate me, don't you?"

Alexandria shook her head. "You frustrate and disappoint me. And honestly, I don't like who you've become. But I don't hate you."

Christian looked down the hall that led back to the kitchen. "I know they all do, probably even Mom and Dad. I can't blame them."

"You've done some really awful things that would warrant it, and this morning is a prime example. But even after the stunt you pulled, they don't hate you either." Alexandria took a deep breath. "The fact that you wanted to swindle our mother was a low-down thing, and then bringing a strange and unstable woman into this house . . . that was such a messed up move. What if that lunatic had been carrying a gun?" Alexandria said, knowing Brandy owned two pistols and a shotgun. "She could've hurt any of us, or even killed someone. But you didn't stop to think about that. You let the drugs take over and make your decisions for you. Our great-great-grandma Allene always said, 'You can never go wrong doing right,' and the same holds true in the reverse. You did wrong."

Christian rubbed his hand across the soft black curls atop his head. "I'm not a bad person, Alexandria."

"I know, but you're acting like one. You need help, Christian."

He nodded his head with a solemn look on his face. "I guess I do."

Christian stuck his hands in his front pockets, a move their father was known for. "Everyone thinks I'm a bad person, but I'm not."

"We're only going on what you show us. Until you own up to being an addict and admit to your shortcomings, you're going to continue to spiral down, and eventually your risky and dangerous behavior is going to cost you your life."

"You're right." Christian looked down the hall toward the kitchen. "I guess I need to go and apologize."

"Yes, and you need to go upstairs and start packing your bags."

Christian looked dumbfounded. "Why?"

"Because Dad said he wanted Brandy and you out of this house."

"He was just saying that in the heat of the moment. He wouldn't really put me out," Christian said as he started walking toward the kitchen.

Alexandria didn't say a word; she simply walked behind her brother, with Allene right beside her. She kept quiet because she knew their father had meant every single word that had come from his mouth, and in just five minutes, Christian would know that, too.

"You ready for what's gonna come next?" Allene asked.

Alexandria sighed. *Yes, as ready as I'll ever be.* She knew that Christian's expulsion from the house wasn't going to be easy, so she braced herself for the volatile exchange that was about to take place back in the kitchen.

Chapter 28
Victoria

Victoria felt as though things were going from one extreme to another, and the highs and lows of the last two days were starting to make her think that this trip to Nedine wasn't such a great idea after all.

Victoria was still livid when she thought about the half-naked stranger who'd called her a bitch right to her face. And now, as she looked at her husband and son, she knew another tense and potentially disastrous moment was about to unfold. "Honey, are you okay?" she asked Ted, knowing he wasn't.

"I will be in just one minute."

His tone was tight and short, and as Victoria watched her husband's eyes narrow in on their son, who'd just reentered the room, all she could do was pray that Ted wouldn't pick this time to go off.

Victoria had always admired the fact that Ted was so cool and composed in nearly all situations. The only time she'd ever seen him appear frazzled was during the birth of their children. He'd been so excited both times that he'd barely gotten them to the hospital in one piece. She knew that Christian had inherited his steady composure from Ted, but as his drug and alcohol use increased, he'd become increasingly dramatic, to the point of unexpected outbursts.

As Victoria's eyes shifted between her son and her husband, she knew right away that Ted was serious about putting Christian out of the house, and even though she felt the odds were against Christian acting as though he had some sense, she kept a sliver of hope, praying she was wrong. But when Ted's body language became even more steely and Christian's held a relaxed, almost casual pose, she knew she was about to witness a display that was going to make her headache grow even worse.

Christian looked around the room and cleared his throat before he began to speak. "I want to apologize for my poor judgment and insensitivity. I created an uncomfortable situation for everyone, and I sincerely regret that." He turned to Victoria. "Mom, I'm deeply sorry. I didn't mean for any of this to happen, and I can't apologize enough for the insult you suffered. I hope you can forgive me."

Victoria wanted to ask him if he was sorry about his plans to swindle her out of the very house in which they were standing. But she decided to let it go because she could see that Ted was about to rip into their son.

Christian stepped up to the kitchen island to prepare a plate, and that's when the fireworks began.

"What are you doing?" Ted asked.

Christian gave him a quizzical look as he shrugged his shoulders. "Getting something to eat."

Now the entire room could sense that something serious was about to erupt, and everyone, including Victoria, held a collective breath.

"You need to be upstairs packing. I already told you, you have to leave this house," Ted said.

"You can't be serious."

Ted folded his arms across his chest and locked eyes with his son. Victoria looked over and saw that Alexandria was standing with her head held down toward her feet, eyes trained on the floor. *Father in heaven,* Victoria said to herself. Now she knew for sure that things were going to get ugly. She knew that if Alexandria couldn't even bring herself to look at what was unfolding, this situation surely wasn't going to end well. Victoria said another quick prayer and again hoped for the best.

"Yes, I'm serious," Ted responded. "This was your last time disrespecting our family. Your mother and I have put up with a lot from you since you were a child, from sneaking out of the house through your window at night while you were still in middle school, to smoking pot in your room, to making honor roll and then ruining it by fighting on school grounds, running up the limit on the credit card we got you when you went to college, and always scheming and lying to get what you want . . . and that's just the tip of the stunts you've pulled over and over, and like fools, we've all forgiven you and tried to get you help, blaming your behavior on the drugs. But now I see that this is just who you are, and this morning you took it way too far.

"You brought someone under this roof without a care about anyone other than yourself. You put all of us in possible danger because you don't know a thing about that woman, who she knows, or what she's capable of. And what has me outraged," Ted huffed as the vein in his temple began to pop up, "is that your mother was called out of her name. That's something I will never tolerate in my presence, as long as I'm living."

Christian raised his voice. "I said I was sorry!"

Ted raised his voice right back. "Watch how you talk to me!"

Victoria shook her head from side to side and leaned on one foot, nervous and afraid of what would happen next. She wanted so badly to step in, but she knew that doing so might make things even worse.

Ted lowered his voice. "I don't care where you go, but you've got to get out of here."

"You mean you really want me to leave?"

"I'm not going to repeat myself. Get your things and get out of this house."

"This is Mom's house. You can't put me out."

Victoria could hear the slight tremor in Christian's voice. Ted was the only person whom she knew her son feared, but apparently not as much as she'd thought. He'd just made a bold and disrespectful statement, and she knew it was going to be met with fury from Ted.

She sucked in an extra breath of air as Ted stepped up to Christian, so close their noses were almost touching. Both men were the same six feet two inches in height, and like Ted, Christian was lean and well built, but with the added advantage of being significantly younger. However, despite Ted's age, Victoria knew it wasn't a factor for her husband when it came to protecting those he loved.

"Watch your step, son." Ted's voice was smooth, calm, and hard at the same time, and it put fear in Victoria because she knew what her husband was capable of. She knew that as calm, cool, and reserved as Ted could be, he could also tear up the entire room if he was pushed. And she prayed again that their son wasn't foolish enough to test fate.

"C'mon, man. Don't do this, let it go," Tyler said as he stepped up beside Christian. "You were wrong and your father has spoken. You need to bounce on up outta here."

Uncle Maxx shook his head as he looked at his great nephew. "You been nasty and disrespectful. You better be glad you got understandin' parents, and if I was you, I'd do 'xactly what your daddy asked 'cause he means business, and ain't nobody here gonna get they ass kicked tryin' to defend you."

"Just go," Alexandria said as she raised her head. She looked deeply into Christian's eyes. "Trust me when I say you need to pack your things and leave, right now."

Victoria felt as if she were standing front and center in the middle of a crazy reality television show. This was supposed to be a happy family breakfast buffet, not a standoff between father and son that had the potential of turning physical.

She knew that Tyler, Uncle Maxx, and Alexandria were all right. Christian was about to be put out of the house. The entire family wanted him gone, and sadly, so did she.

Christian looked at her with a small plea on his face, and it made her heart feel conflicted. On one hand, she knew it was best for him to leave, especially after the cryptic stare she had seen Alexandria throw his way. But on the other hand, Christian was her baby, and despite his ways, she didn't want to see him thrown out of the house.

"Mom, do you want to put me out, too?" Christian asked.

Victoria bit her bottom lip and nodded as she looked at her son. "You brought this on yourself. Your father is the head of this family and I stand by his wishes, as should you. You need to pack your things."

"Fine!" Christian said in a loud, angry voice. "I knew I shouldn't have come here to this miserable little town in the first place. Everybody always wants to judge me. But that's all right. I got this."

Victoria, as well as everyone else in the room, stood still and quiet as Christian practically stomped his way out of the kitchen and up the stairs in a rage. She thought about all that had transpired in less than an hour, and the more she pondered, the more she went back to what she'd originally felt. Maybe this trip was a good thing after all.

Christian had shown his ass and had gotten kicked out of the house. This was the first time his family had rejected him and not stood behind him when his behavior clearly dictated they should exercise some tough love. Victoria thought about the fact that this was part of her family's past behavior that needed to be buried so that new ways of dealing with their family problems could start anew.

As Victoria walked back to the other side of the buffet that she'd set up on the kitchen island, she continued to think about what she'd just witnessed. *I pray this day goes uphill from here,* she said to herself. But as she spooned scrambled eggs unto her plate, the pit of her stomach told her that she needed to hold on tight for more bumps in the road.

Chapter 29

Samantha

Samantha was so mad she wanted to spit. She knew that fighting, especially in front of her son, would have been a terrible thing to do, and a horrible example for a young boy who was already trending dangerously to the wild side. But she couldn't help it. She'd wanted to give Brandy a beat down right there in the kitchen in front of everyone.

She was glad that her levelheaded husband had stepped in and made her act like she had some sense. "Baby, you know that's not the example we want to show Chase," Tyler had whispered into her ear when he'd gently pulled her off to the side.

"He's looking at that hoochie mama's legs and thighs so hard he doesn't even notice that I'm ready to kick Ms. Thang's ass."

"Kids notice everything, Sam. Whether we think they do or not."

Samantha knew Tyler had been right again, and she was glad she hadn't reacted the way she'd wanted to. She knew she had to control her mouth and her actions, and this practice in self-control was good training for when she came forward to her family with the secret she'd been keeping.

She put her emotions to the side and joined in as everyone partook in the delicious breakfast that Victoria and Ted had prepared. Despite the physical incident that had nearly just transpired, Samantha was still amazed by how much she was enjoying this trip. She'd known from the beginning that being in Nedine was going to help her family, but she hadn't anticipated that she'd actually have fun.

After everyone finished breakfast, she and Tyler let Chase know that he was responsible for cleaning the kitchen.

"You mean I have to do the dishes and clean this whole kitchen by myself?" Chase said, surprised and slightly annoyed.

Tyler nodded. "Boy, you act like you have to do hard labor."

"It's gonna feel like it."

Samantha looked at her son and shook her head. "You have no idea what hard labor feels like. There's a heavy-duty dishwasher to help you and an army of cleaning supplies under the sink."

"Yeah, but I still have to do all this work by myself. Eight people had breakfast but only one has to clean up. That's not fair."

Samantha shrugged. "Neither is life."

"You're the youngest person in this house," Tyler said. "So you should have more energy than any of us to get the job done. Now stop complaining and get to cleaning."

Chase wasn't bold or crazy enough to give Tyler any back talk, so he sucked up his attitude and pulled out the cleaning supplies. As Samantha and Tyler walked upstairs to shower and get dressed, she hoped the rest of the day would go as smoothly.

It was a little after lunchtime, and even though they'd devoured a hearty breakfast, Samantha, Tyler, and Chase were eating again. They were sitting outside the Masonic Lodge, finishing their meal of cheeseburgers, French fries, and chocolate milk shakes before going inside to check out the black history exhibit. For someone so thin, Samantha had always had a ferocious appetite, eating anything she wanted without gaining a pound. She loved that there were dozens of food vendors set up at every celebratory event location throughout town.

"Are you two ready to check out the exhibit?" Tyler asked as he polished off the last of his shake.

Samantha wanted to laugh because it was him they were waiting on. She and Chase were fast eaters, but Tyler always took his time. Now that he'd finally finished, they were ready to head inside.

Samantha was impressed and inspired by the attention to detail and obvious effort that the city's African American community had put into making sure the town's celebration included black people who'd made significant contributions in Nedine's history. Having grown up in D.C.'s "Chocolate City," she'd always had a healthy appreciation for and knowledge of black history and culture. But as she looked at some of the pictures hanging on the walls, which spanned from grainy black and white photos of slaves to a colorful canvas of this year's NAACP officers, she felt a new kind of pride. The photos showed that struggle could lead to triumph, and Samantha felt the same way about her life.

If anyone had told her during her late twenties that

she'd be happily married with two children, living in a sprawling suburban neighborhood in the South, she would have laughed and told them to stop drinking. Even with the difficulties that lay ahead involving her son, along with the difficult task of revealing her true paternity, Samantha knew that life was good, and that she'd been blessed in spite of herself.

"This history lesson is better than anything that Chase could learn in school," Samantha said to Victoria as she watched her son and husband walk around the room, taking in the displays. "I'm so glad he and Tyler are spending this kind of time together, bonding and sharing. This really means a lot and I'm so grateful to you for allowing us to join your family on this trip."

"I'm thankful that my beautiful daughter received the vision from our grandma Allene, because that's what brought us here," Victoria said, giving Alexandria a big smile.

Ted nodded in agreement. "Even though we've had a few bumps early on, we're going to put those behind us and enjoy the rest of this weekend. From here on out, it'll be smooth sailing."

Samantha hoped Ted's words were going to ring true, but as she looked at Alexandria, she wasn't so sure. Victoria and Ted seemed not to notice that their daughter looked as though her mind was in a different place. Samantha wondered if Alexandria was having one of her visions or if she was simply tired. She wanted to ask, but she also didn't want to alarm anyone. Just then, Chase and Tyler came up.

Tyler was smiling and she could see that he had good news.

"While Chase and I were looking at one of the photos, a guy came up to me who happens to be head of the local Urban League. We started talking, I told him about YFI, and he's interested in starting a chapter here in Nedine."

"That's great," Samantha said.

"My father's little town is making big connections," Victoria said with a smile.

Tyler nodded. "It sure is. As a matter of fact, he invited us to come over to the Urban League office because they're having a reception that starts in an hour. I figured we could head over there if it doesn't interfere with your plans for us."

"Sure," Victoria said. "We're going to stick around here for a while and then take Uncle Maxx to the old neighborhood where he grew up before we head back to the house."

"Sounds good," Samantha said. "We'll see you later." She gave Victoria and the rest of the family a hug before following Tyler and Chase out the door.

Three hours and hundreds of handshakes, smiles, and two slices of pound cake later, they were back at the house. Samantha didn't realize how tired she was until she kicked off her stiletto sandals and lay atop the cool comforter in her and Tyler's room.

"This has been a full day and we still have the evening gala tonight," Samantha said as she wriggled out of her skirt and summer tank top.

Tyler pulled off his shorts and polo shirt, then walked over to the bed to lie down beside her. "What time does it start?"

"At eight."

"Good, we've got a few hours."

Samantha yawned. "Yes, and I'm going to take a nice long power nap to keep me going for tonight."

Tyler turned onto his side so that he was facing her. "Sam, I need to talk to you about something."

The seriousness in his voice and the intensity in his eyes told her that whatever he wanted to talk about wasn't going to be good. "Okay, I can tell this is something serious. What's wrong?"

"It's about Chase."

Samantha shot up in the bed. She'd been sleepy only moments ago, but now she was on full alert. Her heart started beating fast and she had to remind herself to breathe. "What's happened now?"

"Several things. Not just what's going on at the moment, but what's happened in the past."

Samantha sat in the middle of the bed looking stunned as Tyler told her about the other two pregnancy scares their son had experienced last year. If she hadn't known better, she would have thought that Tyler was making it up as a practical joke. But she knew her husband didn't play around like that, and nothing about what he was telling her was remotely funny.

"I wanted to tell you," he continued. "But I didn't know how."

"How about, 'Guess what, Sam, our son just got a girl pregnant!' "

"It wasn't that easy."

"And why the hell not?"

"Because I've always told Chase that he can come to me, man-to-man, and tell me anything in confidence. I want him to trust in my word, Sam."

Samantha shook her head. "But he's not a man. He's a child. Our child."

"He's growing into a man, and what he's facing right now is a grown-up situation and responsibility."

"I don't care what kind of trouble Chase finds himself in, I'm his mother and I deserved to know what was going on. How could you have stood by, knowing he'd gotten two girls pregnant, and not say a word to me?" Samantha was incredulous. She hopped off the bed and started pacing the floor. "This is the reason why LaMonica is pregnant right now."

Tyler stood to his feet, too. "You think that because I didn't tell you about the others, this is the reason Chase is in this situation? You can't mean that."

"I absolutely do. If I had known about the others I would've done something to put a stop to him going out and getting another girl pregnant."

"If you had known about the others you would've done exactly what you did two weeks ago, which was get upset, start yelling, and then worry yourself into a glass of wine."

Samantha glared at him. "Did Chase come to you about this before he sat down with both of us?"

Tyler nodded.

"This is fucking unbelievable. How long did you know before our little sham of a family meeting?"

"He told me that morning, after you'd gone to work," Tyler let out a heavy breath. "This made his third strike, and I told him it was time for us to handle his mistakes as a family. If I could change things I would. I'd have told you last year after I found out about the first girl. But I can't go back in time, Sam. All I can do is move forward.

"And I promise you here and now, from this point on you won't ever have to worry about me keeping anything from you. We're a family, and I want us to be strong for each other."

They stood far apart in silence for several minutes, Tyler looking at her, Samantha looking up at the ceiling. Her head was swimming with painful realizations.

"Say something?" Tyler said.

"I feel so empty right now."

"Baby, I'm sorry." Tyler walked to her and took her into his arms. "Please forgive me."

Samantha laid her head on his shoulder. "I guess it's me who should ask for forgiveness. Neither you nor Chase trusted me with the truth because you were afraid I'd go off, and that's not right. I have to own up to my shit and start controlling my actions . . . and my mouth."

"Yeah, you do," Tyler said with a chuckle. "I made a mistake and I'm sorry."

"What you did is exactly what I've done for years. I've held on to a secret that affects other people, all because I wanted to protect them from hurt. But now I know it's best to tell people the truth, show them love, and then get through it together, like you said, as a family."

Tyler pulled back and stared at her. "Have you been reading self-help books?"

If the situation weren't so serious Samantha would have either laughed or felt offended. "What? I can't be deep and thought-provoking?"

"That's just such a healthy approach. I'm proud of you, baby."

Samantha was actually surprised and proud of herself, too. "Thank you, I'm learning."

The truth was, taking in the exhibit at the Masonic Lodge, which had featured several pictures of Victoria's grandfather and father, and then hearing a historian talk about the legacy they'd built, had inspired Samantha. And now, standing in the room that John Small had once slept in, in a house steeped in history and a lifetime of love, family, and dreams, she felt hopeful.

Samantha placed her head back on Tyler's shoulder and smiled. "We both dug up and then buried our past, and now we can move on with a new beginning."

Chapter 30
Alexandria

Alexandria and her family, sans Christian, were standing among the large crowd assembled at the Masonic Lodge, which was located on the south side of town and home to most of Nedine's black residents. The unassuming structure, which had undergone several expansions through the years, and most recently a complete renovation, was a time-honored gathering place for the African American community.

More than two hundred people were milling around, inside and out, all there as part of the town's Flower Festival activities which had been organized to observe and pay homage to Nedine's black residents, community leaders and business owners who'd done extraordinary things in the name of progress.

"Ali, even though this morning started off a little rocky, things are looking up. This is turning out to be a great day," PJ said as he stood beside Alexandria and her parents.

As her family, local townspeople, and tourists enjoyed the artful history displays, historical photos, and abundant food stations throughout the room, Alexandria thought about the conversation that she and Grandma Allene had had last night. There were some things that were simply out of her control, and even if she could use her abilities to intervene and change them, it was best to step back, watch, and let things take their own course.

"My great-grandma, Susan Jessup, used to always tell me, 'Everything is as it needs to be,' " Allene had once said.

Alexandria knew her wise ancestors were right, so instead of lamenting what she couldn't change, she chose to focus her mind on what was in front of her. She looked around the room and took in the poignant, complex history that the two-thousand-and-five-hundred-square-foot space held. It was alive with energy. She smiled when a vision of her grandpa John flashed in front of her. She saw that he'd celebrated his graduation from both high school and college here, and that he'd rejoiced with happiness when he and her nana Elizabeth had hosted their simple but elegant wedding reception in this very room, which her great-grandmother Henrietta had personally catered.

"Look at Daddy and his father," Victoria said with pride as she pointed at a picture of Isaiah and John Small that hung prominently in the center of the main wall. They were both dressed in tailored business suits, looking like they belonged on the cover of *Fortune* magazine. "I never knew my grandpa Isaiah because he passed away when I was just a baby. But the stories I heard about him were legendary, and that's why my daddy turned out to be the kind of man he was." Victoria smiled and shook her head. "Daddy was all about business, and you couldn't find a smarter man alive, but he also loved and cherished his family. He was a great man, and I miss him so much."

"Yes indeed," Maxx said. "They was both pillars of this community, respected by blacks and whites alike."

Alexandria nodded in agreement. "Yes, Mom and Uncle Maxx. I've seen all that you say, and I can feel their spirits right now."

"Are they here in the room?" Victoria whispered as she looked at her daughter with hope.

"Their energy is, along with so many others." Alexandria scanned the room. "Every face you see in the pictures on these walls is here, and they're happy to finally be acknowledged."

"I'm always so amazed by what you can do," Victoria said with a smile. "I wish I had your gift, even if for just one day. What a blessing that would be."

Alexandria knew that her mother didn't have a clue, nor did most other people, that her gift could bring a heavy burden, just as she and Allene had discussed last night. Each day was an internal fight to control it. Some days were easier than others when trying to tame the voices and visions that were always competing to be heard or seen. At times like now, when she was both mentally and physically tired, it was all she could do to simply function.

As Alexandria took another glance around the room, making note of each photograph gracing the four walls of the beautifully restored building, she couldn't help but feel overwhelming awe. From the moment she'd entered the historic space, she'd been greeted with the intense spirit and energy of the people whose faces decorated the walls, and the physical presence of those who'd been in this very room from as far back as one hundred fifty years ago, when the original building had been constructed as a small, one-room shack.

Voices and visions from the past shot out at her as if she were watching snippets of a movie. She saw people laughing at celebrations, finger snapping to loud music at parties, and receiving honors at ceremonies held to commemorate special occasions. But she also felt the sadness, mourning, loss, and sorrow that had once filled the great room. She closed her eyes and was instantly transported back to the past. She watched as secret meetings took place in the very spot where she was standing.

The town's black activists had strategized under the cover of night, developing plans to keep their community safe in the wake of lynchings, cross burnings, and other atrocious acts committed by the Klan.

She saw her grandma Allene in these meetings. The only woman in a room full of men, Allene sat close beside her son, Isaiah, who resided at the head of a small wooden table where the quiet group had gathered by dim candlelight. Allene spoke to the men in hushed tones as they listened with rapt attention to every word coming from her mouth. Alexandria strained to hear what they were saying, but try as she might, she couldn't make out a single word.

Grandma Allene, what's going on? Alexandria asked through her thoughts, knowing Allene was close by. *I know I'm seeing this vision for a reason, but I don't know why.*

Alexandria waited for Allene to respond, but she heard nothing except the silence in her own head and the busy chatter of the crowd that filled the room. She looked around for Allene, hoping to see the tall, regal woman who always stood out even when she was sitting down. But she didn't see a trace of Allene's signature silver-white mane that was fashioned into a neat chignon high atop her head, or the flowing ankle-length skirt she always wore.

Alexandria was confused and didn't know what to think. Although Allene was out of sight, she knew the old spirit was in the room because she could feel her.

Where are you, Grandma? As Alexandria concentrated harder, fatigue began to grip her body. The visions were coming too fast, and the fact that she couldn't make sense of them made her feel helpless to what was happening. She made one last attempt to communicate with Allene. She wiped a thin trace of sweat from her brow and reached out through air, space, and time. *I'm seeing things that I don't understand. Please tell me what all this means.*

"Baby, are you okay?" PJ asked as he held Alexandria's hand in his. He looked at her closely. "You're trembling and you're starting to sweat. Are you having a vision?"

"What's wrong, sweetie?" Victoria asked as she looked on with worry.

Alexandria nodded. "I need something to drink. I feel a little light-headed."

"I'll take care of her, Mom," PJ said to Victoria. "Don't worry—this happens from time to time when we're at home. I know what to do."

Victoria looked into Alexandria's eyes, and then at PJ. "Sweetie, are you sure you're all right? Is there anything I can do?"

"PJ will take care of her," Ted said gently as he gave a nod.

Protection mixed with a mother's instinct was layered in Victoria's voice. "Your father and I will be right here if you need us."

Alexandria smiled. "Thanks, Mom. But don't worry. I'll be fine. I just need a few minutes to sit down and rest."

As PJ slowly led her to the other side of the room, Alexandria tried to once again communicate with Allene.

Why aren't you answering me, Grandma? What's wrong? Suddenly, it all became crystal clear to her in what seemed like the blink of an eye. Allene had never been in the room at all. What Alexandria had thought was her great-great-grandmother's physical presence had actually been the strength of the all-too-real vision she'd experienced only moments ago. Allene had pulled her into the past. So much was going on that she could barely keep pace with the speed and intensity of it all.

"Here, sit down," PJ said as he helped Alexandria to a chair in the corner of the room. "I'm going to get you some water and I'll be right back."

Alexandria nodded. "Thanks, honey." She watched PJ walk through the crowd and she felt relieved to be off her feet so she could rest for a moment. But before she could calm her mind and body, another vision appeared. This time, she could barely believe what she was seeing.

She closed her eyes, took a deep breath, and concentrated. She'd been transported again, back in time to a place that felt new and familiar at once. As she squinted to focus in for a better view, she nearly lost her breath when she began to realize where she'd landed. She was standing in a room that felt as comfortable as her own bedroom, and she immediately knew that this was her grandma Allene's house.

She blinked twice to make sure what she was witnessing was real. "How can this be?" Alexandria questioned in amazement. She watched as two people, whom she'd had no idea knew each other, sat engaged in what looked to be a serious conversation. As she stared more closely she was a hundred percent sure that her eyes had not deceived her. Allene Small and Carolyn Thornton—her father's mother—were talking about the future.

Chapter 31
Alexandria

Alexandria fought to regain her breath as she looked around Allene's quaint living room. The furnishings were simple, if not plain, and two antique table lamps lit the small space. The soft glow of light radiated an intimate and cozy feel that made her instantly relax. Allene was obviously a good housekeeper because everything Alexandria's eyes landed on was neatly arranged and had been polished to a high gloss. From the small mahogany coffee table in the center of the room, to the sparkle of the lead crystal vase sitting on top of it, Allene made sure her humble home reflected her attention to detail and care.

Alexandria turned her head to the left as she inhaled the smoky scent of wood burning in an old-fashioned potbelly stove on the opposite wall. The stove's heat helped to combat the bitter cold she could feel trying to push its way through the front door.

She walked closer to the middle of the room where Allene was sitting comfortably in a worn-looking La-Z-

Boy recliner. Her blue gingham print shawl was draped around her shoulders, along with a heavy quilt she'd laid across her lap to create an extra layer of warmth. Alexandria's eyes focused in on her Granny Carolyn, who looked as though she was in her late teens. She was wearing a plain, long-sleeved grey dress, black stockings, and heavy, black winter boots that looked too rough and too big for her dainty frame. Her long, jet-black hair was pulled back into a neat ponytail, exposing the delicate features that made her a natural beauty.

But, as Alexandria studied her, she realized that Carolyn had the saddest-looking eyes she'd ever seen. Though she was so young, her eyes looked as though she'd lived several lifetimes. She was sitting at attention, back straight and shoulders squared, in a chair next to Allene's. The two were engaged in what appeared to be a very serious conversation.

Alexandria had to concentrate in order to control the visions that were flashing in front of her at lightning speed. *Focus! Focus!* She told herself as she tried to stay in the moment.

But it was no use. Her visions were coming too fast. She took a deep breath, centered her thoughts, and aimed her mind on Carolyn. Alexandria needed to connect the dots in order to find out why she was witnessing something that no one else in her family had a clue about—the connection between Ted's family and Victoria's.

Carolyn Thornton had passed away when Alexandria was five years old, but she remembered the old woman as if she'd just spoken to her yesterday. And more specifically, she remembered every detail of Carolyn's wake and funeral because it had been the first time she'd ever communicated with someone who had passed on from the world of the living into the next realm. Alexandria hadn't understood it at the time, but it had been her first glimpse into the powers of the gift she possessed.

As Alexandria allowed herself to give in to her visions, she watched her paternal grandmother's life play out before her eyes.

Her birth name had been Carol Lynn and she'd been born to an attractive young woman named Sally May Turner, whose life had not been her own. Sally May was a nineteen-year-old domestic, living in the opulent home of Jean Paul Millieux, a fifty-year-old wealthy and successful Louisiana businessman who had his sights set on a position in the state legislature. From the beginning, Sally May's tenure and standing in the house had been made shaky by the unwanted advances of her employer. One night he took what wasn't his, sealing Sally May's fate to become an unwed mother and an outcast in her community. She lost her job once the lady of the house learned of her pregnancy, and her own family turned her away amidst the ridicule and shame of her situation.

Sally May packed her bags and went to live with distant relatives in Jackson, Mississippi, who were willing to take her in, but only for a short time. After her baby was born, and she and little Carol Lynn became too much of a burden in an already struggling household, her family's Southern hospitality ran out.

Sally May was forced to go out on her own and make it the best way she could. Living was rough for a young, uneducated black woman in the rural South raising a mixed-race daughter who looked pure white, with no trace of African blood running through her veins. Sally May cleaned houses, took in laundry, cooked meals, and did whatever she could to scrape together a living for herself and her growing child. But her harsh existence became too much for her fragile body and mind to bear.

Sally May contracted a deadly infection, the result of a month-long battle with pneumonia. With no money or access to proper medical care, she quietly succumbed in her sleep, making a five-year-old Carol Lynn an orphan. An already bleak situation was made worse when none of Carol Lynn's relatives would to take her in, lest they have another hungry mouth to feed.

With no mother or family willing to care for her, Carol Lynn bounced from foster home to foster home around the small county where she lived. She was emotionally abused, never able to find a good footing in the black community or the white.

Even though Carol Lynn's life had been filled with disappointments she'd managed to forge a friendship with Hattie McPherson, a young black girl her same age who would become her lifelong friend. Hattie was the smartest girl in their school and she made sure that Carol Lynn studied and received good grades right alongside her.

When Carol Lynn turned sixteen, she decided to create a new life for herself by passing as a white woman. She'd heard about light-skinned blacks who looked white and were able to live as such, so she decided that was what she was going to do. Hattie was the only person she told of her plans.

"If you're gonna do this, you need help," Hattie had said. "My grandma has kin folk in South Carolina who know of an old woman with the gift. Maybe she can tell you where to go and what to do, since you don't know anybody up north."

"You think she can help me?" Carol Lynn asked.

"Anything's worth a try."

Carol Lynn decided to start her new life in the New Year. When the first of January rolled around she set out on her journey up north. But she hadn't realized how dangerous traveling alone could be for a young woman, or how bitterly cold the winter nights could feel once you were out in it for hours on end. She was relieved when, after several days of walking and hitching rides with strangers, she finally landed in the small town of Nedine, where she met Allene Small, whom Hattie's grandmother's people knew. She'd arrived on Allene's doorstep in the middle of the night, tired, hungry, and ailing from a fever and cold she'd caught while braving the elements.

Allene kept Carol Lynn's presence in her home a secret, which was fairly easy to do given that she had very few visitors. She enjoyed having the young girl's company and was glad she could provide a warm, safe place for Carol Lynn to rest and recover.

One night, when Carol Lynn was eating a meal of beef stew and cornbread that Allene had prepared, she asked Allene to read her future.

Allene had known what was going to happen to the young woman even before she had knocked on Allene's door a few nights before. She'd known Carol Lynn was coming, seeking refuge and guidance, and she'd seen everything that was going to unfold in her life over the decades to come if she listened, learned, and allowed the cards to fall into place.

Allene looked at Carol Lynn, who she could tell was eager to know what fate would befall her, good or bad. Allene only read people's futures when her gut told her to, and because she knew that she and Carol Lynn would one day be connected through their children, she felt compelled to tell the young woman what awaited her life.

But Allene also knew she had to warn Carol Lynn. "What I'm 'bout to tell you is very important, and it's gonna happen just like I say it will."

"Okay." Carol Lynn nodded with anticipation.

"In a few years from now you're gonna remember

this night when you see things start comin' to pass that I'm gettin' ready to share with you. But you can't try to change or avoid them. You understand?"

"Yes, ma'am," Carol Lynn said.

"If you try to change even one single thing, you gonna end up makin' a worse mess outta your life and a whole lotta others right along with you. Do you understand me?"

"I do."

Allene looked into the girl's eyes and saw that she was telling the truth, and that she understood more than Allene had given her credit for. Carol Lynn was young, but she was mature beyond her years and she was ready to accept whatever was going to happen in her life. Allene took a deep breath and told her what lay ahead down the road.

"You're gonna get settled into your new life without any problems," Allene began. "You're gonna graduate from a real good college, and you're gonna marry an important man from a wealthy family. He's gonna be handsome and very smart. Most of all, he's gonna be a good, decent person who's kind and loves you. You and him gonna have three beautiful children, and you're gonna be blessed with longevity into your eighties."

A smile lit up Carol Lynn's pretty face, but it quickly faded when she saw the somber look that came over Allene's. "What is it? Is something bad going to happen?"

"It already has, child. The life you're chosin' comes with a price. Running from who you are always does."

"But I have no choice."

"We all have a choice. But I understand that you've made yours, and I know you're not changin' your mind."

Carol Lynn shook her head. "No, I'm not."

"You're gonna have to bury your past, lie to the people you love, and look over your shoulder every day for the rest of your life," Allene said slowly. "You're gonna live a long time, but you're gonna die empty, with pain and secrets. Those secrets will end up hurtin' the very people you love most, and they'll struggle with what you did long after you're gone."

Carol Lynn looked down into her bowl of stew and let out a heavy sigh. "My life's been filled with pain and secrets since the day I was born, Ms. Allene. I guess it's fitting that that's the way it's going to end."

Allene had never heard anyone so young sound so sad in all her life, and as much as it pained her to acknowledge it, she knew that Carol Lynn's words were right. The road she was set to travel held consequences of which even Allene couldn't fully see.

Carol Lynn stayed in Nedine for another week, just long enough for her to recuperate and sell the ruby brooch that Hattie had taken from her grandmother's jewelry box.

"Here, Carol Lynn, take this," Hattie had said as she handed her friend the ornate piece of jewelry before hugging her good-bye. "It's not much, but it'll get you down the road. Be safe and write me a letter when you can so I'll know where you end up, you here?"

Hattie's generosity fetched enough money to pay for a one-way bus ticket to Boston, the city Carol Lynn had decided to make her new home after talking it over with Allene. She left Nedine just as she'd arrived—in the middle of a dark, cold night. Before she walked out of Allene's door, the old woman surprised her by pressing a thick wad of one-hundred-dollar bills into her palm. "Take care of yourself," Allene said.

Tears fell from Carol Lynn's eyes. Other than her mother, whom she'd lost when she was five, and Hattie, whom she'd had to leave behind back in Jackson, Allene was the only person who had ever cared for her or shown her any kindness. She wanted to keep in touch with the old woman and report her progress once she settled in Boston, changed her name to Carolyn Jones, and started living her new life. But she knew she couldn't. Just as she had to erase her time in Jackson, she had to forget everything and everyone in Nedine. Living white meant denying anything black. "You take care, too, Ms. Allene," Carol Lynn said through quiet tears as she walked down Allene's front steps and disappeared into the night.

Alexandria blinked her eyes, fighting back tears of her own as she stood in the past, watching her grandmother seal a fate rooted in lies and pain. She tried to hold on to the moment so she could learn more about a past that was merging with the present, but things were beginning to move fast again. Her head started swimming with flashes of visions, and finally, she had to let go. She took several deep breaths, grounding herself as she came back to the present. She was still sitting in the chair where PJ had left her just a few moments ago, and a wave of comfort enveloped her when the sweet fragrance of magnolias filled the air.

Grandma Allene?

"Yes, baby girl," Allene said. "I'm here."

Alexandria looked to her right and saw Allene sitting in a chair beside her.

"You're doin' real good with your visions."

Thanks, Grandma, but why didn't you tell me that you knew my granny Carolyn, or that you helped her escape to Boston? I have so many questions.

Allene shook her head and smiled. "Some things is best for you to figure out on your own. Doin' that will make your gift even stronger. Don't worry—the answers will come."

Alexandria nodded, knowing Allene was right. She concentrated again, and as if a light had just shone bright on a mystery, she had the answer to something that had been puzzling her all her life.

"That's right," Allene said with a smile as she read Alexandria's thoughts. "Life is about the choices we make and the consequences that come along with them. I chose to use my gift with Carol Lynn because I knew that helping her would help my family. There's some things you just have to trust yourself with."

"This is what you were talking about last night when I asked you about knowing when to intervene in a situation or when not to."

"Yes, it is. You won't always make the right decision, and that's okay because you'll learn from your mistakes. Your gift is natural. It's inside you so you can't turn it off."

Alexandria nodded. "But it's a choice. And I have to decide when and how to use it."

"That's right. Just like your brother's situation. He can drink and use drugs or he can stop. It's all up to him. Like you told Granny Carolyn, 'Everyone has a choice.'"

"That's right, baby girl."

Alexandria looked up when she saw PJ walking toward her with a large plastic cup in his hand.

"Here, drink this," PJ said. "I couldn't find any water—all they have is sweet iced tea, and tons of it."

"That's the same thing as water in the South." Alexandria smiled and gladly took the cup from his hand, gulping it down in just a few swallows.

"I think we should go back to the house so you can rest," PJ said with concern. "You look tired."

"But we came here to enjoy the festival, not lie around at the house. I don't want to spoil your fun."

PJ took Alexandria by her hand and pulled her to her feet. "My fun is wherever you are. We can hang out later tonight at the big gala, but right now you need to rest."

"But honestly, I feel okay. I just got my second wind and I'm not tired at all."

"I want you to rest, Ali. Do it for my sake."

"Go 'head, baby girl," Allene said. "He's right. You're gonna need all the strength you can gather for tonight and tomorrow morning."

After thinking it over, Alexandria agreed, and Percy Jones offered to give them a ride back to the house.

"Here are the keys," PJ said to Ted and then told him where he'd parked his rental car.

"Don't worry," Alexandria said as she looked at her mother. "The vision I just had gave me a new understanding. I'm going to be just fine and everything else will be, too."

After she and PJ hugged her parents good-bye, they followed Percy outside to his car. Fifteen minutes later, they thanked Percy for the ride and told him they'd see him at the gala later tonight.

"I see Uncle Tyler's truck is here," Alexandria said as they climbed the steps of the porch. "They're probably resting up like we're going to do."

PJ nodded. "I wonder how much longer your parents and Uncle Maxx are gonna stay out in town. The temperature is rising and it's been a long day already."

Alexandria closed her eyes and blinked. "They'll be home in another hour," she said as they made their way to their bedroom.

"Let's relax," PJ said as he pulled off his shirt and looked at Alexandria.

Her eyes took in his smooth skin, sculpted muscles, and chiseled abs. Because of his hectic schedule and their planning for this trip, they hadn't made love in nearly five days, and now his body was reminding hers of what she'd been missing.

Alexandria licked her lips at the delicious sight of him, and when she saw PJ flash her a smile that matched the seduction in her eyes, she knew they were on the same page.

"We'll have to be quiet," PJ said as he walked over to Alexandria and started removing her denim shorts and tank top. "Tylor and Samantha are down the hall and Chase is in the room right across from us."

Alexandria nodded as she accepted his warm, tender kiss to her neck. "I can't make any promises," she said through short breaths, "because this is exactly what I need."

They finished removing each other's clothes and lay across the bed, kissing, teasing, sucking, and caressing each other as they prepared to make love.

PJ ran his strong hands along the soft contours of Alexandria's shapely body, causing her to moan seductively under his skilled touch. She was hungry for him, and when she felt his hardness against her leg she grew more excited and ready for him.

Slowly, he parted her thighs and teased her moist middle with his finger. "Oh baby, that feels good," she panted.

"You like that?" he teased.

"Oh yeah. You know I do," she moaned again.

"You're so wet."

"You make me that way."

He gently flicked her delicate folds, massaging her tenderness with gentle care until she begged him to enter her. She breathed deeply, arched her back, and tilted her pelvis forward so she could receive him into her warmth.

He took his time entering her, pressing the tip of his head into what he'd been craving. He moved from side to side as his hardness gently sunk into the empty space that was now made full by his swollen manhood. She wrapped her legs around his waist and moved to his rhythm as he rocked her back and forth, giving her body pleasure that made her want to call out his name.

She tensed her muscles around him when she felt the beginnings of the euphoric wave of sweetness that always gripped her when she was about to orgasm. *"Mmmmm,"* she moaned into his ear, letting him know that she'd reached her climax. Her body slowed its pace as PJ increased his, and a few minutes later he joined her in that same satisfied place.

They lay in bed clinging to each other as they drifted off to sleep for the next two hours. They'd just started a new beginning, and now they were resting their bodies for the night to come.

Chapter 32
Allene

Allene had a perfect view of everything from where she sat, tucked away in a corner inside the Masonic Lodge. "This place brings back memories," she whispered to herself. "Who'd of thought it would turn into what it is today?"

Allene remembered when the now state-of-the-art meeting and banquet facility had been no more than a one-room shack constructed of wood and tin, built by former slaves to serve as a place of worship and learning for the town's black community.

Every Sunday, a small group would gather in praise and fellowship, giving thanks for what they had while praying for better days. Every weekday, an even smaller group would assemble, made up of children who came to receive their schooling, giving their parents hope for their future.

But then there were the nights that no one knew about, when a select group would meet in secrecy and purpose, working to keep their community safe from those who meant it harm. Those gatherings were held in the strictest of confidence by those in attendance, lest they be discovered and meet with a fate that could result in cross-burning threats, near-fatal beatings, or worse.

Allene had always been the only woman present in those secret meetings. During that time, most women's roles were relegated to the sidelines, as the risk of danger was much too great to put them in harm's way. But Allene wasn't the average woman. She was mother to Nedine's most prominent black businessman, she possessed a heart of courage and fearlessness, and most importantly, she had the gift. The determined leaders knew that last asset would help them in their fight against civil and racial injustice.

"My, my, my, how things done changed," Allene said as she looked out on the crowd of people taking in the black history exhibit. Most were black, but there were a few white folks and Latinos who'd come to pay honor and respects. It made her proud to see the large photo of her son and grandson prominently featured on the main wall. They'd loved this town as much as she had, and now they were being recognized for the work and the legacy they'd left behind.

Allene thought about her life and her family, and she was grateful that things were starting to fall into place. She'd been faithful and patient, and now she was trusting and believing that this weekend was going to prove to be healing for everyone.

"Everything's finally comin' to light after all these years, and now it's time for healin' to begin."

Allene had always been a loyal, honest, and trustworthy person. She'd been a confidante to many and a keeper of secrets to more people than she could count, inside and outside of her family. She'd been privy to information that could have gotten some people killed while setting others free, and she'd remained silent on things that she knew had no business ever seeing the light of day.

Keeping quiet had sometimes been a very hard thing for Allene to do. But her wisdom had given her good judgment, and she never made a decision without consulting her gut and trusting that God would lead her on the right path.

Her gut was the reason she'd never revealed her connection to Carolyn.

During the days when her grandson had been living in New York City, enjoying his young bachelorhood as he chased after the wrong women, she'd known from the beginning what would happen long before it came to pass. But she couldn't intervene because she knew that doing so might prevent John from marrying Elizabeth Sanders, or cause Carolyn to overlook Richard Thornton, which would have ended in Alexandria never being born. Changing one set of events could change the others in unexpected ways.

Allene looked back with fondness when she thought about the frightened young woman who had knocked on her door one cold winter night, seeking comfort and shelter. When Allene had first laid eyes on Carolyn she'd known right away that the girl was going to play a key part in the Small family's very existence. And now, as Allene looked across the room at Victoria and Ted, she knew that he was ready to embrace a past that his mother had tried to bury.

"You can never go wrong doin' right," Allene said.

Chapter 33
Victoria

Victoria stood beside Ted in the middle of the Masonic Lodge, and was filled with emotion that nearly made her burst with pride and sadness at the same time. She was proud of her family and she was sad that her own son wasn't there to help celebrate their history and legacy.

After recovering from the drama that Christian had caused this morning, which had been made easier by a down-home Southern breakfast, everyone's spirits had picked up considerably, except Victoria's. She'd wanted to enjoy herself, but her mind and heart had been worried over her troubled child, who always seemed to leave a trail of bad feelings in his wake.

"Don't let him ruin the rest of your day," Ted had told her as they'd prepared to leave the house.

She had tried to put her disappointment out of her mind as they headed over to the Masonic Lodge, where she'd been told that her father and grandfather's pictures were on display as part of the town festival. That happy thought had helped take her mind off her son.

But now as she and Ted walked from one end of the room to the other, looking at pictures that told a story of Nedine's rich past, Victoria couldn't help but think how much Christian needed to be there, more than anyone else in their family.

With each sliver of history written in the narratives that appeared under the pictures on the walls, Victoria felt inspiration by the accomplishments that the brave African American pioneers of the town had made through sacrifice and determination. She smiled when she saw that just like last night, a small crowd had gathered around Maxx, where he was sitting next to the display of Isaiah and John.

"This is what Christian needs to see," she told Ted. "It would help him understand and embrace the hard work and self-control it takes to survive and thrive in this world. I wonder if he's going to come by here today."

"If he doesn't, it'll be his loss."

She looked at Ted, who'd been indifferent toward their son's presence since the beginning of their trip. She was glad that this weekend was bringing her and Ted closer together, which she'd been praying for, and that Alexandria seemed to be making good progress of her own. She'd also hoped Tyler and his family would benefit in some way by being in Nedine.

"V, you've got to stop checking for him every five minutes," Ted told her.

Victoria had kept her eyes glued on the front entrance, looking to see if Christian would walk through the doors. She wanted their son to be there and she wanted Ted to feel the same parental desire. "You act like you don't want Christian here," she said.

"Honestly, I don't."

"I never thought I'd hear you say that you didn't want your own son around you."

"And I never thought my own son would lie, steal, and do God knows what else to me, and you."

Victoria became quiet for a moment. She was about to ask him if they could step outside and talk when she looked at the front entrance again and saw Parker walk in. Her shoulders tensed and her back became stiff like a board. She swallowed hard when she realized that Ted's eyes were trained on Parker, and the two men were looking at each other.

Damn it! Victoria screamed inside her head. Even though Nedine was a small town, she had been hoping they'd be able to avoid Parker for the remainder of the weekend. Last night had been uncomfortable and nearly dangerous, with both men coming short of escalating the tension up to a brawl. She was tired of the intense anxiety and stress she always felt whenever there was a possibility of Ted and Parker being in the same room. And now they were about to be face-to-face because Parker was headed straight toward them.

Victoria watched Ted and bit her bottom lip. On the few occasions when he and Parker had been forced into the same room, Ted's physical demeanor had always taken on that of a slow and steady bull ready to charge. Even though he wasn't giving off a threatening stare as he did last night, she could tell he was on alert.

Victoria's heart started to beat rapidly as Parker approached, just a few feet away. She could see that his body language was confident as always, but he also exuded an edge that let her know he was ready to do battle if he had to.

Breathe, she told herself. She knew if she could get through what happened last night and the blowup between her husband and son this morning, she could get through this moment, too.

"Please don't cause a scene," Victoria whispered to Ted.

"I won't tolerate disrespect."

Victoria was hoping that Parker would walk around the center and look at the exhibit, but instead he came right up to them. "Good afternoon," he said.

Parker's eyes focused in on Victoria and then over to Ted. Victoria could see that her husband was instantly pissed because Parker had stared at her a little too long.

Ted looked Parker in his eyes. "I've accepted the fact that your son is going to marry my daughter, and I accepted a long time ago that you used to be a part of my wife's life. But the one thing I won't accept or tolerate is your flagrant disrespect of my marriage."

"Disrespect is a matter of opinion."

Victoria could see that both Parker's and Ted's body language was threatening and she hoped they would calm down before security had to escort them from the building.

Ted shook his head. "In this particular case, my opinion is the only one that counts. Victoria might be slow to your game, but I'm not, so I'm going to be mindful for the both of us. I love my wife and she loves me. I'm going to keep her happy so there's no room for you in our lives other than when we have to see you at family gatherings in the future."

"Why do you feel you have to defend your love and your marriage to me?"

"I'm not defending it. I'm just stating the facts so you'll know you need to back off."

"You're crazy as hell if you think I'm gonna stand here and listen to you bark off orders to me about what *you* think I need to do," Parker said, raising his voice.

Victoria was tired of all the drama so she stepped in. "Oh, just stop it, you two! You're both acting like geriatric school yard bullies and it's really pathetic. We need to be civil because our actions will impact Alexandria and PJ." Victoria let out a deep breath and turned to face Parker. "My husband is right. You've been disrespectful of him and of our marriage. I made a mistake with you long ago, but I won't make the same mistake twice. Please respect our marriage just as much as you will Alexandria's and PJ's."

Parker looked off for a long moment, not saying a word. The three of them stood in silence as people buzzed around them. Finally, Parker spoke. "I'm going to leave now because I don't want to cause any trouble for my son. But I want to say this." He looked directly at Ted. "I've never hidden the fact that I care for Victoria because doing so would negate who I am. I know you two are married," he said, turning his stare to Victoria. "I respect that institution, and I won't do anything that I'm not called to do."

"You must be out of your mind." Ted fumed. "I should kick your ass right here."

Parker's jaw line tightened. "You give the word and we can do this."

Victoria's eyes bucked wide.

"I said I should," Ted responded, "but I'm not. I'm not going to spend my time fighting a war that I've already won." He took hold of Victoria's hand and squeezed it.

Parker's eyes glanced down at their hand lock and then back up again. He opened his mouth to say something, but then decided not to. He looked at Victoria and smiled. When he saw her look down to avoid his eyes, an even bigger smile spread across his face. "I thought so," he said. "I hear this exhibit is very interesting. I think I'll check it out now." He turned on the heel of his expensive dress shoes and walked away just as smoothly as he'd approached them.

Once again, Ted and Victoria were left off-balance by Parker's presence. She braced herself because she could feel Ted's eyes positioned on her like laser beams. She knew he was questioning her reaction to Parker's stare, along with his last remarks. "Ted, I'm too exhausted to go through what we went through last night."

He nodded. "So am I, V. I don't want to spend another minute arguing, disagreeing, or second-guessing our love."

Victoria raised her brow, hoping this wasn't some kind of trick.

"I trust you, and I have faith in us. I'm not going to let anyone challenge that, ever again."

Victoria's shoulders relaxed. "I'm grateful that you finally realize Parker's not a threat to us."

"I am, too. As I listened to him, everything became so clear."

"What became clear?"

"You and I were standing beside each other, united as one, while he stood there alone. As long as we're standing together no one can tear us apart."

Victoria smiled and squeezed his hand. "You've just made me the happiest woman in Nedine. I can't tell you how much what you said means to me."

Ted smiled back. "I'm glad I made you happy, V. That's all I've ever wanted to do. This weekend has been an eye-opener for me in many ways. Not just for us, but for me, as an individual."

"Is there something else you want to tell me?"

"As a matter of fact, there is." Ted's face became serious. "Being here in Nedine has had a profound effect on me. Being in your grandfather's house and now seeing the rich legacy that he and so many others left behind for future generations has made me think about my own family, and the fact that my mother hid who she was for her entire adult life, even up to the day she died."

Ted had shocked Victoria for the second time today, this time by talking about his mother. He kept in close contact with his sister, Lilly, a few of his cousins, and most of his nieces and nephews. But rarely, if ever, did he mention a word about his mother, whose memory caused him pain and confusion. Victoria listened as Ted continued.

"The brave people honored in this room fought every day to keep their dignity during a time when it could be taken from them without cause. Your father once told me that he'd had to fight against men who looked like me, and work twice as hard to get half the credit. I'll never forget that, V. At the time I didn't know that some of my ancestors could have been your father, in a manner of speaking. I can name nearly every relative of the New York and Boston Thorntons on my father's side, but I don't know one single member of the Louisiana or Mississippi Turners on my mother's side, and that's because I haven't tried to find out who they are. But that's going to change.

"This trip has taught me a valuable lesson about the past, which can serve to hurt or help. For a long time I've looked at the past with hurt." Ted paused, as if struggling to find his words.

"Do you want to go outside?" Victoria asked gently. "So you can speak more freely."

He shook his head. "No, I want to get this out right now while I still can." He took a deep breath and continued. "I was hurt by my mother's deception and her shame crept over into me. I know it shouldn't have, but on some levels it did. And I carried around the hurt I felt about you and Parker, creating stories in my head that weren't even true. But I'm done with all that."

Ted took a step toward Victoria and drew her into his arms right there in the middle of the room. "That was the part of my past that hurt. But the part of my past that has helped me, and has given me life, is the part that lies in you, and what we've created together. I'm ready to bury that old hurt, and I want you by my side when I go to Louisiana and Mississippi in a few months to start a new path toward my mother's family."

Victoria felt as though they were the only two people in the room as she and Ted stood in a warm embrace. She saw a few people stare, but she couldn't care less. Right now she was thankful and overjoyed. "I'll always be right here by your side. I love you, Ted."

"I love you, too, V."

Chapter 34
Alexandria

Alexandria smiled as she looked around the ballroom of the Nedine Convention Center. Hundreds of people had gathered for the final night of the town's fiftieth annual Flower Festival celebration. The men were decked out in tuxedos and custom-tailored suits, while the women wore everything from ball gowns to tea-length dresses. The room was filled with lively chatter, glowing candles adorned each table, and best of all, Alexandria and her family were seated at a table with a prime location next to the mayor.

After Victoria had called Percy Jones to ask him to prepare the house for her family's visit, word had spread that Isaiah Small's granddaughter was coming to Nedine for the grand, time-honored festival. The local newspaper had called Victoria last week and conducted a telephone interview that had run in the *Nedine Chronicle* the very next day. Following the phone interview, a representative from the Flower Festival committee had also contacted her, apologized for the obvious oversight of not extending an invitation to a descendent of one of the town's leading African American business pioneers, and offered prime seating at the gala for Victoria and her family.

Their table of ten was complete with one addition whom Alexandria was a little shocked, but overwhelmingly happy, to see, and that was Parker. He was seated between PJ and Samantha, looking as dashing as ever in a tuxedo she knew had to have cost more than most people's mortgage payments. She and PJ had been delighted when her parents told them that they'd seen Parker earlier that day and had invited him to be a guest at their table tonight. At the time, she hadn't been sure if he'd show up, and now she was glad he did.

Everyone was having a great time, and as usual, Uncle Maxx continued to garner attention from people, who came up to him to shake his hand, take a picture, or simply say hello.

"You're a celebrity," Chase told him. "I'm gonna take a picture and post it on Facebook."

"I don't know what that is, but it sounds good to me," Maxx said as he smiled at Chase's camera phone.

Alexandria was glad that her family was so happy—that is, everyone except Christian. She didn't want her brother to ruin her evening, and she'd wanted to put him out of her mind, but she couldn't because of what she knew. She'd tapped into his thoughts earlier today.

She had seen that Christian had been so furious after being thrown out of the house that he'd packed his rental car and headed back to the airport. But a few miles outside the city limits he'd decided to turn around. A short time later he'd found himself checking into the Nedine Express, wishing he could go back to the family homestead, but knowing he had work to do before he'd be welcomed into his family's fold. He'd unpacked his things and hadn't left his room until it was time for the evening gala.

Alexandria wished he would have arrived at the event sober, but he'd snorted two lines of cocaine while sitting in the parking lot right before he came in.

When he'd walked up to their table an hour ago, well after everyone had been seated, both Victoria and Ted had looked at him with caution, not knowing whether he was there to cause trouble or make peace.

Ted had risen from his seat beside Victoria and greeted his son. "For the sake of family and your great-grandfather's memory, let's put what happened this morning to the side and celebrate tonight."

"Agreed," Christian had said.

She knew that Christian ran hot and cold. He could either sit at the table and behave himself, or jump up and make a scene that would cause her father to handle him physically in public.

Alexandria was about to entertain a fresh wave of worry when a sharp feeling hit her in her gut and changed everything. As quickly as she could blink, all of her fears vanished. In that instant, she knew that no matter how Christian chose to behave, there was nothing he could do to ruin the evening, or the remainder of the weekend for that matter.

She smiled to herself as she looked around the table from one person to the next, and thought about the words Allene had spoken to her in a vision that had started this journey. *It's time to bury the past so we can all start new beginnings.* Each one of them had traveled to Nedine with a purpose, and as they sat around the table eating, drinking, and enjoying the night's event, she knew they would all leave tomorrow with a new path to travel.

Samantha, Tyler, and Chase now had the clarity they each needed to move forward. Samantha no longer had to worry about burdensome secrets, Tyler would no longer keep things from his wife, and after the news Alexandria had delivered to them earlier this afternoon, Chase would no longer act irresponsibly, especially since five months from now he'd have a baby daughter who would look exactly like him.

Parker had traveled to Nedine to protect his only child, and to see if there was any inkling of a chance for rekindling love with the only woman he'd ever loved. He was satisfied and felt good knowing that PJ was going to be safe, and he was thankful that even though Victoria would always hold a place in his heart, he was now able to move her from the forefront of it so he could make room for someone else.

Christian had come to Nedine with the twisted intentions of seizing control of his mother's property and real estate holdings, but now he was leaving a partially broken man, knowing that the only people who'd ever supported him were ready to put distance between them unless he cleaned up his act. He knew that his next step wasn't graduate school, it was going to be a rehab facility, and after that, one day at a time in rebuilding the trust and love he'd torn from his family.

Victoria and Ted had both been hoping that this weekend would give their daughter the understanding she needed, and that it would serve to bring their marriage back to where it had once been. They'd weathered storms that would have torn most couples apart, and they'd forgiven each other for past hurts and misunderstandings. But most of all, they rediscovered what had brought them together nearly thirty years ago, and that was an unselfish love for each other that would never die.

Uncle Maxx had come to Nedine to say good-bye. He was tired, and he was ready to move on to a place where he would no longer feel lonely or have to worry about living in a changing world that had passed him by. The last two days had taken him back to a time in his life that had been filled with good friends and good times, and he was glad that he'd been blessed to come back to where his life had begun, helping him to feel at complete peace in anticipation of its end.

Alexandria was so full of emotion that she could hardly contain the feelings flowing through her body. She'd come to Nedine to protect her family and pay final respects to the ancestors who'd come before her. Tomorrow was going to be a big day that would bring this visit full circle, and as she looked around the table, knowing exactly what lay ahead for every one of them, she felt both joy and sadness.

"You done good, baby girl," Allene said. "Everything's gonna be all right. Just remember to always trust your gut, and know that I'll be here to help you."

Alexandria's heart was full of joy, and as she sat at a table filled with love and hope, she was grateful that even though tomorrow held sorrow, new beginnings had already taken flight.

Chapter 35
Victoria

Later that night after the big gala had ended, Victoria and Ted lay in bed talking about their busy weekend and the events of the day.

"It's been a very eventful weekend," Ted said as he yawned.

"Yes it has." Victoria didn't want to beat around the bush, she wanted to get to the bottom of why their intimacy had disappeared. "I want to talk about our love life," she said.

For the first time in a very long time, Victoria could see that Ted was very uncomfortable, and this wasn't like him. He was always in control of his emotions and the way he expressed his feelings, even when pushed to the edge. No matter how pressing or complicated the situation, he could always manage to find the right words or solution to abate the problem. But now, as he sat propped up on the fluffy pillows beside her, Victoria saw a look on his face that she'd never seen. He was uncertain, and not only that, he was scared.

"Ted, talk to me," Victoria pleaded. "I know in my heart that something's wrong. What you told me about Christian yesterday is just the tip of the iceberg. I know you're upset about what our son has done, but there's something else that's been holding you back from me and making you distant. There's no intimacy between us, and every time I've tried to initiate anything you brush me off. Tell me what's going on"

Victoria hadn't realized she was trembling until she felt Ted reach for her and pull her into his strong chest. Being in his arms felt good, and she wanted to stay there for as long as she could. But that comfort didn't quiet her need for answers. She pulled away from him and looked into his eyes. "We're not going to sleep tonight until you talk to me. I mean it."

Ted inhaled sharply and exhaled loudly before he spoke. "The truth of the matter is that I can't perform the way I used to. I think you noticed that the last few times we were intimate, didn't you?"

Victoria nodded her head. She remembered that it had taken Ted quite a while to get an erection, and then it only lasted a few minutes before he lost it. When she'd asked him if everything was okay he'd told her that it was, and that he still found her stimulating, even though there was physical proof that that wasn't necessarily true.

Ted cleared his throat. "I'm ashamed of the way I've handled this situation, V. I've felt a lot of pressure ever since Parker came back into our lives. No man wants to think that he can't please his wife, and then when there's the threat of another man who can, it messes with the mind."

Victoria blinked several times. "Do you think you have erectile dysfunction?"

"I don't know." Ted looked straight ahead again, as if he couldn't bear to see the expression on Victoria's face.

They sat in bed without saying anything for a few minutes. This time it was Ted who broke their silence. "V, say something. Please."

"If you're having physiological problems why didn't you just tell me, or go to the doctor and get some medicine? Hell, there's an erectile dysfunction commercial on every five minutes. You had me thinking that you were having an affair or that you didn't want me. Either way it hurt me, Ted."

"I know, and I'm sorry," Ted sighed. "I've always been able to please you, and the thought of not being able to any longer sent me into a loop. On the one hand I wanted to please you, but on the other I was afraid to try because I didn't want you to be disappointed like the last few times we made love." Ted let out a heavy breath. "I know I'm getting older and things won't work the same way they used to, but when a man can please his woman it makes him feel like he's still got it. You're so beautiful and loving, and I want to show you that I can still satisfy you."

Victoria put her hand on top of his. "This is something we can work on. When I was battling breast cancer I learned about so many natural approaches for healing the body through holistic medicine. If it could help me heal and beat cancer, it can certainly help you get it up."

Ted shook his head. "You've always had a way with words."

"Yesterday when you told me you were going to make a hard decision that was going to drive a wedge between our family, I held my breath thinking you were going to tell me that you wanted a divorce. So hearing this news is music to my ears."

Ted ran his finger along the side of Victoria's face. "Why would I want to leave the only woman I've ever loved? Not one day has gone by, even during that bad time we had in the past, that I've ever thought about leaving you. When I said I do, I meant it. I don't want to ever be without you, and the only thing that's going to separate us is death. I love you, V."

Victoria moved in close and sank into Ted's embrace. "I'm going to call your doctor and make an appointment for you when we get back home. You need a complete physical anyway. Once we know what's going on physically, we can work on this together.

"Together has a nice ring to it."

They shared a long, passionate kiss and then lay in Victoria's favorite position, with Ted spooning her from behind. This was the first time they'd lain in bed this way in months, and although she missed feeling the hard rise of his manhood against her behind, the love and warmth of his embrace gave her all she needed.

Victoria felt like a new woman when she awoke and found herself still wrapped inside Ted's arms. He was spooning her in a gentle hold, and she wished they could stay that way the rest of the weekend.

"Sleeping Beauty is up," he said.

She yawned. "I am. What time is it?"

"Almost eight."

She could feel Ted's warm breath on the back of her neck and it made her want him. She moved closer into him, pressing her body against his. She was hoping to feel hardness against her skin, but when she didn't, she knew it was okay. She was simply grateful for the closeness and the intimacy they were sharing, which was just as meaningful as their physical lovemaking had always been.

Ted kissed her neck. "We had a full day yesterday, and we were up pretty late last night."

"That's true."

"You must've been tired because you snored," Ted teased in a playful voice. "And you were loud, too."

"Was I?" Victoria let out a soft laugh. "Did I keep you up?"

"I was up most of the night, but it wasn't because of your snoring. I was thinking about us."

Victoria turned to face him. "What were you thinking?"

"That I should've opened up to you a long time ago. I'm sorry that my actions made you think I didn't want you anymore. That's the farthest thing from how I feel. I wanted to tell you two months ago when you first asked me what was wrong, but I didn't know what to say, and I didn't want to disappoint you, although I think I already have."

"The only disappointment I feel is what you said—that you didn't tell me before now. We've been together so long, I thought you knew you could talk to me about any and everything."

"But this is about my manhood, V."

Victoria pulled away from him and lowered the left strap of her gown, revealing her bare chest and a scar that stretched across it. "This was about my womanhood, and we faced it together. I thought you knew that after we beat this, there was nothing we couldn't conquer."

"Yes, I hear you," Ted said with a sigh. "But you're still beautiful, and you can still please me."

"And you're still handsome, and you can still please me, too."

Victoria could see that Ted was looking at her with doubt. Of all the hurdles she knew they might face in their marriage—from being an interracial couple, to raising mixed-raced children, to discovering they weren't so interracially mixed after all, to awakening family secrets, surviving near infidelity, and finally, battling a life-threatening illness—she'd never thought that Ted's virility would be one of the challenges they'd face.

She knew they would both slow down with age, and she'd anticipated that their sex life would surely change over time, but thinking about it and actually living it were two very different things.

She knew she wasn't alone, and that a few of her girlfriends were experiencing a drought in their sex lives as well. Ever since Debbie and Rob divorced ten years ago, Debbie had been searching for someone who could make her feel excited, let alone help her achieve an orgasm. And Victoria's devoted office manager, confidante, and friend, Denise, had all but given up on sex with her husband.

"Girlfriend, I've had my fill," Denise had told her a few months ago when Victoria had confided in her about her diminishing sex life with Ted. "After more than forty years of marriage, all these old bones of mine want is a nice dinner and a movie, and I'm good."

The only girlfriend she knew who was still happily satisfied was Samantha, who didn't mind sharing. "Tyler gives it to me good and on the regular. As a matter of fact, that's how we got the day started," she'd told Victoria yesterday.

Victoria knew she wasn't in her prime, but she wasn't ancient either, and she still desired physical pleasure.

But looking into Ted's eyes, which were filled with unconditional love, she knew that having the type of intimacy, openness, and honesty they'd shared last night was enough for her. They'd been through too much and had loved too strong for too long to let things fall apart over something that could be fixed, either by a holistic approach or with prescription drugs. And even if neither worked, she knew that if this was as bad as it got, she was fine with that outcome, because what they had together could reach the sky.

"Ted, I know you know this, but I think I need to remind you that your manhood isn't attached to what's in between your legs. It's what's here," she said, placing her hand on his chest. "You're a wonderful husband and father. You're strong and true, and you're the best man I know."

"I appreciate you saying that, V. But I still want to please you as a man. I felt you move up against me when you woke up." He paused and let out a deep breath. "I know what you wanted, and it kills me that I'm not able to give it to you."

"Yes, I would've loved to make love to you. But what you've given me is just as good, and maybe even better. I can't remember the last time you held me through the night, and I woke up in your arms. That's a feeling that a lot of women would give anything to experience. I'm lying next to a handsome man who loves me just the way I am. A man who's honest and respectful. A man who loves and protects his family. A man who I know without a doubt I can count on. Baby, you've given me all I need, and more."

Ted pulled Victoria into his chest and kissed her slowly and gently. She moaned with pleasure when she felt him reach under her silk nightgown and run his strong hands along the contours of her body. They cuddled, and caressed, and stroked, and nibbled, and kissed, and laughed, and loved on each other as they lay in bed, knowing that their love was strong enough to see them through anything that came their way.

Chapter 36
Allene

Allene sat in her rocking chair enjoying the hot summer night that blanketed Nedine. The stars were sparkling in the sky like Christmas lights, the crickets were chirping like an orchestra playing a tune, and the vibrant flowers in the front yard provided a sweet fragrance akin to perfume. "This is my kinda night," Allene said as she rocked back and forth, satisfied and happy.

The last of the celebrations had been held this afternoon, and now all of Allene's family who'd traveled to Nedine this weekend were safely back home, resting in their own beds. She smiled as she thought about everything that had happened this weekend and all that she'd witnessed since the sunrise today.

Sunday had always been a holy day of praise, celebration, and fellowship in the Small family. Allene had happy memories of times spent at Rising Star A.M.E. Zion Church, and hearty meals shared with her family after Sunday service. Today, her family's plans were much the same.

Victoria had planned to prepare a big breakfast for everyone, and she'd asked one of the deacons from Rising Star to come over to the house and bless their food before they fellowshipped together, under the roof Isaiah built. Afterwards, they would all travel to Butler's Cemetery and lay flowers on the headstones of their loved ones.

Living two lifetimes had taught Allene that plans can always change, and as soon as Alexandria awoke this morning, that's exactly what happened.

Alexandria had risen early, said her prayers, and then quietly tiptoed down the stairs, making her way to Maxx's room. She didn't knock on his door because it was already open. She walked in slowly, knowing he was expecting her.

"Hey there, Alex," Maxx said in a voice that was barely above a whisper.

Alexandria walked over to his bed, sat down beside him, and held his hand in a warm embrace.

"You came to be with me before I leave for good."

"Yes, Uncle Maxx. You came into this world loved, with someone holding on to you, and that's how you're going to leave today."

Maxx gave her a gentle smile. "I lived a good life."

She smiled back and nodded. "Yes, you did."

"You and your mama been good to me, and I love both of you."

"We love and adore you, Uncle Maxx."

Maxx paused for a minute, gathering his strength one last time. "I want y'all to go 'head and enjoy that big breakfast your mama said she was gonna cook, and have a few drinks for me. I don't want nobody cryin' and moanin' today. Celebrate my life 'cause I'm happy. I'm at peace. And I'm ready."

Alexandria gave his hand a soft squeeze. "You go ahead and rest now, Uncle Maxx."

Maxx smiled, and then let out one last breath before he joined John, Elizabeth, his mother, Grace, his father, Milford, and so many others who'd already taken their journey to the other side.

Alexandria looked out the window near Maxx's bed and smiled as the sun slowly rose, flooding the room with radiant light. She leaned over, kissed Maxx on his forehead, and then walked outside to the front porch where Allene was sitting in her rocking chair.

"It's real fittin' that Maxx left just as the sun was risin'," Allene said. "He was a mornin' person and he loved to see the sunrise."

"Yes, it is. Isn't that a sign of something?" Alexandria asked with curiosity.

"I've heard tell that when a person passes away at sunrise, it means the angels came for 'em to take them on to heaven."

"Then that's where Uncle Maxx is headed."

Allene smiled. "He was a good-natured man, and I'm glad he went peacefully, back here in the town he loved. That's what he wanted, and I'm always happy when people get what they want."

"I was glad I was with him when he went."

"Everything happens exactly the way it should. You bein' there with your uncle Maxx represents the cycle of life," Allene said with a smile.

Alexandria nodded. "Yes, as one life ends, another begins."

"I'm happy for you and PJ, baby girl."

Alexandria smiled and ran her hand across her flat stomach, knowing that in nine months she and PJ would be welcoming a baby to give Gary company. Last night at the gala, when she'd felt a sharp sensation in the pit of her stomach, it wasn't just the overwhelming love she'd felt for her family that had caused the intensely surreal feeling; it was the seed that PJ had planted earlier that afternoon that was already growing inside her.

Allene knew that Alexandria had been tempted to look into the future and find out whether she was carrying a girl or a boy, but she'd decided against it. She knew that because of her ability, many things in life wouldn't be a surprise to her, whether she wanted to know or not. But she knew that this baby was a gift, and surprise gifts were the best.

After everyone awoke and gathered in the kitchen, Alexandria delivered the news about Maxx. Victoria's eyes had teared up as Ted rubbed her shoulder.

"He told me that he didn't want any moaning or crying today," Alexandria told them. "He wants us to celebrate his life and have some drinks in his honor."

Victoria shook her head and smiled. "That's ol' Uncle Maxx, all right."

Although they didn't have a big breakfast as planned, the deacon from Rising Star came by and said a prayer for the family before he headed off to morning worship service.

After Maxx's body was taken to the morgue and the Sparrow's Mortuary was called, the family gathered around to toast Maxx's life.

"This is just the way Maxx wanted it," Allene said to Alexandria, who was sipping sparkling apple cider.

An hour later, Allene watched as the family once again piled into their vehicles. This time they were on their way to Butler's Cemetery to lay flowers on the headstones of their dearly departed loved ones. She was a little saddened by the fact that even in today's modern world, Butler's was still considered the Negro cemetery. The Flower Festival was in its fiftieth year, but the town itself would be celebrating its two hundred and fiftieth anniversary next year. Black folks and white folks ate together, drank together, and even worshipped together, but each time a black resident of Nedine passed away, Butler's was where they were laid to rest. "So much for two hundred and fifty years of progress," she said to herself.

The walk to the section where the Small family members were buried was situated toward the back side of the expansive land. They all walked slowly, and with purpose. Victoria and Alexandria each carried beautiful flowers in their hands while everyone followed behind them. Finally, they reached their destination.

"Here they are," Victoria said as she looked at her parents' headstones, which were side by side. A mixture of joy and sadness filled her voice. "I love and miss you, Mom and Daddy, and this morning, Uncle Maxx came to join you. I'll be here with you all, one day . . . one day."

Allene watched as Victoria placed beautiful flowers on each of her parents' headstones. Ted walked up beside her and held her hand as they stood in silence.

Now it was Alexandria's turn. She took a step over to the left and stood in front of Allene's final resting place on earth.

"Devoted wife, mother, sister, aunt, and friend to all who knew her," Alexandria said as she read part of the inscription on Allene's headstone.

Allene could feel that Alexandria wanted to reach out and take hold of her, but she knew she couldn't. She knelt before Allene's headstone and bowed her head. "I thank God for you. You loved me before I was who I am today, accepting me in every imperfect way. You loved the very idea of me, and for that, I'm eternally grateful. You've guided me, protected me, cared for me, encouraged me, and supported me. You comforted me when I was down and you waited right there by my side until I was able to pick myself up. Whether I stumble to my knees or soar to the clouds, you're always there for me. I love you to life, Grandma Allene. You are my blessing and my greatest gift."

"And you're my heart," Allene said as she hugged her own side, wishing she could embrace her great-great-granddaughter.

Alexandria placed her flowers at the foot of the headstone and smiled. Slowly, she brought her fingers to her lips and then gently placed them on the engraved inscription of Allene's name.

Allene gasped with a rush of air when she felt a warm sensation upon her lips. "Could it be?" She smiled as she watched Alexandria nod her head.

Yes, Grandma. That was a kiss from me to you.

Allene was compassionate, loving, and sentimental, but she'd never been one for shedding tears. Growing up a black woman in the segregated, rural South, there had been no room for such emotion. The last time she'd cried she had been ninety years old, on that late long-ago summer night when Susan Jessup had come to visit her for the last time. Now, standing under the bright sun with her family gathered together in love and purpose, Allene cried again.

"These tears you see," she said through sniffles as she looked at Alexandria. "They're the happiest I ever have shed."

Everyone standing near could see that something "special" was happening, so they remained silent and let Alexandria have her moment with Allene.

Alexandria rose from her knees as PJ held her hand, helping her stand up. "This is a day of loss but also of celebration and love, and I thank God for all of you." She looked directly at Christian as she continued. "We're blessed because we're standing on the shoulders of people who made this day possible. No matter what state we were in when we arrived here this weekend, all of us have changed in some way over these last three days. For me, I've embraced every bit of who I am and I'm walking away with a special gift I'll share with you all very soon." PJ squeezed her hand and smiled as Alexandria continued. "Thank you all for coming, sharing, and loving. Family is the glue that holds us together. It's not determined by blood," she said, looking at Tyler, Samantha, and Chase. "It's defined by love. And I love you all."

As Allene continued to rock back and forth in her chair she smiled again when she thought about her family. They'd made her proud and had filled her with joy. As she gazed at the brilliant night sky, she was excited that she had so many things to look forward to. Her great-great-great-grandchild would be born next year, and Victoria and Ted would be moving to Nedine once Ted retired.

Slowly, Allene rose from her chair and headed inside. She smiled again as she thought about the very reason why her family had come to town, which was to find their way. "You can never go wrong doin' right."

Chapter 37
Alexandria

Alexandria was so excited she could barely contain herself. She'd waited patiently for this day and now it was finally here. Her wedding day.

"Are you ready, sweetheart?" Victoria asked as she fluffed her daughter's tulle veil.

"I was ready last week." She smiled. "This is without a doubt the happiest day of my life."

"That's exactly how you're supposed to feel on your wedding day, and it means you've made the right choice."

"Yes, without a doubt, Mom." Alexandria smiled and looked at herself in the floor-length mirror."

"You're not only a beautiful bride," Victoria said with tears forming in her eyes, "you're a beautiful person. Your father and I are so proud of you. We know that you and PJ are going to enjoy a wonderful life together. The journey won't always be easy, and you'll have a few bumps along the way. But if you keep God first, hold on to each other, and trust in the love you share, you'll be just fine."

Alexandria nodded. "We intend to do just that."

Victoria delivered a perfect air-kiss to Alexandria's cheek. "I'm going to walk out to the vestibule now so the ushers can seat me."

Alexandria looked over to her side and saw Allene smiling. *Thank you, Grandma Allene,* she said in a language that only Allene could understand. *I know this day wouldn't be possible if you hadn't come into my life a year ago, and for that I'm eternally grateful.*

It's me who's grateful, Allene answered back. *Now go out there and marry that handsome man waitin' for you at the altar.*

The wedding directress, whom Victoria had hired, straightened out the bottom of Alexandria's silk-and-pearl laced train. "Okay, it's show time," she said with a smile. "Let's get you married."

They walked out to the vestibule where Ted was waiting. Alexandria smiled when she saw the pride and joy on her handsome father's face. He wrapped his arms around her in a warm embrace. "Other than your mother, you're the most beautiful bride I've ever seen," Ted told her.

"Thanks, Daddy. I think that's the best compliment anyone has ever given me."

"It's true. Your mother and I are so proud of you, and we want you to know that if you and PJ ever need anything, our door is always open."

"I love you, Daddy."

"Love you, too, princess."

The wedding directress motioned to Alexandria. "It's time for you to make your grand entrance."

"All right, let's do this," Alexandria said as she laced

her arm in her father's. They stood in front of the sanctuary door and waited for their cue.

When the sound of Pachelbel's "Canon in D" filled the air and the doors opened, Alexandria was blown away. The fragrant flowers smelled like heaven. Large vases overflowing with roses, lilies, and gerberas were in every corner the eye could see, and looked more beautiful than the displays she'd seen two weeks ago at Nedine's Flower Festival. Candles adorned the window sills giving a warm glow to the ornate space, and the smiling faces that filled each pew made Alexandria feel appreciated and loved.

She walked slowly in her strapless, form-fitting ivory colored gown that had been handmade to highlight her bold curves. She chose to go bare at the neck, allowing the crystal teardrop earrings that dangled at her lobes to accentuate her flawless beauty.

Butterflies fluttered in her stomach with each step she took. She was ecstatic to see Tyler, Samantha, and Chase smiling as they sat together, united as a family whose strength was in their love and commitment to be open and honest with each other, no matter the situation.

Alexandria beamed when she saw Christian smile at her and mouth, "You're beautiful, sis," as she walked by. She could see that the last two weeks spent in rehab had done him a world of good. She knew he still had a long road ahead of him, and was glad that he was going to check himself back into the treatment center after the ceremony ended.

A small tear fell from the corner of her right eye as she looked at her mother, who was bursting with happiness in the front pew to her left, and sitting beside her was Gary, adorable in a black suit and tie that she and PJ had picked out for him last week after he was released from the hospital. She blew a kiss to him as he smiled and gig-gled with joy. Alexandria's heart felt another boost at the sight of Parker, standing at the front as PJ's best man. She knew the love and pride on his faced matched the joy he felt in his heart.

Now, she was only a few feet away from PJ, and she wanted to run up to him and say their "I do's" right then and there. But she knew she had to be patient for a few more minutes. She smiled wide as she walked slowly to-ward PJ, who was smiling back at her.

Alexandria could hardly contain her excitement when she looked at her handsome, sexy bridegroom decked out in his custom made tuxedo. Her body trembled with hap-piness as she approached the altar where PJ was waiting for her.

Alexandria had known that because she was a spoken word artist, she was expected to deliver a rousing and sentimental oration for her wedding vow. But she'd de-cided against it. The words she wanted to tell PJ would be spoken and enacted later that night as they made love as husband and wife for the first time. So when the part of the ceremony came where they were supposed to recite their vows, she was shocked when PJ announced that he'd written something special for her that he wanted to say.

PJ cleared his throat as Alexandria looked on in dis-belief. "Ali, I wrote this for you and I hope you like it."

Alexandria as well as the church full of wedding guests listened with rapt attention as PJ began. He spoke from the heart without a written script as he looked into Alexandria's eyes and smiled.

"I'll never forget the day we met at a Jack and Jill meeting. Even though I was only five years old, I knew what it meant to feel love and be loved. When I looked at you I felt both. You were my very first friend. My best friend. You were the prettiest little girl I'd ever seen, with long ponytails and a smile that made me smile. I was so happy when I found out you were in my kindergarten class. I credit you for the reason why I loved school and was eager to be there every day. It was because I knew I'd see you. We shared sandwiches, candy, traded snacks, and held hands at recess."

Alexandria smiled as tears fell from her eyes and from their guests' too.

"A year later I moved away," PJ continued. "But I never forgot my very first friend because you'd cemented a place in my heart. More than twenty years later God's grace and a meant-to-be love brought us back together. You're still my best friend and the best part of the man I've become.

"Your smile keeps me going when I'm down. Your encouragement and support give me motivation to finish whatever I start. Your understanding nature gives me peace in a world that can be full of challenges. And your love makes me feel like I can conquer the world.

"I'm proud and honored to share this day with you, Ali. I love you. I cherish you, and I can't wait to build a lifetime of memories with you by my side. Thank you for loving me. Thank you for allowing me to love you. And thank you for making me the happiest man alive by becoming my wife and partner for life."

When PJ finished there wasn't a dry eye in the church. Even Parker, who was usually the epitome of cool, had brought out his handkerchief to wipe away happy tears.

Alexandria was overjoyed and more thankful than she could put into words. Right before PJ had come into her life a year ago she'd been in an unfulfilling relationship, but once her grandma Allene helped her embrace who she was, her whole world changed. Alexandria's gift allowed her to see that life was short but precious, and she was determined not to waste a single moment of it on anything or anyone that didn't fulfill her, teach her, or help her grow. She was happy that PJ did all those things and more. She had a lot of living ahead of her, and she was ready to start doing it with her new husband and the children they were going to raise as they walked through life's journey.

A Note to Readers

In this story, Christian Thornton battled drugs from an early age. Substance abuse, whether drug- or alcohol-related, affects millions of individuals and their families. The collective toll it takes can ruin the lives of the abuser and those around them. Addiction is a serious problem, but just as with any problem, there's always a solution. Professional counseling and treatment can save lives. If you or anyone you know is dealing with substance abuse, please get help.

For treatment and referrals please visit the Substance Abuse and Mental Health Services Administration (SAMHSA) at www.samhsa.gov. You can call their 24/7 treatment referral line at 800-985-5990, or reach someone by texting 66746.

Don't miss Trice Hickman's scandalous novel,

Deadly Satisfaction

On sale now wherever books and e-books are sold!

Chapter 1
Dropped the Bomb

The elegantly sleek interior of G&D Hair Design was alive with chatter, laughter, and gossip. Even though G&D was a high-end salon situated in the trendy Arts District section of town, the owners, Geneva Owens and Donetta Pierce, made sure their establishment was as down home and welcoming as sweet potato pie, which they often served their clients as treats. And on this particular Tuesday morning, the salon was unusually busy. It was two days before Thanksgiving, and as Donetta had said, "Every woman in town is tryin' to get their style on for the holiday."

From one side of the salon to the other, each stylist's chair, shampoo bowl, and hooded dryer was occupied, and even more women were patiently waiting in the lobby, sipping coffee and tea from the complimentary beverage station. From blowouts to twist-outs, to full sew-ins, roller sets, and everything in between, the ladies of Amber, Alabama were primed and ready for the royal treatment that had become G&D's trademark. Geneva and Donetta had worked hard to overcome many obstacles to open their salon, and now they were reaping the rewards with their thriving business.

"I've been doing hair for as long as I can remember, and this is the busiest holiday turnout I've ever seen," Donetta said. "You'd think we were giving away weaves up in here."

"Everyone wants to look good when they visit with their families," Geneva said with a smile as she reached for her flat iron.

"Speak for yourself and these other women," Shartell Brown huffed as she sat in Donetta's chair. "As for me, I'm gettin' fly for me, myself, and I. My family is on my last nerve right now, and I'm glad I only have to tolerate them once or twice a year during the holidays."

Donetta made a *tsk*ing sound as she measured a track of hair for what would become part of Shartell's full sew-in weave. "Girl, why're you stressing about your family?"

"'Cause ever since I blew up, they're always coming to me with their hands out and a whole lotta foolishness."

"Shoot, if they know you like I know you, they'll leave you alone before they end up in one of your columns, or maybe even that new book you're writing."

Shartell smiled slyly. "You know, Donetta, that's not a bad idea. I can write a juicy story from all the shenanigans that go on in my family. Real life is much more scandalous than fiction."

Donetta pursed her lips. "I was just joking."

"Girl, that's not a joke, that's a good idea."

"Shartell, that would be flat-out wrong to put your family members' business on front street. That's cold."

"Honey, please. That's business, and it's called being shrewd."

"How 'bout it's called being coldhearted." Donetta quipped in return. "Where the hell are your morals, Shartell? Don't you have a conscience anymore?"

"Of course I do. But if I'm telling the truth, what's wrong with that? Even the Good Book says the truth shall set you free."

"Don't use the Bible to justify your mess."

"I stand behind the things I say, that's why no one can ever accuse me of a being a liar, and that's the truth."

Geneva chimed in. "Just because something is true, that doesn't mean you have to say it."

"You better listen to Geneva," Donetta said as she parted Shartell's hair with her comb. "And don't think about putting anyone in this salon in your book because if you do, you'll end up having to do your hair your damn self, 'cause you know I won't touch your head again."

"Whatever," Shartell said.

"Heffa, you know I barely like you anyway," Donetta teased.

Geneva shook her head and laughed. "You two talk so much junk."

"Donetta knows she loves me," Shartell said with a chuckle. "And hey, I might be a heffa, and I might even be coldhearted, at times, but I'm one of the realest chicks you ever gonna meet, and there ain't a phony bone in my body."

Everyone within earshot nodded in agreement with what Shartell had just said. Shartell Brown, who had once worked as a stylist with Geneva and Donetta a few years ago, at Heavenly Hair Salon, had been nicknamed Ms. CIA, because she was a known gossip with intel on everyone in town. Now she was a respected news and entertainment reporter for Entertainment Scoop, a wildly popular online website that was giving TMZ a run for their money. Shartell had risen to prominence thanks to the most salacious and talked about murder case the town of Amber had ever seen.

Two years ago, Johnny Mayfield, who had been Geneva's ex-husband, had been murdered inside his home. Johnny had been a charismatic but nefarious man who'd amassed a legion of enemies, both male and female. The list of suspects had been as long as a hot summer day, but thanks to Shartell's contacts, inside information, and her uncanny ability to find out the word on the street before it ever hit the pavement, she'd provided the authorities with useful tips that helped them solve Johnny's murder and had cemented a new career for herself in the process.

Geneva shook her head. "Shartell, try to go easy on your family. You should count yourself blessed that you have relatives to spend the holidays with. I'd give anything to share a meal with my mother again, God rest her soul."

"That's because your mother was probably just as nice as you are, Ms. Pollyanna," Shartell teased. "My mama, on the other hand, could drive Jesus to drink hard liquor. And my four siblings . . . let's just say that if the devil needed extra disciples he'd come looking for them, and their badass kids."

"Shartell!" Geneva chided. "That's an awful thing to say."

Donetta threaded her needle and nodded her head. "That's the kind of truth telling she probably shouldn't have said, but you have to admit, it was funny as hell."

"Thank you," Shartell said, reaching up to give Donetta a high five. "My aunt is coming in town for the holidays and I have to pick her up from the train station tonight, but once I drop her off at my mama's house I'm gonna be in the wind and they won't see me again until Thanksgiving dinner, which I plan to cut short."

"You're seriously not going to spend time with your family?" Geneva asked.

"I'm gonna try my best not to. Besides, I have work to do. I'm writing an article about finding love during the holidays, and it's due tomorrow afternoon so it can run on Thanksgiving Day, and I know none of my knuckle head, backwards-ass relatives can help me with that subject matter."

Geneva adjusted her smock as she spoke. "You two are the most jaded human beings I know. Where is your optimism? Where's your hope?"

Donetta sighed. "Oh Lord, we've gotten her started."

"I'm serious." Geneva put down her flat iron and reached for a hair clip as she continued to speak. "Try not to be so pessimistic about everything."

"We're not pessimists, we're realists," Donetta said, hand on her slim hip. "Hell, I know exactly what Shartell's talkin' about when it comes to family. Every time I spend the holidays with mine I end up needing a double dose of therapy. They're just way too much, and that's why I'm not foolin' with them this year."

"Donetta, you know you're more than welcome to spend Thanksgiving at my house," Geneva said, "but your aunt is going to have a fit if you don't stop by and visit with her and your cousins."

Donetta smirked. "She'll just have to have one because my backstabbing relatives won't see my face this Turkey Day. I refuse to go over to my Aunt May's and listen to the bullshit that I know she's gonna be serving. I got my life to live and I'm doin' just fine without them."

"I'm truly sorry to hear that," Councilwoman Harris spoke up from Geneva's chair. "Donetta, I'm going to say a prayer for you, and you too, Shartell, that you and your families will find peace."

Charlene Harris was one of Geneva's favorite and most loyal clients, and over the last two years she had become a close friend and confidant. Charlene was a pillar of the community, and much like Geneva, she was a woman who'd mastered the art of reinventing herself. Two years ago, after putting up with years of infidelity from her husband, she'd ended her long-suffering marriage and had started a new life. She'd updated her look and style from classic conservative to contemporary chic, but she'd kept the same elegant grace and comportment that she'd become known and respected for, along with her humility.

Geneva smiled at Charlene. "You understand what family is all about, and I know you can't wait to see your children when they come to town."

"Yes, I can't wait to see Phillip and Lauren. We haven't all been together since last Christmas, so I'm certainly looking forward to it."

"That's a blessing," Geneva said as she worked her flat iron through Charlene's razor-cut, chin-length bob, putting the finishing touches on her chic hairdo.

Although no one else listening to Charlene speak could recognize the catch in her voice when she'd mentioned her children, Geneva had. And that was because Charlene had omitted any reference to her eldest child, Brad. Brad had moved to Los Angeles over ten years ago, married a tall blonde from the Valley, and hadn't spoken to his family since. It had hurt Charlene to her core, knowing that her firstborn had basically disowned his entire family, but she'd learned to make peace with it over the years through prayer, and the hope that someday her son would come to his senses. But until then, she poured all her love and care into the two who still remained close in her life.

"Yes, it is," Charlene said with a nod. "Lauren's

doing well in med school at Johns Hopkins, and Phillip was just named senior associate at his law firm."

"That's impressive," Donetta said. "You did a great job raising them."

"Thank you, Donetta. But I have to say they made it easy because both of them have always been very focused, self-directed kids who never followed the crowd. They stayed true to who they are, and that's why I'm so proud of them. They're good, kindhearted human beings who care about people, and that's what's most important in my book."

Geneva nodded. "Yes, it certainly is."

"Amen to that," Donetta chimed in, along with Shartell. "Not everybody has the opportunity to pursue their dreams and still remain true to themselves while they're doing it. That takes a lot of effort and sacrifice."

Geneva looked at her co-owner and best friend and smiled. She knew that it was a topic near to Donetta's heart. It had been a little over a year since she'd undergone gender reassignment surgery, commonly known as SRS; or as the trans community called it, bottom surgery, so that her outward physical appearance reflected who she was inside. It had taken Donetta many years, tremendous sacrifice, and at times, painful heartache, to pursue her long-held dream of living life the way she'd always felt she was meant to.

"Your words speak so much truth, Donetta," Councilwoman Harris said with a nod. "Life is a journey filled with many paths we can take to arrive at our intended destination. The key is knowing how to navigate your course, regardless of what anyone else thinks, and then master how to stay on it."

"And the best way to reach any destination is in a pair of Jimmy Choos," Donetta replied with a wink.

They all laughed at Donetta's joke, but suddenly the room fell silent when Shartell looked up at the fifty-inch television screen hanging on the wall and let out a loud gasp. Every eye was glued to the face on the screen that put panic in each of their hearts, for very different reasons.

Geneva stood frozen in place while Donetta reached over her, grabbed the remote, and turned up the volume. The *"Breaking News"* caption rolled across the screen with a photo of Vivana Jackson above it. A hush came over the entire salon as they listened to news that left everyone's mouth hanging open with questions.

Vivana Jackson—formally known as Vivana Owens— had been convicted of murdering her ex-lover, Johnny Mayfield, in cold blood, and was serving a twenty-five-to-life sentence for second-degree murder in the Alabama state penitentiary. But according to the information coming out of the reporter's mouth, Vivana was now being represented by a prominent local attorney who'd taken her case pro bono, and had found compelling evidence that suggested Vivana was innocent of the crime for which she'd been convicted. A murder committed impulsively, and without premeditation.

"I've uncovered evidence that corroborates my client's claim that she is innocent of killing Jonathan Mayfield," Leslie Sachs, Vivana's attorney, said. "I can't go into detail now, but when I present the evidence to the judge next week, it will be clear that Ms. Jackson, formerly known as Mrs. Owens, was not only framed, but the real killer is still at large, and is quite possibly watching this interview right now."

The reporter ended the clip by telling viewers that an exclusive jailhouse interview with Vivana would air tonight on the evening news.

Everyone remained silent while their eyes fell on Geneva, who was still frozen in place.

Donetta looked at Geneva. "Honey . . . you okay?"

Geneva shook her head from side to side. "No, I'm not. I need to go home."

From that moment forward, the salon was filled with voracious gossip, wild speculation, and unfounded theories about the murder case that had rocked Amber. Johnny Mayfield had done so many people wrong that a different suspect had popped up each week after his death. Mostly everyone in town believed that his scorned ex-lover, Vivana, had done it, while there were a select few who believed Vivana's claim that she'd been framed. But there were only four people who knew without a doubt that Vivana was innocent. One of them was dead, one was sitting in jail, one was Johnny's real killer—the honorable and well-respected councilwoman, Charlene Harris—and the last person who knew the identity of Johnny's real killer was the person who'd sent Councilwoman Harris a mysterious text, telling her that they had proof that she'd done it.

Later that night, nearly everyone in Amber was held captive in front of their televisions as they watched Vivana's defiant face and listened to her lawyer's self-assured words. People from one end of town to the other were abuzz with chatter and speculation, and there were a few who were more than a little concerned, namely Geneva, Donetta, and especially Charlene Harris. Each one of the women knew that in the days to come, this would be a holiday they'd never forget.

Chapter 2
Geneva

The two loves of Geneva Owens's life were her loving husband, Samuel, and their adorable ten-month-old daughter, Gabrielle. They added meaning and purpose to everything she did, and she looked forward to coming home to them at the end of each day. But this afternoon wasn't one of those days, and as Geneva drove home—ten miles above the speed limit—she prayed that Samuel and Gabrielle wouldn't be there when she arrived.

Geneva breathed a heavy sigh of relief when she opened the garage door and saw the empty space where Samuel's SUV was usually parked. "Thank goodness Samuel's already on his way to the airport," she whispered to herself.

A small twinge of guilt pulled at Geneva's stomach for feeling that way, but she couldn't help it. She didn't want her husband or daughter there because she needed to be alone so she could sort out her thoughts in peace. She'd been stressed and anxious ever since she'd seen

Vivana's face flash across the television screen at her salon this afternoon. From that moment forward, Geneva had not been able to shake the feeling that something bad was about to happen.

After she removed her clothes and changed into her comfortable lounge pants and matching shirt, Geneva went into her den. She curled her feet under her hips as she leaned back into the comfort of her brown chenille sofa. She looked to her right and picked up a beautifully framed picture of Samuel, Gabrielle, and herself, and let out a sigh. "I've got to keep them safe," she said. "Nothing else matters."

Geneva didn't know what Vivana was cooking up, but there was one thing she was certain of, and that was the fact that nothing good could come of anything Vivana Jackson was involved in. The thought was nearly too much for her to process, and again, she was glad the house was empty. She looked at her watch and noted the time. "They probably won't be back home for at least another hour or two."

With Thanksgiving only two days away, Samuel's parents were coming to town to celebrate the holidays and he'd taken Gabrielle with him to pick them up from the airport. Geneva had been excited about her in-laws' visit. She loved Samuel's mother and father as if they were her own parents, and their love for her was equally sincere. But at the moment, Herbert and Sarah Owens were pushed to the back of Geneva's mind, thanks to her new worries surrounding Vivana.

Geneva picked up the TV remote control and flipped to the local news station that was set to air Vivana's interview. "Whatever craziness that woman is scheming, I know it has trouble written all over it," she whispered as she sat on the edge of her couch, as stiff as a park statue. She stared at the TV in disbelief. "This can't be happening," she whispered again, bringing her hand to her mouth at the sight of Vivana's face on the screen. "What in the world is that psychopath up to?"

Geneva was struck by the change in Vivana's appearance. Vivana had once been a full-figured beauty who had been meticulous about her appearance. But in the span of the two years that she'd been incarcerated, the woman looked as though she'd aged a decade. Her smooth skin had become wrinkled, her vibrant eyes had lost their sparkle, and the apples of her cheeks had begun to sag. She fidgeted back and forth, constantly tucking and retucking her salt-and-pepper strands behind her ear. Geneva knew that was the nervous habit of someone who had something to hide.

Geneva watched without blinking as a haggard but defiant-looking Vivana Jackson spoke freely, proclaiming her innocence. Geneva paid close attention to Vivana's every word and movement, and she noticed that the woman's eyes, now weathered with tiny crow's-feet on each side, still harbored a wild emptiness that was almost frightening. She had the look of someone whose burdens ran deep and whose capacity for ruthlessness flowed even deeper.

"My story has never changed and it never will," Vivana said resolutely.

Geneva gasped because Vivana looked into the camera as if she was speaking directly to her, and it sent chills up her arm.

"I said it two years ago, and I'll say it again," Vivana continued, "I didn't kill Johnny. He wronged a whole lot of people, and that's where the focus should've always been . . . on those other people, not me. I've been locked up for a crime that I didn't commit while the real killer is still out there. But believe me," she said as a menacing smirk overtook her lips, "what's done in the dark always

comes to the light, and that light's about to shine real
bright because—"

"Yes," her attorney said, cutting Vivana off in mid-
sentence. "Ms. Jackson is innocent of the murder of Johnny
Mayfield. She was framed and was wrongly convicted
and incarcerated while the real killer is still at large. Once
I present the judge with the new evidence next week, I'm
confident that my client will be vindicated."

The news reporter launched question after question,
aimed at both Vivana and her attorney, hoping to get
more detailed information about what type of new evidence was going to be introduced that would prove
Vivana's innocence. Although it was clear to see that Vivana wanted to say more, as was evidenced by her edgy
behavior and shifting eyes, she remained silent under the
advice of her attorney. Finally, after several minutes of
unsuccessful probing, the reporter gave up and went to
commercial break.

"I don't know what to think," Geneva whispered
aloud as she shook her head. She knew from firsthand experience what Vivana was capable of, and that knowledge made her feel a little afraid. "I've got to shake this
off. I can't let this get to me."

Not since Johnny's death had she felt so many con-
flicting emotions. But oddly, her anxiety and heavy heart
hadn't come from the grief or sadness that most people
experienced when losing someone; rather, Geneva had
been unnerved because she felt an overwhelming amount
of guilt.

Geneva hadn't been completely surprised on the fate-
ful morning she'd learned that Johnny had been murdered. At the time, she and Johnny had been estranged.
Geneva had left him, and they'd been separated for several months pending divorce. In that time she'd moved
on, met and fallen in love with Samuel, and had been more

than ready to start a new life after the hell Johnny had put her through during their five and a half years of marriage. He'd been a dishonest, deceitful, womanizing dog whom Geneva had grown to detest toward the end of their turbulent union. And even though Johnny had been the guilty party in their relationship, he had contested the divorce and had vowed to fight her to the bitter end.

The week before Johnny was killed, he had come by the salon where Geneva worked and begged for her forgiveness. He'd told her that he was remorseful about the way he'd mistreated her and taken her for granted for so many years. But in the process of his apology he'd caused a scene in front of her clients, and Geneva had no patience for him or his drama. All she'd wanted to do was remove him from the salon and from her life. She told him to leave and she even walked him to the front steps, and that's when things turned from bad to worse.

Geneva and Johnny had exchanged heated words before Geneva made the misstep of telling him that she was in love with another man. Hearing that news sent Johnny over the edge. He'd impulsively grabbed her arm, and as she pulled away, she'd lost her balance, and caused them both to tumble down the salon's steep steps and hit the hard concrete one story below. That single fall cemented both their fates. Geneva had ended up in the hospital, where the doctors revealed that she'd been pregnant and had lost the baby. Her grief had been heavy, and was made worse by the fact that Johnny came out of the accident without so much as a scratch.

That night, as Geneva lay in her hospital bed, she'd prayed for Johnny's death. She'd prayed that he would befall a slow and painful demise, and that he would suffer greatly. A week later her plea was answered. Johnny was shot in the chest at point-blank range, and he'd died slowly, suffocating on his own blood as a result of his fatal wound. When Geneva had heard the news, guilt had crept in.

Geneva shivered at the thought. She turned off the TV and slowly rose from the couch. She walked into her spacious gourmet kitchen, filled her stainless steel teakettle with water, and reached into the cabinet for a box of her favorite herbal tea. "I need this to calm my nerves," she said aloud. She shook her head when she thought about the fact that there was a time not too long ago when a glass of wine would have been her drink of choice to calm her anxiety. But during her pregnancy, Donetta had persuaded her to start drinking herbal tea. "Honey, folks sleep on tea, thinking it's weak. They just don't know that it's the liquid of the gods."

Geneva had to admit that Donetta had been right. Orange hibiscus had become her favorite lately, but as she stood by the stove waiting for the water in her kettle to whistle, the anticipation of the flavorful taste was overshadowed by whatever scheme she knew Vivana was plotting.

Geneva hadn't been shocked that Vivana had killed Johnny; after all, she was the same woman who had deceived Geneva for months. Vivana had walked into the salon where Geneva had been working and said her name was Cheryl, and that she was newly divorced and had just moved to Amber for a fresh start. She'd struck a chord with Geneva, who'd been on that same path and had just filed paperwork to divorce Johnny.

But as time went on, Geneva, as well as everyone else at the salon, quickly realized that Cheryl was unstable and had major problems. She was moody, attitudinal, arrogant, and obnoxiously rude. Geneva eventually found out that Cheryl's real name was Vivana, and that she'd assumed that identity so she could find out everything there was to know about her, and then kill her. During Johnny's murder trial Vivana had even confessed that her plan had been to kill Geneva first, and then do away with Johnny as payback for all the pain they'd both caused her. But she'd said that someone had gotten to Johnny first, foiling her plans.

Geneva's mind kept replaying the look she'd seen in Vivana's eyes when the disturbed woman had been on the witness stand. It was the same look Vivana had during the interview tonight, and Geneva knew that meant that if Vivana got free, she'd come looking for her to finish what she'd started.

As Geneva poured her tea and waited for her husband, daughter, and in-laws to arrive, she knew she had to do what she'd been putting off for the last two years. Tomorrow, while she was out running errands and getting food for her family's holiday feast, one of the top things on her list was going to include paying a visit to Rusty's Pawn Shop so she could buy a gun.